PRAISE FOR
AGAINST INFINITY

"Not since Ahab thrust his lance at the lightning and swore the white whale's doom have I read anything much like it. . . . Benford has just been getting better and better."

—Algis Budrys

"Engrossing . . . typical Benford virtues . . . a gritty, three-dimensional future, a believable hero, and a real flair for the alien. . . . Benford evokes the mystique of the hunt and the link with the prey . . . an element of American literary tradition rare in SF."

—*Publishers Weekly*

"A worthy successor to *Timescape* and a must for the SF collection."

—*ALA Booklist*

"Glows with a rare immediacy and realism, with sparkling descriptions, vivid dangers, and a convincing alien-frontier cast and ambience."

—*Kirkus Reviews*

Don't miss these fine novels by Gregory Benford, available wherever Bantam Spectra Books are sold:

GREGORY BENFORD

AGAINST INFINITY

BANTAM BOOKS
NEW YORK • TORONTO • LONDON • SYDNEY • AUCKLAND

THIS NOVEL IS A WORK OF FICTION. NAMES, CHARACTERS, PLACES, AND INCIDENTS ARE EITHER THE PRODUCT OF THE AUTHOR'S IMAGINATION OR ARE USED FICTITIOUSLY. ANY RESEMBLANCE TO ACTUAL EVENTS OR LOCALES OR PERSONS, LIVING OR DEAD, IS ENTIRELY COINCIDENTAL.

This edition contains the complete text of the original hardcover edition.
NOT ONE WORD HAS BEEN OMITTED.

AGAINST INFINITY

A Bantam Spectra Book / published by arrangement with the author

PRINTING HISTORY

SECTIONS OF AGAINST INFINITY *APPEARED IN THE FEBRUARY AND APRIL 1983 ISSUES OF* AMAZING SCIENCE FICTION STORIES

Bantam edition / March 1991

SPECTRA and the portrayal of a boxed "s" are trademarks of Bantam Books, a division of Bantam Doubleday Dell Publishing Group, Inc.

Library of Congress Catalog Card Number: 82-19324.

ISBN 0-553-29005-3

Published simultaneously in the United States and Canada

Bantam Books are published by Bantam Books, a division of Bantam Doubleday Dell Publishing Group, Inc. Its trademark, consisting of the words "Bantam Books" and the portrayal of a rooster, is Registered in U.S. Patent and Trademark Office and in other countries. Marca Registrada. Bantam Books, 666 Fifth Avenue, New York, New York 10103.

PRINTED IN THE UNITED STATES OF AMERICA

RAD 0 9 8 7 6 5 4 3 2 1

To
James Alton Benford

PART I

BEYOND SIDON

1

They went out from Sidon Settlement in a straggling band, clanking and crunching over the hard-packed, worn-down purple plain. The ice near Sidon had been melted and frozen and remelted again and again by orbit shuttle landings and by the heater exhausts of passing crawlers, so that now it was speckled and mottled with rainbow splashes and big blotches of contaminants. Out over this crusty trampled ice they went, carrying the boy Manuel. Inside their wheezing and huffing machines they sang and shoved each other and early got into the smeerlop and whiskey, as they always did.

The boy was thirteen. He watched it all with wide eyes. For five years now he had waited and listened to the talk of the ice ridges and ammonia rivers of the melting land, quick and treacherous under the feet. Hunkered down around a heater, evening after evening, he had listened, not knowing how much to believe but wanting to trust it all for fear of forgetting anything he might need later, for he knew even then that everything you learned came to use if you waited. What he knew most deeply was the bigness of the wilderness they now crawled into, bigger than any of the puny human Settlements, vast and powerful and with a reason and logic to itself. Ganymede—the biggest moon in the solar system, with nearly as much land and ice as old worn Earth, but fresh and unmarked by man until the last two centuries. Manuel heard the talk and thought of the big trackless wastes and knew the talk was empty, no matter whom it came from—from the new Earthers who'd swarmed in a few years back, eager to hack and chip away at the vast ice mountains in search of metals and seams of rare elements; from the biotechnicians who brought the metaformed animals, sure the beasts would find here a new place to yip and labor and take the burden from the humans; from the older settlers (like Petrovich), who had heaved up the big hydroponics domes and now hummed away inside them, growing the food and weaving the organics, and were fatuous enough to believe they had any more hold on the huge cold wilderness than the ones brand new off the shuttle; from the olders, men and women who'd sent out the first fusion-busters to put the land to rake and fire; from the survivors older still, of whom Manuel knew only Old Matt Bohles, with his gravel voice and slow, stooped walk, who talked little but whose eyes were liquid and rheumy with tales; from all the waves of humans who had washed over the face of Ganymede and then seeped away, most of them, leaving behind only those who had the strength to endure and the humility to learn the skills and to fight the awful and unforgiving cold.

In the first hours the wise-ass veneer rubbed away from him. He watched the smeerlop going down and even tried a drab, grinning, but it was not to his liking yet and he thought with some relief that that was about right anyway. In the thick, close air of the cabin the stench and sweat of the men seemed to tighten around him, and he contented himself with watching out the big ports, where the augmented and servo'd animals rumpused about on the pocked plain. A dime-sized sun struck colors from their carapaces, steels gleaming blue-green, the ceramics a clammy yellow. They frolicked at being out of Sidon Settlement again, beyond the domes where they bent their backs at agro work, their reward being the blunt pleasures of food and sex and cartoon stories and sensos in the off-hours. But none of that gave the zest of romping free in the thin air outside, scampering around the lumbering crawler treads, whistling and chattering and sending their clipped cries to each other in the stinging cold. They had been in their multiplex servo'd pods so long that Manuel could hardly remember what their basic bodies were. Short Stuff was a chimp, maybe, and The Barron a kind of thoroughbred dog as near as he could make out. The others were pigs or dolphins or something else. Often the animals themselves did not know. With their truncated bodies and regrown cerebella and cerebra ballooned into a nearly human 40 IQ, they were confused, yet far smarter than before, eager to use their abilities. They had been Skinnered into mild, subservient behavior. They gladly did jobs a robot couldn't or a man wouldn't, and were taintless in their ardor for the work.

"Good to let them come," Manuel said to his father, Colonel López.

"Ay. Watch they don't get seized up in the treads. Or trip one of the walkers."

Up the crumpled ridge they went, rising with a wrenching sway above the big plain so that, looking back, they could make out the sprawl and glimmer of Sidon Settlement like a jeweled handkerchief thrown down by a passing giant. The talk began again. It was, as usual, about policing the jackrabs and rockeaters and the ammonia-soaked scooters and the crawlies that processed methane, for that was the ostensible purpose of this annual expedition. But soon the talk drifted, as though drawn by the same current that ran through all of them, to the best game of all, the best subject for listening and the best for thinking as the blue-white wastes tilted by outside. He had heard it before, the voices at first quiet and filled with weight and with a deliberate easing up on the subject as the Settlement fell behind, recollection floating up in them like bubbles breaking on the surface of a deep pond. Even though still a boy, he had heard the tales in squatters' shacks hardly able to hold their pressure; and in agro domes; in work sheds rank with metal shavings and sour spit; in living rooms where the women who had been on the hunt in the past would talk too, but not the same way; and in growing tanks where men chopped at the ever-expanding mass of inert turkey meat as big as a walker and steaming with fat-glazed ooze—had heard the frightful stories and seen the occasional well-thumbed fax photos and known that what came down to him was from an age long before anything he could know. He sensed that something was waiting for him when he would at last be allowed to come out from the small and insignificant encrustations that man had spattered over the mute face of Ganymede, come out to take part in the pruning of the small creatures and find in the vast wastes the thing that waited, that was a part of what Ganymede held for humans. Because he was born here, he had inherited more than the Earthers who had come late. He had left to him, without ever seeing it, the big luminous artifact with the jagged beam-cut slash and the V-shaped runners that in the millions of square kilometers of Ganymede had earned a name that held respect and some terror, for it was not like the other ruined and timeworn pieces of alien handiwork that were strewn through the whole Jovian satellite system. They called it Aleph. Some Jew had given it that, a blank name that was the first letter of the Hebrew alphabet: a neutral vowel that bespoke the opaque nature of the blocky, gravid thing, the bulk that humans had tried to write upon with their cutters and tractors and on which they had left no mark. A neutral name, and yet it was the source of a long legend of domes cracked open and rifled, of walkers and crawlers and even whole outposts caught up and crushed and trampled as it moved forward on its own oblivious missions, or else homes and sheds ripped apart as the thing rose up out of the ice where it dwelt, walls split by the heaving of the land as it broke free of ice and poked its angular face—eyeless, with only sawtoothed openings to mark what men chose in their ignorance to call a face and so to take away some fragment of its strangeness—breaking freshly again into the dim sunlight, seeking, always seeking materials men also needed and had compacted into their homes and factories, and thus were forced to futilely defend against the legend that came for the metals and rare rock, the Aleph making no distinction between what men held and what the bare plains offered, so that it took where it found and thus engendered the continuing legend of alarms ignored and traps brushed aside and servo'd armaments smashed and animals mangled and men and women injured and laser and even electron-beam bolts delivered at point-blank range as though into nothing, the alien absorbing all and giving nothing, shrugging off the puny attempts of men to deliver death to it, and without pause it kept going—down a corridor of ruin and destruction starting back before Manuel's birth and even before Old Matt, the massive thing lumbered, not swift but with a ruthless determination, like a machine and yet like a man too; moving onward eternally on some course humans could not guess, it ran forever in the boy's dreams, a vast immemorial alabaster shape.

To Manuel it rose above the wilderness of ice and stone and became bigger than the barren blankness, more significant than this slate-gray moon that men had begun to scratch at. He had seen the ruts in the ice and even, once, clearly cut into the hard rock, a delta-shaped print the Aleph sometimes left, where an appendage that might be a foot or might be a kind of feeder—no one knew—bit down and took something from the soil wherever it went, moving by means that even high-speed cameras could not fix, gliding at times and at others just lumbering, seeming to shift the huge weight from side to side of the irregular chipped and scoured body, grainy and yet unlike rock in that its color changed through the years, so that the old prints showed a custard-colored wedge of fast-moving luminescence, and then as the men tracked it better and brought faster optical instruments and the scientific teams came down from the research satellites nearer in to Jupiter, they got it more firmly fixed. It was bigger than five walkers together and used many things to move: quick, strong leglike extrusions; electromagnetic repulsors that sank fields into iron-rich meteor fragments and hurled them behind it; hole-borers for traversing the ice; a thing like a propeller that would carry it into the deep slush and liquid that lay beneath the seventy kilometers of sheet ice that encased Ganymede; treads on one side; levitating fields—all used when needed, carrying the thing stolidly through gangs of hooting men and packs of servo'd but useless animals, through metal and rock as though they were butter, through teams of scientists with carefully wrought deadfalls and immobilizing streams of electricity, through generations of futile plans and expeditions that tried to study it, slow it, stop it, kill it. Revenge was a part of the legend, debts that needed payment for Settlements ruined and limbs severed and lives wrecked and torment suffered, human misery spreading endless in its wake. But after generations the scientists discovered more interesting artifacts on the moons far out from Jupiter—or at least less dangerous ones—and they went there to study things that did not move or hurt or shrug them off. The Aleph was beyond them and they invented a theory that it was a mindless marauding thing, damaged but still dangerous, fulfilling no function beyond naked existence, left over from the millennia when the still-unknown aliens came. The aliens had built a mechanism for seeding Jupiter with simple, edible life—reworking whole moons, laying down a foundation for some future use that had not yet come. Once labeled, the inert artifacts could be forgotten by the men and women who struggled to live on the moons. They were alone at the rim of the human universe, pressed against an infinity that did not bear contemplation. The scientists left the Aleph for a later time, perhaps hoping it would simply wear down and die and become a safe numb object for study, like the rest.

Petrovich called out to him, "Hey there, little López! Let's us see some frittins, hey?"

Manuel went to help with the food. He didn't mind work. He knew that was a quality which would get him through times when merely being clever would not, so he bore down on that and made it his own. Hail rattled on the hull of the crawler. He watched the landscape as he worked as cutting the stock tubes of vegetables, feeling the warm kitchen blower while outside a slow drizzle came in from the north. This was the way he would later remember going into the wilderness for the first time: an endless oncoming wall of water, hail and ammonia drops—less ammonia now than years back, now that the scooters were eating it and farting out water-soluble compounds less hostile to man. The sun was rising, only twelve hours into the weeklong extension of Ganymede's "day," stretching blue shadows across a flat vast crater bottom. He was in the lead crawler, which except for its creaking seemed suspended, as a sole boat hangs alone on a placid sea and awaits the tide. The crawler rocked the way he imagined ships did, though he had not seen an ocean and never would. Old Matt came forward to get some soup and saw him watching the far rim of the crater come nearer, seeming to rise up out of a blank flatness and throw arms out to embrace the small party.

"You brought the potshotter." Old Matt did not make it a question. He had the quality of knowing the way things would be, no matter how small, so that his questions were just statements that you acknowledged with a nod.

"No good against it," Manuel murmured. "Don't know why I brought it."

"Practice. Always you need practice. The shot will be no use, but the aim is."

Petrovich overheard and called, "Don't tell us you think you get a chance so soon? I am laughing. Only I should be crying."

Manuel said, "Come on. I didn't mean—"

"Sure you did! Ever' boy comes out here, he means to *kill* it. Only, you lissen to me." Petrovich leaned forward, bottle on his knee, the air rank with him. "You'll freeze solid as iron when you see it. Which won't be for long."

"Microsec, maybe," Major Sánchez murmured.

"Right! But lissen. Be lucky if you even *see* it."

"I know."

"It comes, *zap*, it's gone."

Old Matt said softly, "Not always."

"Oh, sure! Sometimes it takes its time, tramples somebody."

"Not what I meant."

"Not true, anyway," Colonel López put in. "It doesn't hurt people on purpose. The statisticians showed that."

"Lissen, it's a lot smarter than those statis—statis—" The green-and-brown liquid had hold of his tongue. Petrovich blinked and closed his mouth and let the smeerlop work on him.

"No sign it's smarter, none at all," Manuel said.

"I think the point is that we are not out here to settle the question," Manuel's father said clearly. He was the leader and it was up to him to put a stamp on the conversation. "We are to test the new mutations, prune them, and perhaps to take some live samples."

"Or dead ones," Major Sánchez said.

"True. Or dead ones. But you all know the Survey does not permit hunting for sport."

"Plenty crawlies," Major Sánchez whispered, so that

the words could be heard but did not have to be acknowledged by the Colonel.

"Crawlers are still needed. There is a lot of rock for them to break down." The Colonel turned to Sánchez. "We shoot only muties, *sí?* Not good crawlies."

"Hey no, I was just thinkin'—"

"Think otherwise," Colonel López growled, and the talk was over for a while.

They went on. Over the ruined, once-jagged ramparts of the ancient crater. Through a wrinkled valley of tumbled stone caught in russet snowdrifts. Across a jumbled plain, still pitted with craters that the thin, warming atmosphere had not yet erased. And finally to the first camp, the boy passing through the wastes as though they were opening momentarily to accept him and then closing behind him, sealing the lip of the world so that in all directions there was only the splotched ice, rocks nested in the hills, and the steady hail and rain that brought to this moon the first hint of what having air would mean, when the humans were through. None of this was strange to Manuel, since he had often thought of it and sensed what it must be like. The camp was a rambling shack, with seams welded crudely and compressors that grunted and whined into life. It took hours to warm it up, and he labored with the rest to patch fresh leaks and fix circuitry, all with the odd seeping sensation of foreknown acts, of living something he already knew. He ate the field provisions the men swore over, but he found them tasty, different from the Settlement ration, gamy with spices the Cong cook put in. He slept in rough-fiber bedrolls left over from the days when they had killed the heat at night to save ergs, and found them warmer than his bed at home. The shack snapped and popped with the cold relentlessly seeping in. He felt it as a weight trying to crush and break through the thin layers men carried with them. It kept waking him. A thin wind moaned at the corners, and he listened for the sound of something else beyond it, and while he strained to hear he fell asleep. After a timeless interval morning came. The men began to grunt and cough and started to finally get up and stamp their feet to bring the circulation back.

2

For breakfast they had sharp-root and coffee and lurkey. The heavy smells mingled, stirring Manuel's stomach until it growled. The lurkey was good—thick slices cut from the old slab at Sidon, meat that still had cells in it from the first turkey to survive the voyage out. For years the original Settlement families from old Mexico had lived on it and very little else.

The men ate with concentration, smacking their lips and hardly talking, until the Colonel started outlining the day's jobs.

Petrovich murmured, "I rather throw sights down on crawlie mutations, Colonel."

Before Colonel López could reply, Major Sánchez said irritably, "You heard what he said last night."

"Uh. Cannot remember it."

"You remember pouring smeerlop down that gullet, eh?"

"Best Swedish stuff. Trivial alcohol content."

Major Sánchez grunted. "Nice word, 'trivial.' Means you got it—*cojones*—you got no worry. If you don't—"

"Lay off him," the Colonel said mildly.

"I don't want Hangover Head here shooting at crawlies around *me*."

"I say it again, for last time." The Colonel's voice had a firm edge to it. "Scooters we're paid to prune, scooters we do."

Petrovich muttered, "Ugly things. Centipede with armor, color of pile of shit."

Major Sánchez said, "Hiruko makes 'em to work, not for pets."

"Ever smell one? Get some on your suit, come back inside, make you puke—"

"You can get sick on your own time," the Colonel said. "We're not paid to criticize."

Major Sánchez laughed. "*Sí*, or we might remember those street cleaners you wanted Sidon to adopt, eh Petrovich?" There was low chuckling around the table. "Big as bear, knock over people to get trash—"

"We can get started now?" Petrovich said abruptly, standing up. "Too much dumb talk."

They spread out from camp, into the territory south of Angeles Crater. The Colonel supervised the sample-taking, which was fine by the men because that was the worst job, dull and methodical, and they got enough of that kind of work at the Settlement. They went after the scooters. BioEngineering had put out a Spec Report on the long crawly things five months back. Scooters had been designed to soak up ammonia-based compounds and digest them into oxy-available ones. They searched out their foul-smelling foods in streams and pools, or chewed ice if they got desperate, and then shat steady acrid streams that Bio said would be good for plants and even animals in the long run. Trouble was, the scooters' long-chain DNA didn't make good copies of itself. They mated furiously. Half of the broods lately were deformed, or demented, or didn't eat the right compounds. Bio was picking up variant, unwanted varieties living off the shit of the others, like pigs rooting through cowflop.

There were two ways to counter that. Bio could make a new third animal that would compete with the warped scooters. That would introduce a further complication into the biosphere, with further unforeseen side effects.

On the other hand, Bio could hire the Settlements to knock off the mutations by hunting. The Colonel had gone through negotiations with Hiruko, the central authority on Ganymede. The bookkeeping between Sidon and Hiruko was complicated. Manuel could remember his father staying up nights at the terminal, frowning and pulling at his mustache and swearing to himself. When the boy saw his father that way it was hard to think of him as the Colonel, a distant figure who commanded an automatic respect in the Settlement. Manuel unconsciously felt that it was his father who fretted and worried late at night, and another figure entirely, The Colonel, who finally made the deal with Hiruko Central. He had gotten a fair price for Sidon to go out and hunt down the mutes. The hunting won because it was cheaper than engineering a third animal.

That morning Manuel went with Old Matt, who was slow and had the patience to teach. A walker dropped them off fifteen klicks from the base shack. They got out in an ice arroyo. They bent over to secure their vacuum seals, and a fog rose around them as the walker thumped away. The thin air was thick with rising orange fumes as the midget sun struck the far wall. There was not much life here, only some rockjaws scraping at gravel. They were like four-legged birds with chisel beaks, pecking away at ice, swallowing automatically, animals like engines, beyond the time-locked dictates of Darwin. They had few defenses against predators; the awkward gray forms did not even look up as the humans clumped by. They scattered, though, when Old Matt scuffed up pebbles; they were blind but could hear dimly through their feet.

Manuel saw the first scooter, but it was all right—normal, a low, flat thing with crab legs and a mouth that was a blur as it slurped at a runoff stream. It ignored them. They marched for an hour without seeing more than gray sheets of rock and ice and a gully scraped out by a fusion crawler years before and now run dry. The hills slumped down and the valley bled away into a plain and there they found a flock of scooters, all furiously sucking at the ponds of condensed vapor far back in the blue shadows. It was a quiet, placid scene. Old Matt pointed. Far away, skittering among the hummocks, Manuel saw pale yellow flat shapes.

"Bring up that potter gun slow. Slant it up and stand fast."

"Pretty far off. I don't think I can hit 'em."

"They'll come to us. Following the normal ones, so they got to pass by over to left. Stand still and they won't skit off."

Sure enough, the low fast forms came, dodging among the normal forms, eager amid the rocks and ice bulges. There were five, all marked a little differently with red and black stripes and dots. They jerked with energy and random momentum.

"Fast evolving," Old Matt murmured softly. "Got their own mating crests—see, on the first one?—and look at the steam rise from that shit of theirs."

It was a pearly pink vapor. "Converting the scooter crap back into ammonia-based?" Manuel asked.

"Or worse." Old Matt eyed them. "You take the last one."

"The lead one's closer."

"Sure. And when they see it fall they'll scatter. Always work from their rear."

Manuel brought the little popper up slowly, so as not to startle them. He aimed, squinted, and got the form in the sights as it ducked and bobbed, snatching at each morsel of excretion. It was disgusting to watch, the boy thought, but when you thought about it everything alive was eating the shit of something else, in the long run.

He fired. The warpscooter crumpled. He shifted to the next and saw it disintegrate as Old Matt got it. Then the group must have heard or felt something because they dodged this way and that, skipping along on their fast little legs, scrambling into the blue shadows. Manuel led one of them and fired three times, kicking up a quick jet of vapor from the ice each time where he missed. He caught the thing just as it got into the shadow of a boulder. The bolt went clean through its brown armor. *Good,* he thought. He swung the gun back and there was nothing left to shoot at. Old Matt had hit the rest.

He felt proud on the long march back to the camp. They got another flock in late afternoon, surprising muties in a gully, but then the mutants ran and got in among the regular scooters and Old Matt pushed the boy's popper aside before he could shoot any more.

"Bio's strict about killing the reg'lars."

"Okay." Manuel walked on, cradling the gun, watching the dumb forms scuttle for cover.

"Safety."

Manuel replied, "I might get a squint at one if it breaks cover."

"It's then, when you're trying for the one extra, that bellies get sliced and feet blowed off."

Meekly he powered down and slipped on the safety, deliberately looking away from the jittering, mindless flock still seeking shadow. He sloughed on, a half step behind the man, through the glinting Ganymede morning, homing on the endlessly beeping directional for the camp.

It was more than a week before he and Old Matt heard the animals. They were out on their own, running flocks of scooters when they could find them, the man teaching Manuel how to move and where the crusted-over deadfalls were that had been hollowed out years before by the fusion caterpillars and how a man could fall through the thin ice and break a leg even in the fractional gravity of this moon. A flock of scooters had sprung up in front of them and the boy had got two of the warped ones—discolored things, ugly, that lurched away and scrambled over the others to get away—before the mutations got in amongst the rest.

"Bad sign. They already know enough to do that."

"Why doesn't Bio program the reg'lars to turn on the muties?"

"Don't want to give them highly developed survival traits. Be just that much harder to kill them off when we introduce the good lifeforms, the ones we want to make the stable ecology."

"Ah, well," Manuel said, full of himself and with an elaborate casualness, "that just makes for more huntin' and—"

"Listen."

Over their short-range came a sputtering, a low murmur, almost blending with the static of Jupiter's auroral belts. Yet Manuel caught the fervid yips and cries of the pack, a chorus blurred but with a high, running keening to it, each voice a distinct animal but each responding with its own fevered energy. He did not need to ask what drew cries from them. He reached down and thumbed on his gun, though he knew it was useless and a mere gesture. But it was important to make the gesture, just as it was to wait breathless and see in his mind's eye what the yelps and grunts and chattering pursued: the thing that moved smokelike through the icefields, running with blind momentum, the shifting alabaster shape. Old Matt had taught him to tilt his gun high and wait, motionless, watching by using his peripheral vision, not moving his head. He stood and tried to sense an expectant tremor, a rumble, some twinkling of the light that would tell him, warn him. The animals were louder now, but not stronger—their cries had risen too high and had taken on a tone of confusion and submission to the inevitable, not tired yet but flagging in some way the boy could not name but felt.

He touched his helmet to the man's and whispered, not awakening the suit radio, "It's coming?"

The blended murmur of the cries peaked without ever resolving into a clear voice, and the sound dissolved as Manuel listened. Old Matt did not answer. He gradually turned his head so that Matt could see his face and he shook his head, no, with a look of quiet watchfulness. The animals were now a dull drone, defeated, fading. Old Matt smiled.

"It never noticed them. It didn't even speed up this time."

"It's here, though! First sighting in—how long?—nearly a year."

"First one we know of. Lots times nobody says anything."

"It's looking for something?"

"Could be. Some mineral it needs to supply itself, regenerate itself, I don't know. Doesn't seem to need energy. Unless it's got a fusion burner inside and filters isotopes out of the ice."

"Yeah, and if it needs something around here—"

"It doesn't need anything that bad." He surveyed the rough valley before them, inert and plain, and looked at Manuel. His worn ortho'd face held large, luminous eyes that moved liquidly. The replacement jaw and cheek were shiny even in the dim sunlight, and his original skin was wrinkled like an old piece of crumpled paper. It was the eyes that seemed most alive in him, least weathered by the long decades that face had endured, the century mark it had passed almost without noticing, the injuries and radiation and the sweat and ache of toil it had taken and survived.

"Truth is, it doesn't need anything. It's trapped here, far as I can tell. No boosters to take it off surface. Can't get into orbit. Must have been hurt a long time ago and now it has to move through the waters under us and across the ice like a man pacing a cell will do, wearing a path in the stone of the floor but not stopping. I'll bet it looks up at the stars and thinks and wants to go up there. But it can't. It's not complete, or else it would. So it wanders. Not because there's anything it needs but because it wants to have a look. See who's new. See what kind of men there are out here this year and what they can do and if there's a servo'd animal or a machine we can put up against it this year that is any better than all the ones it outran or smashed or rolled over year after year before. It's curious maybe, or just keeping track." He shrugged. "But those are ways of talking about it that make snese to us, and one thing I'm sure of: it doesn't make sense. And it won't, ever." The animals were gone now and there was nothing on short-range radio. "They'll run on after it until it sees what they're worth. Then it'll burrow down, drive straight down seventy klicks or more if it wants to, directly into the slush and water that this ice is just the scum of—and that's it. Gone. Until it wants to come back."

When they reached the camp the animals were already there, huddled together as if to keep warm, bunched up against the wall of the shack. They had all come in an hour before, all except for Short Stuff. A gray rain came down and small puffball clouds swept overhead, blown from the warmer regions to the south where vast volumes of methane and ammonia were vaporizing beneath fusion caterpillars. Old Matt squatted beside the mound of animals and touched the yellow ceramic flank of one. They all stirred, scraping against each other, eyes rolling and flecked with blue, and a muttering came from them, growls and whimpers and a low persistent chippering that the boy could not place as coming from any particular animal. They trembled all the same way: Earthlife returned from meeting something it had not known. Two hours after supper, after the whiskey ration was already gone, Short Stuff came scuffling up to the lock entrance and scraped at it. It chattered weakly, forming words in no particular order, thick-tongued and droning: *hurt . . . fast big . . . fire . . . break . . . hurt . . .* Manuel and Petrovich and Old Matt led it into the service shack and stripped the crushed manifold in its left side where something had brushed by—just a glancing and casual blow, not intended to kill or else Short Stuff would not be here.

"Look, see. It tore the flesh," Petrovich said. Blood oozed from beneath the crumpled steel.

"No bones broken," Old Matt said, feeling along the animal's ribs. The matted hair reeked with fear and sweat. Manuel saw that Short Stuff was a small ape, harnessed well into the transducers and servos that engulfed the lean form.

"Lucky to live," Petrovich remarked as he applied locals and patched up the raked flesh, stemming the seeping, wiping away the cakes of dried blood.

Old Matt murmured, "It just got too close."

Petrovich said, "I saw a fastfilm, once. It picked up animals, smashed them down. It will kill."

"Not this time. Not without reason."

The chimp kicked and howled softly, probably from pain, but perhaps also from the memory of running hard and fast at something it could not hope to catch.

Old Matt patted Short Stuff fondly. "He's seen it before. Knew it. Just like a chimp, smarter than most of the rest and thinking himself to be more like a man. When he saw it he didn't wait, or else he'd never got that close. He had to have thought about it a lot and known that one time or another he would have to run toward it and not away like the rest. To be like a man. Even though it was pointless and he would be paying a price." He rubbed and soothed the animal, talking to it softly. The boy helped him fashion a replacement of curved sheet steel and insulation for the rib section.

It was dark when they left the service shack. Jupiter was eclipsing the sun. The small bright orange ball slipped behind the cloud tops of ammonia cirrus and a rosy halo slowly crept around the squat, watermelon-banded planet. Near the poles the boy could see a violet auroral glow, hanging curtains of gauzy light where atoms were excited by downrushing streams of energetic electrons. Across the slowly churning face of the dark world, lightning forked yellow and amber, strokes thousands of kilometers long, bridging clouds and ammonia and water far larger than Ganymede itself. The men stopped and peered upward at the passing of noon in the seven-day-long alternation of sun and shadow that Ganymede kept. The halo shifted slowly, rimming the huge world in diffused, ethereal amber and pink. The view was better here than among the lights of the Settlement and the men paused, watching the slow certain sway of worlds as gravity gently tugged each on its smooth, unhurried path. Then the glow broke free of the planet's waist and became the fierce, burning dot of their sun, bringing a return of noon. They bent their heads back down then and began to think of other things, of rest before the hunting would begin again tomorrow, and scuffed their boots free of ice and dirt before going inside to the rank smell and buzzing talk and pungent cycled air of men.

3

The boy did not see Old Matt leave the next morning, early, while the cooking was still going on and Manuel was cutting onions for the broth.

"*Madre*. That one goes off, says no word," Colonel López said. His stern jaw clenched. "Thinks he is too old for rules."

Petrovich said, "Get himself dead alone. He falls into a gully, no one to seal his suit if it holes."

They hailed Old Matt on directional, but he would not answer. He was making slow but steady progress toward the west, into the rock hills called Halberstam's.

"I could catch up to him," Manuel pointed out, though he suspected that Old Matt could slip away from him in the hills easily enough.

Colonel López made a rough sound of exasperation. "Then we have two missing. No. He has done this before, I remember, on other hunting teams."

"He may lose function in that arm of his," Petrovich said. "Or the face. Could die before we get him back here for the medical."

"That is his choice," the Colonel said. He shrugged.

Later in the day the Colonel said to him, "You miss not going out with Old Matt, don't you?"

"*Sí.*"

"You couldn't show better taste, son. He's the original."

"Then why don't you go after him?"

"I'll do just about anything to keep a man or woman alive out here. Only I won't smother them."

Manuel said nothing. He had seen the hard edge in his father before, but this was the first time he understood it.

Manuel went out with the other teams for the next three days, each morning arising and hoping to find that the old man had returned in the night. Each day the pulsing orange dot of Old Matt's indicator showed him moving in a sweeping pattern of arcs, pausing often, probably to rest. Manuel teamed with Petrovich and then his father and showed the Colonel how he could shoot. They got some variant scooters and on the second day found a new variety of rockeater, one that had taken to drinking from the ammonia streams and not digesting the more difficult stones as it should. The Colonel checked with Bio and they killed the thing. The animals went with the Colonel, so there was a lot of activity that Manuel was not used to on the hunt. The animals would scamper up the ridges and drive down scooters of all kinds, and the men would try to shoot the warped ones before they got away. The third day they nabbed a big bunch of them in a dead-end valley and shot twenty-two mutated forms and three more of the warped rockeaters. Manuel helped gut them for Bio samples. He had gotten five of them himself, and missed only twice. He felt high-spirited on the hike back.

He came clumping into the cabin, hungry, and flopped down on his bunk before he saw that Old Matt was squatting in a corner, passive and remote and spooning soup into his half-metal mouth, grave and thoughtful. Manuel talked to him, asked questions, but the old man answered only in short sentences, or not at all. The men did not bother with him. After supper Manuel was invited into a card game and forgot to talk to Old Matt again, and then got tired and went to his bunk.

The next morning was dim. Ganymede's night was dominated by Jupiter, reflecting sunlight so that shadows were blurred and uncertain. The moon's shadow crawled across the orange and brown bands. Without any discussion Old Matt took him out again. The old man got a two-seater cycle rider and they went sputtering and muttering their way across glassy-rimmed craters and into the Halberstam hills. Manuel had never seen them before. They were new, thrust up by ice tectonics, the great plates shifting and butting against each other like living gravid glaciers driven by the churn of currents deep within the moon. In places crags and jagged peaks of ice split the rock, and then scarcely a kilometer away the battle turned and iron-gray shoulders of an ancient meteorite ruptured a slick sheet of ammonia ice, ripping through to build new heights. There had been no time here yet for the sway of the seasons to freeze and unfreeze liquids in the cracks and cleave rock from rock, popping slabs of it free and then grinding it, pulverizing it through the centuries, down into dust.

Here and there the heat released by the clash had melted ice and now thin rivers carved snaky lines in the rising valley floors. In time there would be cañons and boulders and grit beneath the boots of men. They left the cycle and went on foot into a narrow, snow-choked ravine where icicles dripped and ammonia fog rose in wreaths about them. In the heavy gloom of night, Jupiter-light struck dull amber reflections from snowdrifts. Old Matt stopped, peered ahead. Then he gestured silently, and the boy saw a channel dug through the ten-meter-deep snow, big as a crawler and bottoming out in black-streaked gray rock, scraped and ravaged and bearing on its scoured face the large delta-shaped print. No ruts led away from the deep channel, and the boy could not see how the thing had come and gone and left no trace beyond this. The delta lay in the rock, mute, and he felt a trace of what he had heard in the murmur and cries of the animals as they met it, some of them too for the first time. He looked around the cramped white ravine and felt trapped. He turned uneasily, fighting the sudden leap of fear that there was something, some movement, just behind his back, where he could not see it in time.

"You found this?" he said unnecessarily, just to be saying something and not have the silence.

"No. I saw some ruts over in the next valley. Looked like they came this way. I was taking you there."

Manuel nodded. He felt an anticipation and also a thick dread, a scent in his nostrils like hot copper in the metalworking shops. The smell swarmed up through him and brought a sensation in his stomach and bowels, a tightening, as he saw for the first time the sign that this was a mortal thing, living and actual, not a mere form that lumbered through his dreams and moved in the stories the men told when they were half-drunk and could not be trusted to get it right—not a fragment of his world but bigger than it.

"You think it's still here?"

"Might. The scientists said it stays in a place for a while—searching, they think. Dunno. Maybe it comes to have a look at us, then it goes on."

"Tomorrow, we can all come. Maybe corner it."

He laughed. "Corner it? Might's well trap a man in a box of fog."

"We can *try*."

"Sure. We can try."

That night Petrovich fell into a political argument with Major Sánchez and the two men got loud, the whiskey doing most of the talking. The news had come through that Asteroid Conglomerate United wanted to push development of a petroleum-synthesizing capability on Ganymede, and the moon as a whole had to vote on the measure.

Major Sánchez said it was trouble enough to grow the food for the goddamn 'roids and what did Ganymede get out of the trade anyway except doodads nobody wanted except the townies, and they weren't the ones who'd have to bust their butts building a goddamn petro plant.

Petrovich thought that was stupid and not forward-looking, or did the Major want to forever be buying petro from Luna or even, God-help-us, from Earth itself, paying percentage on percentage for every middleman between here and Brazil?

What-the-hell, Major Sánchez bellowed, there wasn't a liter of petro in the Settlement that hadn't been squeezed out of seeds or stems, it was sure enough all right for their purposes, and if the 'roids wanted higher-quality stuff they could buy it. What'd they need it for anyway, when they used servo'd animals for their work mostly, and animals didn't need lubricants like machines anyway—that was the reason for developing good servo animals in the first place, to save on lubricants out here, as any damn fool knew if he studied any history instead of pigging it up with the smeerlop every night to scramble his brains every minute he was off work—right?

Petrovich opened his mouth to shout back, but his eyes were glazed and he had trouble thinking as fast as Sánchez because of the smeerlop, and at that moment Colonel López stepped in and broke it up, telling them both to get to bed.

Petrovich sat on his bunk and shook his head for a while, muttering, knowing he should sleep but not wanting to seem to be following the orders from the Colonel, and then he saw Manuel and asked in a slurred, gravel voice, "You thinking you hit it tomorrow." When the boy did not answer Petrovich prompted him with "Eh?"

"No point."

"Sure is point. Learn to shoot. Maybe get lucky, hurt it."

"Don' know what to aim at."

"Nobody does. It is round, like an egg. Nothing to fix eye on."

"No, it isn't!" Major Sánchez sprang up. "*Mierda!* It is blocks, three blocks stuck together. The legs they come down from the corners, each block with four—no, not at the middle, so there are eight legs."

"Is round," Petrovich said. "I saw it three, four times. Round and rolling."

"There are pictures! We get back to Sidon, I show you fast-frame; they—"

"It crawls, blind man. And on its belly, not on legs," a voice drawled from the bunks far back. "I seen it drag itself up a sheer cliff using grapplers, just five years back."

The Colonel stood up and waved the voice into silence. "There are many forms. You forget that the cameras showed different results from time to time."

"Each time *I* see it," Petrovich grumbled, "is the same."

Major Sánchez said slyly, "Perhaps the good machine is simply trying to make things simple for you, my friend."

Petrovich grunted in dismissal and rolled onto his bunk. Low talk continued among the bare pipe frames of the bunks, muted now, desultory, amid the stale, sour fumes left from supper. Old Matt had come into this part of the rambling shack to get closer to the burbling heaters, and he sat down beside Manuel. "They argue over nothing."

"Seems to me it's important to know what to look for," Manuel said.

"It changes. Not to confuse us. For itself."

"Should be some vulnerable spot, you'd think."

Old Matt shrugged, his face wrinkling into a fine-threaded map as he chewed on a hemp slug. "There are holes sometimes. A mouth or an ass or nothing we have a name for. It doesn't matter."

"There's got to be something we can do. Those scientists—"

"They are hunters of a different kind. They never knew."

"With e-beams and all those traps—I looked at some of them when I was in Loki Patera—they sure gave it a try."

"They never hemmed it in enough. Tomorrow, if it comes up on us sudden and we box it in—well, sometimes in the past it's not taken the time to burrow down through the ice and get away. Don't know why. So it might go right through us, fast as a bat out of hell. That's when you got to watch."

"What . . . You mean me in particular?"

"Right."

"It would pick me out?"

"Might."

"You mean, I never been here before, an' it knows me anyway?"

"I don't know. But there've been times before, people who were new, and it . . . Look, maybe it remembers everything, never forgets a man or a crawler or an animal or anything. So somebody new comes along, it gets interested."

"Why?"

"It's been here a long time. Millions of years, they say from dating the stuff on the outer moons. Maybe it's bored."

It seemed to the boy that boredom or any other simple

pathetic human emotion was not the way to think about the huge shape, and that its indifference to them meant it shared none of their values or illusions. Old Matt would say no more about it. He just shook his head and told Manuel to get into his bunk early; to rest; and the next day would be soon enough to see.

4

The land was vast and empty beneath the storm that had moved in from the south again, bringing a slow drizzle of methane-cloaked and ammonia-steeped droplets, all swirling in the still-thin mongrel chemlab gas that was the new air. Hovering just above the ice point, the sluggish vapor rolled in—ruddy banks of fog that clung to the sheets of ice as if the wispy stuff longed to return to the original and stable existence it had known for billions of years, to sink down and freeze and rest, and not be tortured by the harsh warmth that men had brought to boil the elements into a blanket of gas, to cloak the old dead world now resurrected. There were thirty-nine men and women on the hunt that day, three having already gone back to Sidon to help with some hydro processing. (Or so they said. Petrovich and some others muttered over the steaming plates of breakfast that the three had been jumpy when they heard about the Aleph, and had discovered the rush job to be done at Sidon awful fast when they'd called home the night before. The Colonel told them to shut up talking about men behind their backs, and sent the two loudest out to flame the night's ice off the crawler treads, a job nobody liked.)

The thirty-nine included some olders, though none who dated as far back as Old Matt, and some men out for a holiday who had never really hunted a lot and knew little more than the boy even now. Still, as they dismounted from the carriers at the foothills of the Halberstams, there was less of the hooting and high spirits and aimless moving about, less arguing over who would carry what and what routes to take into the craggy wastes that loomed above them all. Storm clouds swept the harsh faces of rock and stole warmth from their suits, making a temperature differential across a suit big enough to stress the multiple-ply insulators, so that their seams popped and creaked. They marched. The crawlers and walkers fell behind, waiting at the edge of the glassy, pitted plain as the men climbed up the rugged hills and split into parties that fanned through the skinny valleys and arroyos. Manuel went with Old Matt, the Colonel and nine others, the men tramping stolidly up the veiled valleys, watching for ruts in the snow or scrapings on the outcroppings of ice. They had six animals with them, frisking at the head and tail of the column, pouring forth more energy than the men in their spirited dashes and leaps and continual tangled games of chase and tag. Old Matt struggled to keep up. He puffed along, head up to the sky, face contracted with effort, listening to the light babble of the animals over short-range and the occasional muffled words of the men, and yet the boy could see that Old Matt was not paying attention to the words and yelps but instead was concentrating on something else, turning his head this way and that so that its steel and copper caught the dulled light. Above, stars were hazy jewels lingering above thin cirrus.

Colonel López tracked each party on his faceplate display, ordering them to drop a man into each promising branch valley as they came to it. The hail stopped and then the pall of rain fell below them. The teams made good time despite the deepening blue-green snow as they worked their way higher. In the light gravity they loped easily, hitting the ground in three-second-long strides, their boots clutching the ice or snow as they landed to ensure a purchase. Where an iceslide or crevasse blocked them and they could not leap it by themselves, they powered up their lower servos and, with some effort, made the jump with augmented muscles. The boy panted at the hard places and could not hear over short-range whether the others did too, but he was determined that they would not have to slow for him. The Colonel set the pace and kept a watchful eye on Old Matt, and the boy saw that his father was restraining the younger men so that they would not get straggled out and the old man would not push himself to keep up. His father was like that, gruff and hard and yet forgiving when you were up against your limits.

They surprised some scooters, slurping away with idiot persistence at the ammonia streams. The men picked off the deformed ones, everybody firing fast before they were all gone. There was not much life this high, and pretty soon they saw nothing but rockjaws munching stoically at pebbles and, higher still, crawlies searching out methane-rich ponds, their carcasses puffy and distended with the storage sacs where they would process the carbon-rich residues into better compounds when they hibernated.

The men dropped off singly at each branching of the valley, taking an animal with them, until there were four left. The Colonel waved Manuel forward as they came to a place where the valley wall split as though a huge hand had pried it apart with a stone wedge. Up that divide a shallow ravine worked back among some jagged peaks.

"Satellite time-step map shows that one is pretty clear of slide debris now," the Colonel said. "Lot of rain here last few weeks. Washing it away."

Old Matt caught up to them. "Where's the pressure ridge around here?"

Colonel López glanced to his left, where his helmet flashed the needed plot in contour lines of green and crimson. "Runs down from that crag."

"Think there'll be any slippage?" the old man asked.

"Fracture fault lines fan out to the north. Don't look like any on this side."

"Satellites can't see everything."

"*Sí*. You go with Manuel, eh? Up that cañon. Keep him from blowing his leg off and bringing down a slide on himself."

"Sure."

The two took Slicky with them and headed up the ravine. A small stream tinkled and chimed, echoing from the ice-crusted walls. Rosy ammonia vapor steamed from it. The boy sloughed along, thinking of the crushed steel plate of Short Stuff and of the high keening cries the animals had made before. Melting snow and ice fed the stream and squished under his boots. The man spoke to Slicky and let it romp a bit and then spoke again, and it stopped moving and quivering so much, and fell into step at their heels, the yellow ceramic sliding and clicking now and then as it leaped over a streamlet but otherwise without noise, patient and eager both. Blocks of shagged-off rock had tumbled into the ravine, and now, as they went on, slabs of ice covered the floor, shortening the ravine until it was a trough. Old Matt kept studying the steep snowdrifts and rock walls. He paused, puffing, and said, "Quiet from now on."

"You think . . . ?"

"There will be nothing, not even rockjaws, this high. Anything that moves means something, here."

Manuel nodded. He stamped his feet to warm them. Old Matt popped a vent in his own suit and said, "Take care of this now."

Urine jetted out and spattered on rock. Manuel did the same. He thought it was to save distraction later, but in the stillness of the cañon the crackling and sputtering of the urine as it froze boomed in his ears, and he saw it was to avoid noise at the wrong time.

He asked, "What about suit sound?"

"Nothing for it. Reverse osmosis is as quiet as you can

get. Only thing we could do would be turn off the warmer, and this high your lungs would freeze solid in half an hour."

Manuel nodded. They went on, walking now rather than loping, to keep down the clatter of rocks beneath their boots. Every few minutes his suit would exhale excess carbon dioxide it could not handle and the gas puff would snap loudly as it froze and fell to the ground. Otherwise a strange silence descended over the boy and he heard only his own breathing. His external micromikes did not pick up even a murmur of a breeze; the atmosphere was too thin here to carry enough. He toted on his back a new gun, given him by his father this morning; a double-bore fan laser, used for engineering back at Sidon. He had fired it only once, at a boulder, to learn the recoil and that it pulled to the left a little, as the Colonel had said.

They went two klicks, until the ravine gave out at a tilted sheet of ice, studded with red-gray rock. Old Matt said, "No point going more. Here's where we separate."

"How come? Won't we be safer if we stick—"

"There's no safe or not safe to this. It'll run down two just as easy as one. You go over near that gorge, where the ice turns purple. Keep your back to the gorge. Not likely it'd come at you from that way. It'd have to come out of the gorge itself, and why should it go to that trouble when there's softer stuff up here?"

"All right." The boy hefted the double-bore.

"I'll be a few hundred meters upslope. That way we get two angles on it, probably."

"And if one of us gets hurt, the other likely won't."

"Yeah." The old man peered at him, blinked with the copper eye, and smiled. "Turn off the short-range, too. Sometimes the Aleph, it gives off a lot of electromagnetic stuff. Just noise, the scientists said. I dunno. It'll overload your set, though."

"Okay."

"And stay still."

"And Slicky?"

"He's a porpoise. Wrong instincts for this, never mind what they say about IQ-boosting making them the same."

"He can distract it."

"I kind of think that's what we're all doing, distracting it. At best. All right. . . ." He bent down and told Slicky to take a position downslope of the two of them.

Manuel liked the first hour. It gave him rest and he became used to the utter silence. An occasional faint *ping* came as a grain of dust, falling in from some askew orbit around Jupiter, struck his suit, making it ring. The unending hail of high-energy protons could not reach him, though, through the tight-wound magnetic fields that blanketed his suit, the superconducting coils with their eternal currents brushing aside the deadly sleet. Old Matt had taught him how moving would in turn make magnetic ripples in the iron-rich rock nearby, faint surges that the Aleph could pick up, and so he stood absolutely still. Ganymede was swinging more into the sun now, and as he waited the dawn came on with infinitesimal slowness, gradually brightening the blue drifts of snow and pushing back the shadows. Above, the dark sky absorbed everything and would not yield. This high the atmosphere that man and his machines labored to bring had no effect and the land was as it had been for billions of years, inert and cold beyond any human sensing, yet with slow inevitable forces of its own that thrust up mountains and tortured the ice. It was in the third hour now and he was becoming tired, even though he had his knee servos on lock and was not carrying his weight at all. The boy felt he could sense the potential in the bulging rock beneath him, and the gathering strength it brought to even this high a place.

Only slowly did it come to him that the tremor and silent pressure was not from his thinking but was real, steady. He blinked and the rock was rising, shifting. Old Matt was a distant figure that had long ago blended into the terrain but now was waving, pointing at the bulge that grew in the ice sheet, and Slicky moved nervously, one foot forward and another back as the first crack came, a jagged line drawn quickly across the purple ice, widening even as it spread, snow tumbling in, and then a second crack and a third, as fast as he could see. Rock groaned under him and he brought up the double-bore, but there was nothing to aim for. The land had risen a full meter now. Pebbles and then boulders began to roll, slowly and then faster and then crashing down, smacking the ice and keeping on, some falling into the spreading web of cracks that split and popped and split again, boulders now tumbling into the fissures and wedging there. The growing yawning blackness echoed the emptiness of the dark sky. Manuel turned, holding the useless gun. He leaped out of the way as the rock split under him with a deep-bass snapping around. Old Matt was struggling down the slope, trying to keep his balance. The boy yearned for a target, something to act against. Slicky yelped and chippered and began to run, away from the growing bulge that centered on the triangle made by the three of them.

Manuel stepped cautiously forward, toward the bulge. The land groaned and heaved, nearly throwing Manuel from his feet. He smelled the hot, coppery scent. Fresh gaps raked across the ice sheet and he leaped to avoid one. Slicky ran, its back to them, and did not see the crack coming. Blackness rushed under the slipping, frantic form and in one instant had consumed it, swallowing the steel and ceramic as though it were nothing and then moving on, the cracks stretching down the shallow ravine like ever-lengthening arms. And then—stopped. The grinding hollow noise that the boy had not separated from the other sounds now abruptly faded, and the ice ceased its motion, pausing, and with aching slowness then began to settle, subside, stones crashing again as it tilted, gaps narrowing, the bulge sinking back.

In a few moments it was gone. Manuel stood with his

gun high and ready and waited, breathless, but there was nothing more. The fissures did not close up fully. He was still wary, studying the ground near him, when Old Matt picked his way to him and touched helmets.

"No short-range, not yet," the man said.

"What . . . It, it never showed itself . . . just . . ."

"Sometimes it's that way. It came to have a look."

"But it never came out, never . . ."

"Doesn't need to, I guess. It could tell we were up here and it let us know we had been looked at."

"Slicky."

"It got a morsel. I don't think it came for that. Could be that's what made it break off, even." The old man shook his head. "No, that's probably wrong. The worst thing is to start thinking about it the way we think about everything else. The worst."

"Slicky was trying to get away."

"Right."

They went back down the ravine in silence, the boy's mind aswarm with mingled thoughts and emotions and confusions of the two. Next time he would act differently, do something, find a way—but he could not think of anything he could have done otherwise, and the flat hardness of that fact itself made him feel better. Whether or not he did anything different, at least he was sure there would be a next time. It might come tomorrow or sometimes beyond, but it would come, and in thinking of it he discovered something that absolved him of his fear, for there was no guilt in fearing what was beyond you and ran, blind and remorseless down through the years, shrugging off the mortal weight that a human had to carry. He tasted the coppery scent in his nostrils and knew it and was no longer afraid of that itself.

The reports came in from the other men and animals: plenty of scooters potted at and a rumble felt here and there, but nothing sighted, nothing engaged. He felt good about that too. It was arrogant to think he had been singled out, but he had been lucky—the dumb luck of the beginner. From now on he would not depend on luck. Someday he would see the thing, of that he was now sure. If it could be done by keeping on, then he would see it. Perhaps tomorrow and perhaps next week.

As it turned out, it was more than a year.

PART II

ALEPH

1

Building the biosphere was a long-term task, almost an act of devotion performed for the generations to come, and so it had an ebb and surge ruled by the abrupt necessities of the present. The asteroid economy was expanding and demanded ever-greater supplies of water, food, nitrogen, carbon. The asteroids were rich in metals, but had few of the carbonaceous-chondrite chunks that could make the simple compounds for life. Ganymede supplied those and food, ferried in huge robot freighters on minimum-energy orbits. The Settlements melted ice, separated it into usable fluids, and grew food, all in exchange for industrial goods from the asteroids and beyond. They also supported the labs and outposts around Jupiter and Saturn. So the work was always piling up, there were rush allotments and long hours, and Manuel was of an age now that meant he had to put in a full man's hours even though he didn't have the strength of a grown man. He learned pipe fitting and thermonuclear-hydro plumbing and worked just behind the construction gangs as they raised the new vapor domes. There was little time for potting at scooters, especially since the things were learning to avoid humans and were seldom seen now near the Settlements. The constant proton sleet made the mutation rate high; the rockeaters started showing big inflamed warts, and some began to prey on the jackrabs, finding some chemical addiction to the stringy jackrab flesh, and in turn working mischief with the delicately balanced and still experimental biosphere.

More than a year after his first time, the boy got to go out again on a pruning operation.

Petrovich and Major Sánchez led two separate parties, and they spent a good fraction of their time sitting at a makeshift metal table and playing cards and arguing over which territory to hunt the next day. Manuel realized that it was their arguing, a kind of comfortable trading of insults and timeworn political clichés, that bound them together, and that despite the occasional flare-ups they were good friends. The Colonel just smiled when their sudden arguments flared up. Petrovich had started to develop a potbelly, the kind of protrusion that on a strongly muscled man almost seems to be another source of strength, bulging down and resting on his belt. Major Sánchez made this a point of fun, and the two men spent themselves trying to outmarch or outshoot the other. They made a pair of hand pistols using plumber's lasers and on the hunt would go off together to find scooters or rockjaw-muties and then would pot away at them, betting on the score.

Manuel was glad this kept them occupied, because he wanted little to do with the parties who went after the rockjaws. He had his own ends in mind and the parties made too much noise, were rowdy with the freedom of living under the empty black sky and not having to work, and got a goodly number of rockjaws only because the dumb things could hardly hear and ran only if they picked up the metallic slap and scraping of boots on rock. He told the Colonel and Petrovich that he would rather go after the scooters. There were far fewer of them this year. Fatal mutations had killed many, as Bio had predicted, and there was less ammonia in the runoff now. The theory behind Bio's plan was that the atmosphere and ice fields would change more rapidly than the scooters and crawlies and rockjaws and the rest could adapt. They were temporary, self-liquidating species, designed for transitional jobs. The changing atmosphere and the greenhouse-induced rise in temperature would eliminate them before they became a problem. The final stage, when the atmosphere changed over to oxygen-carrying, would wipe the entire bioslate clean, leaving room for new species, quasi–Earth-like but able to tolerate the low temperatures. Then the entire moon would be farmed, with engineered fauna capable of withstanding high radiation and other threats.

The boy left each morning right after breakfast, shouldering the single-bore laser his father had given him. He would own it all his life and fire it nearly every year (with only one major six-year interruption), because the biosphere always needed pruning, and would replace the stock twice (once because he dropped it to save himself on a ledge of a crevasse) and the lasing tube five times, each time with a higher-power bolt-generating mechanism. For now the gun felt heavy and awkward in his hands, but he knew he would have to master it to have any appreciable firepower at all, though in truth he did not expect that for his ends mere power would make any difference. What he needed now was knowledge. He set out the first day with a cycle rider and went into the Halberstam Hills. He had not told them he would go that far, because he knew his father would not let him, not without more experience. He shot two ugly, mutated scooters that morning. The slowly rising temperatures had scalped the hills of their snow, leaving iron-gray massifs to poke at the banded crescent of Jupiter. He hiked into the hills, loping in long easeful strides, landing smoothly and navigating by the satellite-guide program he had bought for his suit. It took him three hours to find the narrow ravine where he and Old Matt had found the deep gouge in the snow. The ravine was hard to identify now because nearly all the snow and even some of the ice had been drained off by a stream that clattered with stones and had already cut a deep gorge. The rock here was mostly nickel-iron from some ancient meteorite, and it colored the stream a lurid rust. Slides now clogged the ravine. He walked through it three times before he found a slab of rock that looked somehow familiar. Near the base of it he saw the delta-print pressed deeply in, mute and indomitable, a testament to what was a mere passing moment in the movements of the Aleph but which would be here, sunken in hard rock and testifying, he knew, when he was bones and ashes.

On the second day he ranged in the region south of the hills, among the flow plains of purple-orange ice. He was learning the land without knowing quite how, simply by immersing himself in it and getting the feel of the vast flat plains, the hummocked and water-carved terrain, the stress-torn troughs and gorges and cañons where the melting of snow and ice had shifted weight and brought disruption. In one hollow where the thin winds twisted in a perpetual breeze, he found thin sculptures of blue-black ice, taller than a man, wind-carved, spindly, glinting in the wan sunlight.

He came in late that day. His father studied him as he clumped in from the lock, tired and chilled, stamping off the ice from his boots. The shack insulation was poor and the temperature gradient was steep; standing up, you could wipe sweat from your face while your feet went numb. Colonel López got his son a plate of the thick turkey stew with chunks of baked corn in it. Manuel went through the first plate without talking much, just eating with that intensity the young have when the body asserts its demands. He finished and clumped stolidly into the steamy kitchen and came back with a second. He was a few mouthfuls in, going slower now, hunkered down and head bowed over the table, when the Colonel said mildly, "If you're going to look for it you should have some equipment."

Manuel's head jerked up. "How'd you . . . ?"

"I know it is hard to credit, but I was a boy once."

"Well . . . what'd you mean?"

"The thing's got metal in it. The research reports from back thirty, forty years ago say it's most likely iron and copper. Ferromagnetic, anyway."

"Looks like rock."

"Sometimes, *sí*. Others, not." The Colonel's eyebrows rose as he stared off into space, as if remembering. "No matter. Any big piece of iron moving, an antenna can detect it. Fast Fourier components in the magnetic field."

Manuel nodded. He knew "Fourier" meant some kind of frequency analysis. That could pick up when the Aleph was moving. "They ever track it that way?"

"Sure. Never learned much, though. I looked at twenty years' worth of maps once. Big three-dimensional ones, some from back before all the ridgelines and mountains were exposed by the melting. There—"

"Really? That old?"

"Sure. Two centuries ago, Ganymede was smooth. We been melting and gouging, making terrain. Thing is, the scientific types spent a lot of effort plotting where the Aleph went—figured it had a place to hide out maybe, down in the core or something."

"What for?"

"Repair itself. Rest up, maybe. Any—"

"Ha! *Qué gente estúpida!* It doesn't need—"

"I'll thank you to not interrupt your father again," the Colonel said precisely, each word carrying its own weight. He paused, and between the two flashed a challenge, a hint of the tension that was coming into their talk more as the years advanced, but that neither wanted to acknowledge. The boy twisted his mouth and looked away.

"To continue. I studied their maps. The Aleph goes everywhere, lingers seldom. The trajectory, it filled the moon's volume like spaghetti in a bowl, all through. Up to the crust, down to the core, swimming sometimes and running others. No sense to it."

Manuel's expression tightened. "No help in knowing that."

"My point is the method, not the results. They followed its movements with satellite triangulation. Detecting the ripples of magnetic fields as it passed."

"I don't know as I want to track it."

"No, but I want you to know when it's around."

"How?" Manuel went back to chewing, more pensively now, thinking.

"Carry some loop antennas with you."

"Weigh much?"

"Five kilos, maybe."

"How'll an antenna tell the difference between me, walking, and anything else?"

His father nodded with grudging respect for the boy's technical sense. "You have to stand still and take a reading. Squirt it up to Satellite; they'll process it."

"Uh-huh." He went to get more coffee. When he came back, his father had unpacked a locker from the equipment room and was laying out some rifle antennas on a mess table.

"You had this all ready."

"*Por cierto*. Brought it out from Sidon."

"I'm that easy to read, huh?"

"At times."

"Goddamn, I can't do a single thing without—"

"Son, you talked of little else these months. I do not want you to think you must sneak off and do it. And your mother, she is very concerned." He patted Manuel on the shoulder gingerly, defusing the tension between them with the gesture, reminding them both of the short time ago when they had wrestled on the living-room carpet, when physical contact between them had none of the edge it carried now. He smiled, his lush black moustache catching the light. "Every boy knows he is immortal, but his parents, they are not so sure."

Manuel nodded. His irritation at sharing this dissipated. He listened carefully to the description of how the directional antennas worked, how you had to keep the impedance matched when you took them from the warm cabin into the cold of the plains, how the induction coils could freeze up on you if you kept them on the shaded side of your body for a while. Petrovich volunteered some advice, and some other men picked up the antennas idly, as if remembering something they had felt and done long ago, and then put them back down and returned to their card games or arguments or simply to drinking their throat-searing ration around the heater, staring at the blue-white filaments that glowed like the center of a star.

He went out with the gear the next day, and the next. He ranged to the south, where he surprised a flock of mutant crawlies and got most of them before they could scatter. The antennas worked all right, and Satellite Relay gave him two-second response. But he detected nothing moving under the wrinkled hills. He was learning the small tricks and lore of stalking, absorbing it without thinking. He could tell now at a great distance if a small, skittering form was a mutant, or if a blur of tracks made by passing rockjaws was an hour old or a week, or whether something was hiding in the lee of a rock outcropping, where the ruddy snow gathered. His suit made little noise, and so he became used to the eternal silence of the moon's rawness, marred only by the thin whisper of winds that were slowly claiming the land. A week passed. He returned to camp later and later, knowing the men were watching him with a certain nostalgic affection, seeing him shuffle in each time with a report of how many scooters or crawlies sighted, how many slain, all for the Bio update, though knowing that the central fact would go unmentioned because there was nothing to say about failure. Decades of research had shown that the Aleph might come to a hunting zone because of the increased activity, but it was a weak correlation and many doubted it. The boy might go the rest of his life without his luck turning.

One late afternoon he came in early for the first time, toting the antennas listlessly, and passed by a walker where Old Matt was replacing a blowoff valve. Manuel waved to him silently and had turned away when the man said quietly, "I don't think that's the way."

Manuel whirled, something unleashed inside him, and said, "How come? Just the looking can't change what it does."

"Maybe so. I'm not so sure."

"Well, my father says he picked it up three times this way, when he was trying. Three times."

"And saw it, too."

"*Sí,*" Manuel said, his conclusion stolen.

"Those antennas, they've got resonant frequencies themselves, you know. Something wants to find out if they're around, it can send out a little signal. If your circuit starts to ring, that's a giveaway."

"Why'd it do that?"

"*Why* isn't the right question. No point in asking that. Maybe it got used to those scientists poking at it with those antennas and beams and so on. Got tired of it, even. So it's not interested in that."

"You don't know that."

The man's lips formed a wry expression Manuel could not read, with some amusement in it and a certain strange sadness too. "You're dead right. I sure don't."

Old Matt said nothing more, and the boy stood there awkwardly, not wanting to go on inside. The man did not go back to the valve job either, so the two of them just waited, the boy staring down at his boots and tucking his hands into his pouchpockets. When he saw Old Matt was not going to say anything no matter how long the silence went on, he looked up and murmured, "You think maybe it's watching anyway."

"Could be."

"I don't . . . don't know . . ."

The man said firmly, "I don't want to tell a boy to go against his father's advice. You know that."

"Sure."

"And you're right. Nobody's sure of anything in this and never will be." He leaned against the big legs of the walker, bracing his bootheels on the waffled stepping pads slick with ice. Ganymede was coming out of its long murky night, and the camp—the big rambling shack, the walkers and cycles and crawlers parked every which way, the discarded manifolds and cowlings from repairs, the stunted prickly antenna tower, all collected here in a clump against the spreading cold wilderness that stretched to all horizons—seemed flat and insubstantial in the twilight, unreal. *Resonant frequencies. Ringing circuit coils*, the boy thought.

The man pursed his lips, metal shining. "Your choice, m'boy."

"Guess so." He squinted at the old man, who seemed now to seep into the dusky seamless wilderness and smile fondly out from it, leaving for the boy the next step.

He was one of the first ones out the next morning, loping into a light, misty dawn as the sun broke over the far range of hills, stretching blue shadows on the mathematically flat plain below the cabin. He went twenty kilometers without needing to consult his faceplate map to find a way through the rutted valleys and fresh gorges of the continually working land. He left the antennas in a hollow, a dark depression on an otherwise unblemished blue-white mesa. He felt freer as he loped steadily along, coasting on his long parabolic arcs which gave him a good view of the terrain ahead, making better time without the long rifle antennas. He moved with graceful speed but quietly, landing solidly well free of rocks that could turn beneath him and start a clattering slide. He surprised flocks of scooters and bunches of the stolid rockjaws, picking out the muties as he skimmed over their confused flight, aiming and firing by well-learned habit now, almost casually. He had worried once, back at Sidon, about the ethical matter of killing, especially considering how many people had strong views on vegetarianism (including his mother, who sniffed and obviously withheld comment whenever he ate real meat). He had finally settled his mind when he realized that these beings were inventions pure and simple, not things brought out of the matrix of a world on equal terms with man, with equal ancient origins, but made fresh and sometimes badly in a test tube, engineering miracles on a par with walkers or shuttleships, running well for a while and then breaking down, for that was the way the boy thought of mutation.

The leaving of the antennas was an act of surrender to the emptiness of this world and what it had to yield of itself. He went forward, carrying his fear—for his father was wrong, and his mother; he now felt fear as a presence which should be endured, and in that had left behind the essential state of boyhood. Yet he was without real hope.

He went that way for three days. Each was the same, and he fell into a kind of rhythm of searching, potting at the muties when he saw them but not now seeking them out with craft. By noon of the third day he was further from the camp than he had ever been. He had taken a cycle for the first fifty klicks, both because the area was pretty well picked clean of muties and because he wanted to get free of the chance encounters with other parties. He knew there was no place more likely for the Aleph to turn up than any other, but he felt that fresh terrain was better, somehow. He had already relinquished what he could, and now it was a matter of patience, the running out of the odds. He loped steadily through cañons and river valleys, over low mesas studded with boulders, across kilometer-wide sheets of ice as markless and fresh as if made yesterday. The rhythm of his running absorbed him and he gave himself over to an endless course of ice and snow and rock, all flooding beneath him as he soared and landed, perpetually in an onward-pressing tilt. He stopped only when a comfortable fatigue came into his legs. He found himself in a gorge that played out into an alluvial fan of pebbles and ice chunks, newly swept down from a jagged ridgeline. He recognized nothing around him that corresponded to the faceplate map. He took a leap as high as he dared, but saw no prominent landmarks that would help. It was a matter of pride that he should learn the land, because satellite systems could not always be doing location fixes for each person on the surface. Old Matt had taught him that, and had talked about the days when men first moved on Ganymede and you could wait an hour for a directional fix from the overloaded systems. He started to backtrack, then, to learn this new territory, pay more attention, not let himself get caught up in the endless hypnotic rhythm of the open vastness and his progress through it. Yet in that lay his own transition, for it was in the slow backward trek that he sensed something he could not name and which caused him to slow his pace, to pause in his loping and look out over the yawning vistas of plain and ridgeline. At one outthrust arm of rock he stopped, panting, blinking back sweat. He vented his urine sac, the thin yellow stream sputtering and foaming green as it struck a slab of ammonia ice. He looked down, muzzy-minded, and saw a few meters away in faceless rock the sunken delta print. He did not move. He looked up, slowly and without hope, and saw ten meters beyond another delta impressed upon the pitted iron-gray stone. Looking beyond, he saw the next one and with it a rut carved deeply, slicing down a meter into the rock and scooping out a boulder-sized volume. He went forward, counting—three, four, two together, another—and each had a burnished brown scar around it, as if cut by flame only a moment before, the marks seeming to come out of nothing as he trotted after them, panting, pulled forward, gasping almost as though his suit yielded no more air, up a fan of slide ice and onto a slope—where he slipped in gravel and almost lost the trail. He struggled up and onto a ledge, then over that into a clear spot of barren rock and purple ice, rushing now, breathless and aware of the utter silence around him, his isolation, a black infinity above and no shelter anywhere; and that was when he saw it.

The thing came out of a sheer cliff of stone. It was alabaster in parts and in others oozing an amber, watery light that refracted through his helmet. The ground trembled and the cliff face fractured into thousands of facets as the thing worked its way out, turning by some unimaginable means and groaning, working against the rock that did not confine it but only supported. Splinters of light broke from it, and a harsh rasping rattled up through his boots. It was big—how big he could not say, because here perspective was lost, and he could not pull his eyes away to compare it with anything as shards broke from the cliff and rained down before him, sharp flakes glinting as they turned in the yellow sunlight. It moved up the vertical face and outward at the same time, not struggling but coming steadily, without haste, now suspended above the drop by means he could not see, its form still hard to make out because it reflected the new biting sun into his eyes and carried in its bulk a restless blue glow that fogged the air nearby. It stopped. He had the distinct feeling that it was looking at him, had meant to study him in just this way. This lasted only an instant. Then, so quick his eyes overshot and he could not be sure how it happened, the Aleph was gone. A blue steam churned the air, crackling with phosphorescent orange flakes. He thought it turned and reentered the pitted rock, but a moment later when he tried to recall the act, it seemed that perhaps it had simply faded into the gray mute face, gliding backward into parting rock, with a final crack and groan of weight released. The damaged cliff remained, its oval wound like a screaming mouth. Stirrings trembled up through his boots. He began to breathe again. Only after a long moment in the absolute silence did the boy realize that he had not even raised his gun to it.

2

They returned to Sidon Settlement four days later. The boy was glad of it. He needed time to think and feel his way through that momentary but powerful contact, coming the way he had always known it would, with him alone and confronting the thing without moving, riveted in that single arching instant when it revealed itself, as it had shown itself before to countless men and then gone on, unconcerned, oblivious of the puny attempts to even momentarily deflect it from its unknown course. Manuel needed time, and his father understood that, just as he understood why his son had discarded the antennas. Manuel had forgotten that his calls for interpretation to the satellite system would be billed to his family's account. The Colonel saw the falloff in use and knew, without mentioning it, why it was necessary to the boy. This was a time to ease up, let go, in the rearing of a boy, and from now on the loosening would be more important than the constraints. "Don't let it go to your head," he told Manuel one evening over supper, after his wife had gone to her work shift. "That thing doesn't care about you. It won't reward you when you take risks. It is simply indifferent. That's the fact about it that most never learn. They hate it and fear it and finally ignore it. Because of that. It would be easier if it hated us. Maybe even if it hunted us. But it doesn't care. Remember."

Manuel knew his father was right, but that did not change how he thought about the hunt, or about the huge chunky shape that still swam and towered, absolute and luminous, in his dreams. The form would return to him in sleep every few weeks. He would waken early, sweaty sheets twisted about him in his narrow bunk, the ventilator whirring patiently, and drift up from muzzy lands where the shape always waited, knowing he would come again. Lying there, halfway into the world, he could not fix the form of it in his memory. He relived the momentary brush, and at the center of it was a blank, a space filled with color and sound but no residual image. He knew now the reason Petrovich and Major Sánchez and the others quarreled over this, for he too had only an impression, a faint memory of darker places in the sides and a muscular, ponderous weight. This puzzled him, and he finally went to Old Matt to ask about it.

The old man lived in back of a machine shop on Tunnel D, in an old storage room he had claimed because nobody wanted it. He did odds jobs around the Settlement now, light manual labor, and when his ortho'd arm kicked up he made up his labor increment by contracting himself out, or putting in time at computer inventory.

The room was cluttered and dim, packed with equipment older than anything Manuel had ever seen. He wondered if any of it worked. Old Matt sat Manuel on a creaking cot and poured cups of strong tea. "It looked long, kind of tube-shaped to me, all the times I saw it."

"Petrovich said it was like an egg."

"Petrovich says lots of things."

"Some of the men, Flores and Ramada, say they saw it like a tortilla, flat and saucer-shaped."

"They had been at the smeerlop, I remember that time. Lucky they didn't blow off a leg, the way they were."

"The scientists, their pictures—they show it in chunks. But long, as you said."

"They would know more than I. They had the cameras."

"Were there any mouths or ears on it?"

"Why? What does it matter?"

"We should know as much as we can," Manuel said indignantly, his voice rising.

"Pointless knowledge, unless there is a way to use it." The man slurped at his tea and smacked his lips, relishing it. Manuel had noticed that he always took a long time over his food and concentrated on the flavor of it. Now Old Matt's coppery, grainy eye squinted at Manuel, as if sizing him up. "We haven't got the tools to make use of what we already know, I'd say."

"Like what?"

"It's too fast for a man. Too big, too. Only servo'd things could stay with it, catch it."

Manuel asked wonderingly, "Use the animals?"

"That's what dogs used to be *for*, boy."

"Do the dogs know that?"

"Somewhere back in the brain they must. Far back, after what we've done to 'em."

"We could train them!"

"Maybe."

"What about The Barron?"

"Maybe."

"Next pruning operation, we'll go out and—"

"If they let me."

"Why wouldn't they? And who's 'they,' anyway? You can do what you like. It's a free Settlement."

"I can't keep up the way I used to. The others, they don't like hanging back, waiting for me."

"You can help me train The Barron. That'll do more good than just fast running."

Old Matt smiled. "Sure. Might help."

"Good!"

They worked with the animal in the hills beyond

Sidon. The Barron had a lot of the old instinct left, buried deep in the genes, locked into a time-honored arrangement of long chains of enduring carbon and phosphates and hydrogen. It fetched sticks and chased little servo'd imitation rabbits Old Matt made up for it. Manuel found from the old file on The Barron that it had been a bloodhound—a piece of good luck—and within a week he had it baying as it scrambled over rocks and snow after the fleeing cottontail rabbit-robo. When it caught the thing it bit down and yelped in surprise at the metal and ceramic, expecting juicy flesh well laced with a prey's adrenaline. It became, through Old Matt's patient training and the boy's energetic urgings, a fleet-footed dart that careered round the hills in a steady, almost automatic lope, scattering rocks as it veered, doggedly—Manuel had to look up the word; it was ancient and long out of use—baying and wailing and claiming dominion over the vacant lands and all the mechanical rabbits they served up to it.

Colonel López viewed this with a distant amusement, until it occurred to him that Bio might like a way to delegate the pruning operations to animals, especially the servo'd hounds. He did not like the idea. He was glad to find that there were few hounds among the animals, not nearly enough to turn over pruning to them alone. Still, the next year Hiruko Central mandated that they use The Barron and a few others, in league with men.

Manuel didn't like it. The Barron was his now, his and Old Matt's, in the old sense that dogs belonged forever to the men who trained them, and nobody was going to change that. Hiruko Central had ordered the pruning, this time from a cabin seven hundred klicks from Sidon. The boy was grateful to get out again so soon, to spend weeks in the wild beyond the grinding labor of the Settlement. The base camp was much like any of them, crude and hastily thrown up, first as an emergency station a century before and then as an occasional layover spot for prospectors and now finally as a temporary set of rambling shacks barely able to withstand the pressure differential, with wheezing pumps and sparking generator and a fusion tank that shuddered and burped and kept you awake unless you were pretty tired. He was glad of the chance, and doubly glad that The Barron gave Old Matt a new leverage with the other men, who now grumbled to themselves but held their peace when the old man was the last in the column to climb a ridge or finish shucking off his ice-caked leggings. They scared up big flocks of rockjaws and scooters. There were even a fair number of crawlies, still living on the now-vanishing methane in the swollen streams. The crawlie flocks followed the big, lumbering fusion caterpillars, sucking up the methane that burbled and effervesced from their exhausts. There was a goodly fraction of muties among them, and the men laid ambushes for them, waiting in box canyons, knowing the muties would be the first to run. Evolution had already taught them that they were different, vulnerable, mercilessly tracked and killed—and as always, the hunters credited themselves with a prowess and valor they had not earned in this wasteland, for in the end they were challenging only their own products, their own genetic legacy to the barren moon; there was no deep and natural antagonism between them and the scuttling spawn they had engendered, no fine-honed instincts of hunter and hunted that might have made even the huge advantage of firearms indecisive, as it had once been back in an old lost time on Earth.

The boy hung back from this and used The Barron whenever he could. The dog that was buried far down in the mechanical augmentation and intelligence-modification could sense his steady hand, his reassuring voice—deepening now, becoming more nearly a man's—and gave itself over to the pursuit of the muties, following the old knowledge that came welling up within it. Manuel had gone to Bio, interrogated its compfiles, and worked, under Old Matt's tutelage, to find the patterns in the foraging of the muties. From the data came likely sites to find them, clustering points where the warped and evolving forms met to mate or feed or be together, for mutual defense or simple dim comradeship.

The dogs did well, particularly The Barron. They ran with a taut eagerness and never tired. The old man and the boy, with The Barron and two other servo'd hounds, surprised flocks of muties in arroyos, streambeds, gorges, and water-hollowed caves, killing them with quick hot bolts that cracked in the thin stillness, taking no pleasure in the act of finality but firmly asserting their dominion over what they had made. Manuel tolerated this, learned from it, and bides his time. It was for him training, an exercising for the bigger things which would come in time. He found the new territory far from Sidon no different: vacant and demanding, yielding itself to the same skills he had wrested from the land. He was now as competent as many men in the party. He could track the blurred markings of the flocks, pick up over his micro-mikes the distant hum and murmur of their feeding, know which calls they made in the mating and which odd *chirrup* or *screee* was that of a mutie and not a norm.

He knew, too, the small scratchings and snow ruts of the Aleph. He would never forget the delta-print, but it was the telltale collection of repeating ruts and scrapes that told more about the movements of the thing. He learned the deep incision it made before lofting itself up onto a sheer rock face, the long, skinny, wavering trail it left in ice, the splashes of brown where it burned its way through rock, the way it gouged the land in trenches where it feasted on some mineral it wanted. (The moon was acne-pocked with such marks. An old statistical paper he found used the frequency of such scars to judge how long the thing had been mining and scouring the wounded face of Ganymede, and came to a conclusion that was obviously wrong: 3.9 billion years, a number pressing on the very age of the solar system itself, older than Earth's own biosphere. The alien artifacts buried deep in the outer Jovian moons were scarcely a billion years old. Occam's razor led many to reject this method of dating. The Aleph was too similar to the other artifacts—except for the fact of its movement, its life, its motivating power and response. They dismissed the doubtful dating method. Until something could blast a fragment from the Aleph to test its isotopic abundance, its age would remain a conjecture.)

It occurred to the boy that the Aleph had known this moon far longer than man had even had a rudimentary self-awareness, and yet had left the land intact all this time, merely taking from the terrain what it needed and letting the ceaseless butting of iceplate tectonics replace and heal the scars, never trying to convert it into something it was not, as men did. Whether this made the Aleph better or worse than mankind was not a question to him; it was the simple, immense fact of the difference that mattered. He found the delta mark twice in the new territory, once on a rock wall and again in a crevasse where a scooter had fled. He had assumed now, lacking much true experience, that he would see it only by himself, in some catechism between them. This was an arrogance of youth. His father, sensing without concretely knowing, saw that the boy would have to go on believing it for a while. He let his son have more slack, allowed him to go out on two- and even three-day treks with the old man and the dogs, sleeping overnight in their suits with a generator lugged along to keep their reserves high, seeking the flocks of muties in nominal fashion but, every man knew, waiting solemnly and without great hope for something more.

It came fleetingly at first. The two of them were resting, panting after a pursuit of scooters across a dry plain, at the funnel mouth of a cañon. Old Matt saw it first, crossing three klicks to the north across a narrow neck of the cañon. It did not ride over the jumble of boulders and jagged ice that jammed the point, but instead tunneled through the tangle as if a straight line were to it no trouble, unmindful of the grinding rasp of immense wrenching that it brought and that ran up the legs of the two even at this remove, a rattling of rock giving away and splintering with a thousand small crackings as the shape passed through. Old Matt had shouted—the boy had not expected that—and they set off, the servo'd dogs speeding ahead, crisscrossing cañons and ravines and arroyos in pursuit, clattering and tumbling down slopes, leaping high over outcroppings of rusty rock, feeling the shuddering slow vibrations the Aleph made as it crashed through obstructions, pausing to cut a trench and devour some lode of mineral and then lumbering on, not fast but deliberate, leading the yelping dogs and sweating, panting men as though it knew how to pull them in its wake, always seeking. The other parties were too far away to call in time, and the boy did not want to, anyway; in fact, he was even then sure that with Old Matt present the thing would elude them. He still unconsciously assumed his solitude was necessary, and so was astounded when, as he loped along a ravine, an ice floe exploded with a roar, showering fragments that tumbled glinting in the piercing sun, and the snout of the thing thrust out, turned away from them. He had to tell himself it was not a face—the jagged lines, the sawtoothed mark like a shark's smile—and he saw clearly the holes aft, a full two meters across. He memorized it this time, ready despite his shock. The dogs surged forward at the first dull splintering of ice and leaped after it. It labored away from them, the shape of it shifting in the mind of the boy and of the old man as well, and Manuel thought, *Big. Too big,* even as he ran flat out after it, drawn forward. It turned. This was a recognition that only later struck the boy, but it stopped the dogs dead still for an instant to see the thing grind against shattered ice and swerve, rising. The boy put on a burst of speed and caught up to the dogs, all but The Barron, which had paused only an instant and now, the boy saw, was not going to stop or even slow down. It rushed straight at the thing without plan or true anger, but with ancient instinct, sure of its master behind it, running out of old imperatives born on dusty plains billions of miles beyond. The boy cut in his augmentation. He ran with aching legs after The Barron's high keening cry, into the face of it—beneath the blocks of glowing alabaster and depthless amber. He rushed under bulky, ridged things like enormous treads.

The Aleph moved. The Barron barked and leaped against a crystalline slab, smacking into it, falling and floundering and rising again, furious but aimless. Manuel felt magnetic fields seize at him. Diffuse forces clutched and tugged, seeming to thicken the air in his chest. He ran after the yelping dog, head low, and the ground wrenched under his feet. Above, a hexagonal pit in the side dilated. In its blue depths he saw movement, deliberate and carrying weight, like huge stones moving inside. It moved. Chunky blocks came smacking down, groaning, sending out forking white ray patterns in the ice under the boy. Cracks tripped him. The hexagonal opening turned abruptly black and squeezed down to fist-sized. He snatched at the dog and caught it, then lost it, then snagged a leg again, and was under the shadow of the thing now as it reared up—smelling, he sensed, of burning brass—towering as he had dreamed and thus familar, any sound it made lost in the hysterical cries and yelps of the dogs. He closed his eyes and pulled back on The Barron. When he opened them, it was . . . gone. It had moved in a blur, into a bank of pink snow, Old Matt told him, faster than an eye could follow.

Again the boy thought, *I didn't raise the muzzle of my gun to it*, and this time he knew why. If he did that, it would put him in the same class as the other legions who had gone up against it, generations that had plucked and shot to no effect. The Aleph would think of him that way; and worse, he would too.

The Barron wailed and struggled against the boy. Old Matt talked to it, and after a while the dogs quieted down and they could go on.

"That dog's got everything a dog can have," Old Matt

said, "but maybe this needs more than a dog can give. Even a hyped-up dog that can do arithmetic."

He shook his head, and the boy remembered that Old Matt came from a time when animals weren't like this and lived only on Earth, where they had their old roles and were being squashed down into extinction, before the augmentation came along.

Manuel saw then that he had not found the quality that would make these times different, and single him and the dogs out from all the scientists and hunters who had gone before. There was something more needed. The Barron and, in fact, any dog would need a certain foolish bravery, yes—but more too; and the boy did not know what that thing was.

3

Five months after Manuel's second encounter with the Aleph, a rockhopper changed the fundamental economic balance of the outer worlds. She had been drifting from chunk to chunk in the asteroids, checking known sites to see if she could turn up traces of iridium or platinum. She was a marginal operator. There was no prior claim on the rocks she visited, because they were worthless—jumbles of iron and other cheap metals. She found a cleft on asteroid MKX 349 that ran deep, and, curious, worked her way down it. She took her core sample there, boring farther in. Less than a hundred meters in, she found pure carbonaceous chondrite.

MKX 349 was moderate-sized, 9.6 kilometers mean radius. By some quirk of its formation, it had a sheath of low-grade ore wrapped completely around a core. That was why the immensely valuable center had gone undetected. There was enough carbon, hydrogen, and oxygen there to supply all the asteroid community for decades. They would no longer have to pay to have it shipped slowboat from Ganymede. They still needed food, but the loss to Ganymede was about 30 percent of their total export.

The Settlements were big farms which had made a steady profit from food, selling their already-separated fluids as a lucrative sideline. That trade trickled to nothing within a year of the MKX 349 discovery. Along with it went the little extras the Settlements bought to soften their lot. They still ate well, but did without the latest 3D programs, Lunatic fashions for the women, and carbide-stressed additions to their tunnel-homes.

The long-term prospects were worse. With MKX 349 to mine, the McKenzie asteroids planned to begin large, whole-world farming. Whether they could compete with the Settlements would hinge on economies of scale and how well the Ganymede biosphere worked. Economists predicted a protracted struggle, decades long. The Settlements had the early advantage, and there were fair odds that they might be able to knock the McKenzies out of business if they improved their own profit margins quickly. Everyone knew this, and prepared.

"It's not a matter of working harder," Colonel López told his son, "it's working smarter."

"Don't see why that means deffies."

His mother looked up from her threading. "I do not like to hear that word in our home."

The Colonel said sternly, "They are *not* deformed. They are men, women, children who have been unlucky. They were badly injured. Some even died for a while."

"They're in boxes," Manuel said sullenly.

"Servo'd, yes."

"Like animals."

His mother said, "I do not want my boy to think of animals when he sees them. Suppose it was your sister—remember when she broke her leg on the tractor? Suppose it had been worse? She might be servo'd. And you would call her that name?"

Manuel pressed his lips together and said nothing. His mother spoke quietly, but for her to say that much meant a lot. He had better cut his losses and not mention the deffies again. Anyhow, he didn't have to work with them. They were better than animals, faster too, and worked by themselves, the Major had said. He resolved to ignore them.

As it turned out, he couldn't. One drew assignment in the same tunnel. That was not so bad, even though when it worked inside there was a rank smell from it unlike any animal he had ever known, and far worse. Even that he got used to. Then he got a call on his morning shift and was told to help out with a special job, this time outside, on the surface.

There was a carry-module standing on a splash-melted landing grid, the last of a cargo run from Hiruko Central. Old Matt was there. He waved Manuel over to the side of the module. The boy said, "We got to move that; I'll get the forklift from—"

"Come here."

There was a network of bars on the far side of the module. Manuel bent down and peered in and saw something red and gunmetal blue and coming at him fast. It was already in the air when he bent down, and it crashed into the bars. The whole module rocked. The bars of the lattice—which the boy saw were of steel, and a good idea, too—rang with the impact. Then it was down, scrabbling, and abruptly smashed into the bars again, without seeming to have taken any time to gather itself. It growled or spoke—he could not tell—and thrashed against the bars. Two blue servo'd hands gripped the steel and tried to tear it free. The thing grunted and heaved against it for a moment and then abruptly let go and crashed into the bars again, furious without letup.

"Back off," Old Matt said. "Give it a rest."

They walked away, followed by the steady, heavy thumps, the module shaking each time. "What *is* it?"

"Human. Badly damaged in some accident—up there." Old Matt gestured toward the pinpoints of orbiting stations. "Been years getting it this far."

"A *man*? I don't—"

"Human. Could be a woman. Nobody at Hiruko said. He, she, *it* lost a lot of the left brain in the accident. Can't talk. Sure can move, though."

"What's it like *that* for?"

"How'd you like to wake up, find out you're going to be a side of meat inside a box all the rest of your days?"

Manuel grimaced. "Why in hell's it here?"

The old man shrugged. "The Colonel made a deal. Traded some equipment we hardly use anymore, or can't fix. Got back from Hiruko a bunch of work animals, and this."

"*That's* not going to work. Kill, maybe, not work. And a human. I—"

"Don't try to think it through just yet. Make out like it's an animal and you won't be so far from the truth."

"Why'd they let it live?"

"Don't know. Medicine does a lot of funny things. I do know you can't let a man die just because he's not got enough of a brain to suit your taste. They do that back on Earth, but not out here."

"Maybe we should too." The crashing had slowed but not stopped.

"Not when they're useful. The Colonel, he thinks we need all the hands we can get. Boost productivity."

"That thing's not useful."

Old Matt's face crinkled and his eyes moved liquidly, studying the boy. "I figure it may be important to us."

"How? You'll never get the murder out of that thing."

"Maybe. Your father gave me the job because he feels it's a long shot. Could be. But I figure the two of us can do it."

"How?"

"Watch."

Each day for three weeks they suited up and went out to the module and fed it. Manuel would climb up on the top and slap open the little door there and throw the thing's food down. It couldn't jump that high, but each day it tried, and when it failed would commence slamming itself against the bars again, adamant and tireless. It growled less as time went on, but it never let up its hammering at the walls. After three weeks it stopped leaping at him. It still stood watching, as if trying to figure out a way to get up there but knowing that it should save its energy when it would do no good. But then it would crash again and again into the bars as soon as the door clicked shut, as if to say, *See. See.* Manuel peered down at it in the brief moments when it stood still, glaring up with two wide-spaced black eyes. It was a hodgepodge of parts attached to a gunmetal-gray carapace, bigger than any servo'd animal he had ever seen and powerfully made, bristling with heavy motors and big treads and bulging manifolds. He could not imagine a man or woman deep down inside the thing, tapped into the metal world that had swallowed it whole, raging in an awful silent pocket somewhere. He waved to it once, and for the first time in a week it jumped then, stretching itself, arms tearing at the air, black eyes glaring. Yet after he had hastily—despite himself—slammed the door shut, the thing did not throw itself against the bars. It stood, staring out as the two men walked away.

Old Matt started to starve it then. He cut the ration to half and then a third. After two weeks it lay on its side and did not get up right away even when the food and water came. A week more, and Old Matt took a tractor beam in his best hand and made as if to go inside.

"Wait!" Manuel said. "I'll get my father and some of the men—"

"If it hits me that'll be too late already. Just slam the door after me and get back."

Manuel did as he was told. The old man stepped into the big module from a side portal. The thing studied him but did not move. The black eyes followed Old Matt, gazing with an impersonal opposition to everything, silent. Old Matt approached and tapped the ice-crusted carapace with the tractor rod. No answering rustle from inside. But the thing ground its treads into the ice, shattering a crusted stump, letting the sound speak for it.

The next day Old Matt put his gloved hand on the carapace, closer to the thing. On the third day he beckoned the boy inside. They rested hands on it and Manuel felt a faint tremor, a curiously high kind of vibration without words or form to it but going on, making a cadence that was not that of some machine part but instead carried a feeling of sorrow and anger and yet wanting, too.

It was useless to try to talk to it. The medicos at Hiruko had tried. It wouldn't answer. One of the Sidon specialists did a tap on it—Old Matt had to implant the probes; the specialist wouldn't even go into the module—and shook her head, muttering. There was a strange kind of neural and cerebral activity, but she couldn't make much out of it. "Obvious patho," she said, and gave up. The file on the thing said nothing about what the complex tracings meant. Old Matt sucked at his teeth, thinking, watching the wavy lines on their scope. "I've seen men come apart when they lose a piece of themselves. This one's not like that. This is something different."

"Yeah, crazy."

"Crazy like a fox, maybe."

"What's a fox?"

Old Matt just sucked at his teeth some more, the sound reverberating in his metallic face. Manuel persisted, "You think you can made it so it'll work?"

"Don't want it to work."

"Well, then, let's tell my dad and we'll get rid of it."

"Nobody'll take it."

"*Some*body's got to. Hiruko can't just stick us with—"

"There are things better than working, anyhow."

The next day Manuel went out to see if the thing had enough liquids and power to run, which was one of his chores now, and it was gone. The cage was empty. He ran to tell Old Matt, but the man already knew.

"I let it go."

"*Go?* It'll run back to Hiruko or somewhere, we'll never see it."

"Maybe so."

"It'll kill somebody."

"Maybe." The old man would not say anything more.

But five days later it came back. It was worn out. The days in the open had run down its power reserves, and it was chilled. The life-support index showed the mass of flesh inside was healthy, though, and in fact had a better pulse rate.

"It's fair rundown," the old man said, "but gained a little body mass."

"How'd it . . ." Then the boy understood.

"Scooters, prob'ly. Maybe jackrabs."

"But that, that's a *human* in there. Nobody'd stoop to eating *that*."

"It doesn't give a damn about human or not. Been too long by itself, sealed up in there."

"Still, I . . . Jesus, how's it digest that slimy stuff?"

"The techs insert a universal biotract in most of these. Simplifies the work. Just drop in a standard unit, hook it up, you don't have to worry about what the animal's supposed to live on."

"It's not an animal."

Old Matt studied the form behind the bars, his face half-shadowed and sagging and folded with age, except where the timeless metal moved. "I don't see a whole lot of distinction any more," he said softly.

He took food into it and hooked up the charging leads to its back terminals. The black eyes followed him as he pushed the food closer, glinting and intelligent eyes that did not change or give warning before it sprang. It was weak, and the power leads popped free as it leaped, so there was not much energy in the attack. Old Matt brought the tractor rod around from the harness on his back, where it had been concealed. He caught the thing in midair. The rod mashed in its left buttress, and Old Matt turned to the side, almost like a matador, to let the shape rush past him, still in the air but now twisting and already doubling up with pain. It struck the ice heavily, landing wrong, and cried out—a strangled grunt of surprise and dismay. Old Matt stumbled out the door and slid it shut before Manuel could reach him, and the module rocked again with a heavy thump and right after it a crash and more thumps, rhythmic and shuddering, the way it was on the first day.

"Sonabitch!" Manuel cried.

"Still got spirit. Learning, but keeping the spirit." The man grinned, creasing his face deeply so that the radiation-born blotches stood out as blue-black scars.

"You'd think it'd be grateful."

"No. Grateful would mean it was ours. Mean—bone-deep mean—then it still can hold its head up. To anything."

Colonel López heard of the incident, not through his son but from a crop-tender who had seen it happen at a distance. He came out to look at the thing, now strong again and prowling the modular cage, glaring out hot-eyed and unbroken. It reared up when the Colonel came close to the bars, not to leap but to display its huge belly—groined in scarlet ceramic and molybdenum, cracked and pitted—as challenge, exposing its weakest point to invite attack. The Colonel pursed his lips. "You two have invested considerable time in this creature."

"It's coming along." Old Matt stood with hands in his pouch-pockets, his suit catching the slanting sunlight, showing its creases and stains and mended rips.

"It escaped."

"He let it go," Manuel put in. "And it came back on its own."

The Colonel shook his head, not taking his eyes off the cage. "A lot of work."

"Could be a good return, too," Old Matt said.

"You'll never get it to follow orders."

"Slaves follow orders, Colonel. You want something done a slave can't, you don't ask for a slave to do it."

"What we need now is grunt labor. If we don't keep the price down on our wheat, our soy, our corn, the Settlement will have to mortgage out to the Luna brokers first, and then some Earthsiders later. What we don't need is things like this with mouths big as buckets, trying to chew up one of my best men."

Old Matt said quietly, "Let me run him."

"What for?"

"Keep down the rockjaw muties."

"Got ordinary dogs can do that."

"This one'll be cheaper. Don't have to feed it."

The Colonel nodded, still looking at the big ponderous thing as it padded monotonously around the enclosure, puffing, its breath an orange steam that crackled and fell to the ground, depositing a thin snow. "I heard about its feeding. *That's* the thing you want me to let run loose?"

Manuel said quickly, "We've got to take a *chance* on it, Dad."

"Man doesn't have to take a gamble just 'cause it's there. You got to learn that."

Manuel felt a stab of irritation and started to talk fast: "Damn, that's a swole-headed—" but Old Matt interrupted, began giving the Colonel some specs on the creature. Manuel saw what the old man was doing, shunting the talk aside for a moment before the Colonel got into one of his moods and took a stand and then couldn't back down from it. Okay. Manuel turned away, muttering to himself, the lukewarm anger in his chest like a physical presence, a smoldering he got when he had to skate around the Colonel. He grasped the bars and leaned forward, cooling off. The creature came over to him as Manuel listened to the slow, almost casual way Old Matt drained the hard-nosed stand-fast part out of the Colonel's voice. His mouth twisted. It irked him somehow to see his father being soothed like that; and then he noticed the hunched-down form tapping against the bars with its head, *ding, dingding,* a pattern that varied but seemed intentional. Manuel frowned. *Ding, ding, dingding* . . . He saw suddenly that it was a code, maybe a way for the thing inside to talk. He rapped his glove against the bars in response. It answered, *dingdingding, ding*. Manuel reached down and knocked a patient rhythm on the burnished steel skull. The huge head tilted up, peering out for a stilled moment. Manuel felt something pass between them, something that tightened his throat. If there was still a human fragment left in there, if he could talk to it . . . He knocked on the skull again. Suddenly it reared up. It smacked against the bars with fierce energy, snarling. Manuel jumped back. Arms clawed at him, missing but snatching out again, jerking with lightning-quick anger. Manuel blinked, dazed. For an instant a small trapped part of it had broken to the surface. Only an instant. Now the muscled form prowled the cage again—glaring, snorting.

The two men noticed the momentary eruption. Colonel López grunted. "I've got gangs putting up more domes. Teams outside, working the whole twenty-four."

Old Matt nodded. "It'll have to operate a long way out. No rockjaws near Sidon now, anyway. What I thought was, we put a tractor sting on it. It comes inside a five-klick perimeter, it gets a jolt."

Colonel López grimaced. "Risky."

Manuel noticed for the first time that the corners of his father's set lips were a grid of fine dry wrinkles. He looked from one man to the other and found a similar tone, skin like paper crumpled and then smoothed out. He softened his voice and said, "Dad, it won't be that way when it's loose. It didn't jump anybody when it had a chance, out there."

"I see." The Colonel smiled at his son despite his continuing frown, the learned look of a parent allowing himself to be talked into something. "You think it is merely objecting to being penned up."

Manuel answered crisply, "Right."

"That's so now," Old Matt said. "Earlier, it had things to work off. We let it do that."

The Colonel pointed between the bars at the left buttress of the thing. It oozed green pus from the tractor rod's wound. "Some still working out, I gather?" He smiled. "But I take your point. You can try the scheme—provisionally. Only provisionally."

Manuel beamed. He forgot the passing moment before, the fleeting connection. His father was right: the thing was dangerous. But it could be controlled. He was not sure why he felt a sense of accomplishment and anticipation, but like a boy, he did not puzzle over it.

The Colonel nodded, still studying the big shadowy form in constant motion, and began walking back toward the bright stretching bulk of the Settlement. Ultraviolet from distant domes reflected off his helmet, darting rainbows of color into Manuel's eyes. "By the way," his father called, "what you call it?"

"Uh . . . nothing."

"Even animals get names," the Colonel said.

"We'll find one," Old Matt said. "You give them a chance, most things name themselves."

4

"The way we want him is like he came to us," the old man said to the boy.

"Mean?" Manuel asked. It seemed to him you needed more than that, but he was willing to believe.

"Yes, mean, but all the rest—proud, and mad as all hell, and confused enough to want to make something out of that anger and find out who he—or she, or it—is."

"Uh-huh." Manuel looked doubtful.

"Still, to teach it to use the anger, the madness—it has to learn the rod, sure 'nuff." Old Matt nodded to himself, somber and distant, as if recalling something. "It's not really human any more, but it has to learn—or relearn—some human things. Not be just a crazy thing. But not too human, no. Not too."

They ran it. It would be gone for days, even weeks, and then come lumbering back to the five-klick boundary, and send a mournful long bass note over the comm the way Old Matt had showed it. It preyed only on the muties; Old Matt had taught it the differences, and something told it that the deviant forms were proper game. The boy never discovered how the old man had done the training, but it worked. Bio reported a slow but steady drop in the mutie population near Sidon. Colonel López was guardedly pleased with the result, since the Settlement received transfer credits from Hiruko for work done "in the general interest." The dogs alone could not have done it without humans to keep them to the task.

When it came in from a run, Old Matt or, later, Manuel would fetch it in from the perimeter. There was an increasing work load, and the two of them fell into a routine, tending to the thing when necessary and counting on time to wear it down some. It never attacked Old Matt, though it made a rush at Manuel one time. The boy jabbed the rod at it, missed, and swung full force into the yawning face that seemed to fill his vision, making no sound. The rod hummed with unlocked energy and jolted the thing back, stunning it without doing real damage, and the boy poked it, just enough to keep it backing away, and too late saw the trap the thing had laid for him. He was too far into the cage to reach the door in one long bound, so he had to stand as the thing rounded on him, slewed to the left, and came in low, under Manuel's raised guard. It hit him. He was on the ground and rolling before it registered that anything had happened. He twisted and looked up and it was towering over him, hot-eyed and massive and immobile, merely studying him. *Enjoying it*, the boy thought, *getting the most out of this before it*— and he struck upward hard, turning the rod so its point caught the thing in the right nerve nexus. It howled and jerked away, eyes glaring and mouth gaping. Manuel scrambled up, rod held ready, and backed out, already recovered enough to think of his pride so that he did not hasten, but solemnly stared the thing down even as he retreated.

Later, he was not sure what the thing had been trying to do. The attack might have been a way for it to come even with him. He would never be certain. He hoped no one had seen the incident and after a week was pretty sure Old Matt knew nothing of it. Only months later would the old man refer to it in passing as merely another matter Manuel and the thing had to go through. He learned that Old Matt and even his father had known. They had said nothing, because no talk would underline the point better. It took even longer before he saw that the lesson's point was indeed its ambiguity, and talk could take away from that, too.

After the attack, Manuel walked nearly even with it as he escorted the heavy form out on its runs. He felt himself able to handle it better now; the brush with extinction (so he thought of it) had proved he could move as fast and well as he needed to. There had been a fear in him— not the coppery fear he knew would never leave him, but a milder one that could be banished and now was slowly seeping away. It was after Old Matt saw him walking beside it, still wary but with a jaunty lift to his step, that the old man said, "We should call it Eagle."

"What does that mean?"

"A large bird. Lived on Earth long ago."

"Huh? It's no animal; it's—"

"We should name it Fred? Elizabeth? Carmelita?"

The boy said nothing for a while. Then, "*Sí, sí*, I suppose you're right. But Eagle? It can't fly. Not even with air could it fly."

"The important thing with the eagle was not its flight, but its heart. That was why it died out, I remember. It would not give in, become a barnyard thing."

Manuel shrugged. He did not care much about the ancient past. He accepted the name because in the end one name was as good as another. It meant nothing to him until some weeks later when he returned with Eagle—it was difficult to remember to think of it that way—from the perimeter, across the glassy plain of gaudy splash-landing pits. They loped over blotches of burnt gold, crusty crimson, searing orange. Eagle paced beside him, and Manuel kept the tractor rod cradled easily, casually. Some animals were working on a hot-water feed line, laying it on supports above the ice between two looming gray domes. They chattered among themselves as they labored, hoisting struts and tape-fusing joints with the bright blue arcs, and then caught sight of Eagle. They hailed the two and then broke from the work gang as men shouted after them, five animals clanking and rolling across the purple sheen of ice, glad of a break in their work, chattering loudly. Four of them slowed and then stopped as they got a better look at the thing that walked with the boy, but the youngest had never been beyond the Settlement before and in its fuzzy world knew no enemies, so it came on. It ran up to Eagle, yipping. Eagle hardly took notice of it. It didn't even break stride or engage its treads. It simply smacked the animal in the side and kept on, sending it rolling, tumbling and flailing across the slick surface and down an incline, where it slewed to a stop. Eagle went on, indifferent to the silent wake it left among animals and men alike. They stared after Eagle as it ambled lazily homeward, yawning. The young whined and mewed and sulked. The men muttered amongst themselves, stunned and with a grudging admiration. It was not the act—which was no more cruel than the day-to-day wrestlings of the animals at play—but the way it was done, without anger but with a lofty sense of what Eagle was and what the animals were.

Manuel started to think of it as his own. That ended when again it jumped him. He had left Eagle in the cage for two days when he was busy and did not have time to let it out for another run. This time Manuel clubbed it right away, not allowing himself to be drawn in. The attack was swift, but without the great power the boy knew Eagle could muster. A complaint, then—nothing more. But it served to relieve the boy of the sentimental notion that he had made Eagle his own, as submissive as any of the animals, or as friendly. Old Matt smiled gently when he heard of it and said nothing, but Manuel knew what he thought.

There was more labor to do now that the Settlement was thrusting up more domes, filling them with hard-won soil, blending human waste with cornstalks and old plant fiber ("the honey-bucket brigade," Major Sánchez called it), and extending the tunnels back into the neighboring hillsides for access to more lodes of water and ammonia-saturated ices. There was less time for recreation now, fewer communal dances and meetings, more of the small card games and drinking bouts snatched from time between shifts. Worse, the new works took energy, so the heating budget got cut back. Men and women stayed close to their homes carved out of the ice floes, bundled up. To cut down on drafts, blankets hung in the connecting corridors. The younger kids, including Manuel, spent long hours adding thick gray insulation to the pipe networks, all in the eternal battle against the cold that seeped in, despite magnetic insulation and the steady gurgle of hot, fusion-runoff water in the walls. But the Colonel knew the limits of the community and arranged with Bio for a new expedition out to distant regions, to cull the muties and give everyone a break. It had been some years since a woman had gone on one of the hunts, not from any design but from simple preference. While the men and boys were gone, the women too felt a curious release that brought some renewal. They worked at private gardens and other projects, made entertainment holos to exchange with the other Settlements—not imitations of the slick sensodramas from Earth, but storytelling, tales of Ganymede itself or the asteroids, people like themselves—and dreamed of the day when the families could begin to split off from the Settlements and make their own way in the new land, safe from the deadly proton sleet beneath a shielding blanket of air, owing no one a tribute of taxes or indentured labor. That time would not come soon; probably would not come at all in their generation; but that did not matter: they could see the promise unfolding, and for the moment, leaning forward always on the promise, that was enough.

The party that set out from Sidon was larger than usual, louder, high-spirited with anticipation and smeerlop. During the long ride down to the Prometheus Plateau, Manuel felt a weight lift from him. The routine months of labor had been relentless and grinding. To him the dulling months had smudged the sureness of the things he had experienced out beyond the insulated human-scale pocket that bounded them on every side. Their super-conductors made possible the thin wedges of vacuum that insulated them from the awful cold, and only plain hard work would make of Ganymede a human place, but under its unending hammer they lost the flavor of the open, endless plains that they so seldom crossed now. The early explorers had truly lived here, where treads now ground across the melt-sloped craters. The dome-hemmed farmers had a smaller compass. He was glad to stop being a farmer and take on some fraction of the explorer's role again, tingling as he suited up in the morning for the biting chill only centimeters away.

On the morning they reached the Plateau, six strangers met them. They were from the territory near Nelson Settlement and Fujimura Settlement, a full thousand klicks away, and had been traveling for days. They had a job order from Bio, but what had drawn them was the story of Eagle, now well circulated, and the prospect of a real hunt. They were swarthy and dirty, not the best. Most did not have solid contracts with a Settlement at all. They were stragglers and outbackers, men who worked in their own patched-together domes in river valleys, or else outpost agents (old, most of them, hermits almost, with ancient grudges);—all came with their bore-guns and one even with a heavy e-beam emplacement, towed by a run-down old crawler. They were the kind of men who never fit well in the enclosed Settlements. They were there to settle a debt: "Wonder if we could run wi' yer after it"—none even imagining that they should deal with the Aleph in the TwenCen way: one sunburst of fusion and be done with it. That was unthinkable. Old Earth and Luna had gone through hell to make that a horrifying idea, and so they came as always, yet hopeful, with the same ineffectual weapons their fathers had willed them, the beams and missiles the thing had withstood or brushed aside countless times before. What drew them was Eagle.

The six of them squatted in a cold slow-falling drizzle outside the camp, ready before the bigger party had even finished a breakfast of hot sour corn and lurkey steak. "Thought we might just come along; won't even shoot if you say not to. Providing it doesn't come after one of us, that is."

Colonel López nodded. He could scarcely turn down a team that Bio had rubber-stamped. "You seen much of it?"

"It busted up my first 'ponics dome," a wiry man said, thumbing his bore-gun.

Another said, "Killed my wife, th'ty years ago."

The Colonel studied them and said clearly, "We're here to clean out the muties."

"You want to do that, send some of these boys you got," the wiry one said.

"We're not freezing our asses out here to get run over by the Aleph," Major Sánchez put in. "You got that idea, *mierda*, you can go home."

"Maybe you soft Settlement guys don' see 'nuff a it," said the man who had lost a wife. "It don' come 'round the big places much any more. But us"—he gestured—"we're contract farmers. It dunno we're there, even."

The Colonel squinted at them and said, "You're here on a job order from Bio, *sí?* You see rockjaw-warps, scooters, you get as many as you can. No good stuff, though. You see something else, you shoot—*sí*. But that's not the job."

The men grumbled, but it didn't matter anyway. Nobody got a shot at the Aleph that day, or even that week. It came and went on its own strange routes deep in the ancient moon, and the odds were against even seeing it in a whole season. Manuel found trenches and gorges that might have been marks of its passing, though with the endless melting and refreezing it was impossible to tell. He could not find anywhere the delta-print. But in the second week one of the animals heard something, it seemed, toward the south, and the main party headed that way. Eagle would not stay with the file of men and animals, and so Old Matt gave it the sign that it could stray off farther to the south and try to find something. Neither he nor Manuel had been able to tell Eagle much about the Aleph, though they had shown it pictures.

They were tramping stolidly down a ravine where a big gray slab of ice butted against an iron mountain, forming a kind of waffleboard of alternately stretched and compressed rock. There was no premonition, no tremor of intent. The ravine wall just buckled, showering the lead animals with shards of ice and lumps of snow, and there it was: lean this time, snakelike and undulant, streaming with soft amber light, alabaster chunks bobbing under its rough hide like bergs afloat in some interior fluid. It churned out of the massive ice cleft as if unaware of any resistance—much less of the men and animals that scattered before it, yelling and scrambling in all directions, none taking aim or even looking for a potential vulnerable spot to shoot. All except the boy. He was in the rear of the party when the ice wall ripped open and boulders crashed down. He stood very still. The debris rained around him or tumbled past, crunching over snowbanks or smacking near his boots, and he was the only constant point in all this motion. He studied it. The Aleph twisted its long form as it descended to the ravine floor, ponderous, sheets of ice creaking and splitting under its weight—*wiry this time,* the boy thought, *like it's swimming*—and helical waves pulsed along it, watery amber light refracting from the peaks of the ripples as it crossed the ravine with a liquid writhing grace—*only it's not touching the ground*—and with a huge unconcern slammed into an iron bluff, the blunt head (now without features) entering the rusty cliffs with a grinding noise, the whole side of the mountain seeming to flinch at the attack, shock waves fanning out from the contact. With indifference it nosed in, dust and pebbles spewing out from the hole it made, and then the boy saw the spots. They formed and re-formed along the snaky body, some bigger than a man, not mere floating blue spots but actual openings that shifted and deepened—*that hexagonal again, sure enough*—and gave forth a somber blue-black glow, like looking far down into an ice mountain and seeing through it the pale glow of the sun rising on the other side.

Eagle rushed by him. The Aleph was almost buried now in its oval tunnel, and Eagle rushed on, never breaking stride as it dodged among the fleeing men and rushing animals, not slowing as it passed Old Matt—who was bent over, squinting—and leaped ahead, so fast Manuel could hardly follow it. The nub end of the Aleph was bone-white, coiling with a kind of muscular surge, hanging a meter above the ground, as if held aloft by magnetic fields—and Eagle jumped on it. It clawed at the surface and managed to get a toehold on some minute break in the otherwise smooth-seeming skin. Its sharp hand-servos slashed at the glossy sheen, and Manuel thought he saw a red, searing mark spring from the hide, but before he could be sure one of the amber ripples coursed down to the tip of the body, reflected, and on its way back toward the head caught Eagle by a foot and deftly, effortlessly tumbled it off. Manuel rushed toward Eagle and while running saw that it had left a scar, a definite scar, turning deep red as he watched. Then the white tip of the thing slipped into the tunnel and was gone.

Eagle shook and pawed at the ice, a little dazed. Old Matt came trotting forward fast as he could and gradually other men came up, talking to each other and looking at the tunnel—some even bravely venturing into it, shining lamps upon the walls that were bored out with a screwlike pitch—and relating the way they'd seen it (no one had taken a fax picture) and what Eagle had done or tried to do. The boy did not hear them. He tasted the metallic liquid scent that swarmed up, prickling, into his nostrils—not fear this time, but something stronger, because it settled into him and would stay: a certainty, a sense of things coming, a foreknowledge of what could be—acrid and final and uncompromising in its ferocity, claiming him.

5

The next year stragglers came into the camp, some because they were out of work and wanted to get out into the territory, and others for bigger reasons. Four months earlier the Aleph had popped open a dome merely by brushing against it, killing more than a dozen, and there was talk of nuking it for the protection of everybody. The Luna science council overruled Hiruko, saying the Aleph was like an archeological site on Earth, to be kept for future generations who might be able to learn more from it. None of this mattered to the lean, silent men who pitched their own tiny domes near Colonel López's shacks. They had a debt to get paid, and though they knew it was hopeless and had been hopeless for their own fathers, they kept on. This time there were two men from the McKenzie asteroids, fresh down into Hiruko—to learn ammonia farming, they said—but knowing about the Aleph and even of the mutie hunts that struck it now and then. One had heard in Hiruko of Colonel López and the great gunmetal-blue Eagle. He came without even a laser gun, and the insulated suit he wore had been in an expensive fitter's stock three days before. The Sidon men ignored all these people as best they could.

The McKenzie men were even less welcome, because to the farmers they were the first of a new era.

"I say we not associate with them," Petrovich said one evening over supper. He had as usual tried to talk the Colonel into letting them shoot crawlies, and just as usual the Colonel had slapped him down. Now he wanted to change the subject. "They come here, look around, take our ideas."

Major Sánchez, always quick to contradict, said, "Treaty with Earth says we got to share knowledge."

"Earth!" Petrovich snorted. "Always siding with the 'roids 'cause the rockhoppers, they have them by throat."

The Colonel said soberly, "Earth has enough troubles without getting into our squabbles."

The table fell silent. A new War of Redistribution had flared up in Asia again, and Sydney had gone in the first few hours. It was impossible to be indifferent to Earth's old disease even this far away. Manuel could not understand the fatalism of the way everyone talked of the Wars, steadily raging between the historically poor and the relatively wealthy. He wondered how you could know you were in a period of history, all bracketed and figured out by the metasociologists as if you were dead already—and knowing it, still go on in the grip of history's laws, futile and predetermined, following the same zero-sum game down to a remorseless end. Maybe being able to see Earth and all its blood-steeped riddles as a mere blue glimmer made it easy to misunderstand; or maybe he too was like a shuttle gliding down a smooth and utterly fixed orbit he could not see, and was just as laughable. He shrugged a boy's shrug and listened to Petrovich again.

"—it'd tear their hearts out if they came over to where it sleeps and laid on it for warmth." He was discussing Eagle, which always slept alone, often tunneled into a snowdrift. The animals invariably piled atop one another.

"It's not an animal," the Colonel observed.

"Not a man, either," Petrovich said adamantly. "Hiruko, they brought that brain lobe up to max capacity, yes. Access all the neural connections left. But not a man, still."

"Why not?" Old Matt said casually.

"More to a man than connections."

"What is there?"

"Half a man isn't a man."

Major Sánchez slapped his palm on the hard-fiber

table. "Ha! The neurophilosopher will now tell us how he knows a man."

"Well, humans have bigger, bigger aims."

"Like what?"

"Aleph! To animals, to Eagle, it's just a big rockjaw. Something to hunt, if only they had guts."

The Colonel said, "And to us?"

"Well . . ." Petrovich chewed his lip, cornered. "To us, it's something to learn from."

Major Sánchez said slyly, "You've never been so strong on learning before now, Petrovich."

"I learned something this last year. Something you don't know. Systemwide has a bounty on it."

The Colonel said, "What? For killing it?"

Petrovich grinned, having deflected the talk where he wanted it. "No killing. Capture."

Major Sánchez frowned, outflanked. "You sure?"

"Found it in the old records. Ought to scan those sometime yourself, my friend." He added, deadpan, "Learn a little."

"You have hard copy?" the Colonel asked.

Beaming, Petrovich produced a stack of slick sheets. "Reading for the long nighttime."

It was there. The men passed the records around, calling out snatches of official directives nearly a century old, laughing at the stiff Earther terms and mush-mouthed way of talking. Few of them ever wrote anything down, so anything in hard form was fancy and fussy and unnecessary. Old Matt got hold of the original directive and showed it to Manuel. "Made up about the time the scientists discovered the stuff on the outer moons," he pointed out.

"When they gave up here?"

"Approx'ly, yes. Guess they figured somebody might find a way to slow it down or stop it so they could study it safely. I seem to remember something like that—I mean, why people started hunting it down."

"You were around then?"

Old Matt grinned; his metal cheek creased and rasped faintly. "Still up in the orbital labs, and then out at Titan—but around, sure."

"*Madre*." To the boy, the old man and the Aleph both came out of a faceless time before anything he knew for certain, both from origins lost forever to him, and with the conserving blinkered concentration of humans, he was blissfully secure and at peace in his ignorance.

"See in this one?" Manuel pointed at an old fastframe picture. "The text says they had to go real fast to see the spots on the side."

"Ummm."

"*I* can see them easy."

"Right."

"It must be slowing down."

"We saw it take its time, is all."

"Maybe it's getting weaker."

Old Matt laughed. "Chew up a mountain in a minute, if you think that's weak."

Undaunted, the boy stuck a finger at the print. "What're the spots? They don't show on many frames."

"Holes."

"Anybody know what kind?"

"They change all the time."

Manuel nodded. Old Matt was tired from a day of potting at sleppers, the new bioform introduced to fill in a step in the biochem chain that led toward an oxygen atmosphere. They were efficient, big and bulky and ugly as sin. They mutated easily and were hard to chase down. Manuel stayed up long after the old man had slumped into his sleeping bag. He peered at the old prints, read the data. It had not occurred to him to study up on the Aleph. Studying was to learn pipe fitting or thermodynamics and the Aleph was like none of those—no formulas or procedures: just a fervent running wildness that could be claimed only by sensing it and feeling your way. But as he frowned down at the frozen images of amber and alabaster he nodded to himself, concentrated and intent. The next morning he spoke to Eagle, not knowing if he was understood, but trying anyway. And each morning thereafter trying again.

For eleven days they ran down slepper-muties, with Eagle making the most kills, always far faster than the animals and always quick and remorseless in the killing. The McKenzie man had a partial insulator breakdown from his own ineptness and within five minutes got frostbite in a leg, the skin frozen to the suit wall so that it tore off when they dragged him out of it.

Eagle was leading them all now, with an instinct made sure by time, so that without discernible sign it knew which cañon to choose, which purple-shadowed pocket sheltered the growing communities of muties, where the scattered and warring lifeforms preyed and mated and died. Eagle ran with an unthinking ferocity that daunted some of the men. The kindly and condescending affection that evolution had forged between men and the domesticated animals surely did not apply to a thing like Eagle, and the men stayed away from it.

Eagle found the Aleph alone this time. It was in the last days of the expedition, and Manuel was ten klicks to the west of the main group, scouting out a nest of slepper-muties that were chasing down and eating the normal rockjaws and crawlies. He heard the excited shouts and cries over short-range. Eagle had run onto the Aleph on an open plain. Manuel listened, loping in the general direction of the party, imagining: the men and animals after it, the huge thing surging over the ice, its passage blowing up a fine dry dust of crystal ammonia, and Eagle pacing it, not leaping this time but biding its time, careful and yet growling with a pent-up rage. The boy ran flat out, expending his servo'd energy, gasping. He heard Major Sánchez swearing, Petrovich whooping, animals chattering and mewing in mixed fear and blood-lust. He heard the sudden sharp crack as Colonel López fired two laser bolts at it point-blank. Manuel climbed a bluff and looked down on the plain where the darting black motes swarmed about the huge thing, pursuing, lunging in and then pulling back, although the liquid moving shape had done nothing to stop them. Then one came too close and the Aleph moved over it and onward and left behind a mashed stain of red and steel. The Barron hurled itself at the shape, but slow, uncertain. Something caught it in midair, and the animal twisted in pain and then fell, broken in half.

And Eagle: running alongside, snarling, watching the shifting blue-black opportunities until in a blur it shot in, up the alabaster flank, plunging on and leaping from some unseen purchase, up, to the lip of a triangular hole, and then in, swallowed, gone in an instant, so that the yelping and shouting from the black dots around stopped suddenly and a strange silence descended. The boy felt his heart thump once, twice, and on the third the side of the thing contorted, turning ruddy, and Eagle struggled out from the triangular spot which shrank even as it wriggled free, snarling and spitting and chopping at the Aleph with puny servo'd human hands. Struggling. Then falling. Eagle hit the ice solidly, starring it, and rolled. The boy gasped and leaped downhill, letting his shocks absorb his clumsy, hasty jolting falls. By the time he had reached the plain, Eagle was on its feet, wobbling but fundamentally unhurt, and the Aleph had vanished, burrowing into a rock flat in a blur of energy.

"Hit it both times," Colonel López said as his son approached. "Both times, and not a puncture, not a mark."

Old Matt stood with his hand on the back of Eagle. The men milled around it, though the animals stayed back. Eagle puffed and stood silent, haggard, its ceramics and manifolds rasping hollowly. The boy saw it held something in one hand.

"Piece of the thing," Old Matt said. "Tore it out, somehow. Way back in that hole, I guess."

Major Sánchez stared at the thin shard like rosy sheet metal. "First time I see that. Ever."

"The records have nothing like that," Petrovich said.

In camp that night Petrovich called into Sidon and confirmed: no trace of the thing had ever been recovered. "So the secret all along," Old Matt said, "was in those spots. Goddamn."

The men laughed and slapped one another with a fervent relief that surprised even them, and drank more, and even invited in the straggly bunch from the contract farms, still terrified and subdued, who in the end had fallen behind and never come close to the Aleph. Two of the animals dead and a fragment won: a price paid. The boy knew that night, as he fell into exhausted sleep, that he would not see it again this year. That was just as well; they were all worn down, despite the temporary euphoria. Yet they had done what the scientists could not, and they had done it without fine instruments or a lot of money. He smiled to himself in the warm, musty smell of the bedclothes. It was the end of one time and the beginning of something greater, though he could not know exactly what, and did not care.

6

It was well more than a year before they returned to the wild territories again. The party was larger but no more expert, being larded out with men from Fujimura and Zanatkin Settlements. There were three from Hiruko who had to be watched or else would pop their tanks wrong and freeze their lungs solid (an expensive replacement, and sometimes fatal), or fall into a crusted-over crevasse, or walk alongside Eagle and put a casual hand on it, thinking it was another animal. The extras were useful, because the Colonel and Major Sánchez, by being formal and forthright and simply expecting it, got them to do a lot of the drudge jobs around the camp.

Manuel appreciated that part of it, because as a boy he always drew more dull grunt labor than the men—in the fourteen-percent Earth-norm gravity, even he could lift and manhandle huge crates—and now it was pleasant to graduate up a notch and watch somebody else hustle at it. Still, the ferret-faced interest and comic ineptitude and plain ignorance of these others robbed the long journey out from Sidon of some of its joyous release. The boy did not like it any different than it was before, and in this early disgruntlement, this stand to black the path of change, lost one more piece of his boyhood.

"Hope you don't expect me to go out shooting with 'em," he said to his father the first day in camp.

"We'll share jobs, as usual," Colonel López said. "Share out the new men into our teams, too."

"They're not even from Sidon!"

"Bio gives us the credit for their task-hours, though."

"A measly dab of credit."

"We need it," the Colonel said mildly. He was less stern with his boy now, relied less on discipline and more on a quiet display of steadiness. "We're selling less ammonia-mix to Mars-General. Have to scrape by somehow."

"Not this way. There's plenty—"

"Plenty is exactly what there's none of. Now you go help unshank those treads, same as the rest."

Manuel did as he was told and inside of an hour had put away most of his resentment. It helped that the Fujimura men took to admiring Eagle—its size and strangeness, and its graceful intricate lope as it cleared the hills nearby, going out on its first run. They had never seen anything like it, a thing that resembled a servo'd animal and yet bristled with energy and nervous, repressed intelligence, eyeing everyone and everything with a straight, unafraid, assessing gaze. The new men had felt nervous when they sensed it watching them, as though the hot-eyed intensity found them wanting.

The first night in camp was always cause for more

drinking and sniffing than usual, and the new men fitted into that fine, some even passing out from the smeerlop early and having to be given a dose of oxy to bring their cardio systems back up to full. The Major toured casually through the connected quonsets, keeping an eye on the more raucous and checking to be sure the oxy didn't ignite anything and burn them out.

Manuel sat on his bunk and watched, drinking a little of the brown liquor that the Settlements made easily as sourmash side-product and shipped, with a hefty tax, across the solar system. As usual, the best went for export, but the Settlements had gotten used to the harsher, throat-scraping variety and now even preferred it. The boy sipped and talked to whoever came by and then, tiring of the stories of improbable marksmanship and endless near-fatal accidents and discovered-but-now-lost metal lodes, went looking for Old Matt. He found the old man already asleep, stretched out and looking smaller than a man, his clothes loose on the body, worn and filthy in spots where chemicals had dried and collected the dust from metalwork. He breathed shallowly and his face seemed dried out, burned deeply by UV, the nose blistered and reblistered, the seam where flesh joined to metal warped and lined like old reused paper. Manuel studied the thin, loose-jointed form for a moment and was turning away when a whispery voice said, "You've been thinking."

Surprised, the boy said, "Tomorrow, I'll show you."

"No, tonight. I'm never sure I'll be here tomorrow."

"Hey, you can march half these jokers straight into the ground."

"Maybe. Maybe." Old Matt sat up smoothly, without carrying much weight on his arms, even though one was syntho'd and the other servo'd. "I had to be humble and a little sly, even, to come out here this time."

"Huh? Anybody can come so long's they want."

"The Undue Risk Rule, you know it? If I get injured again, need a new leg or whole abdomen, who's to pay?

Sidon can't do major overhauls. Has to come from Hiruko, maybe even Luna."

"They'd keep you back at the Settlement? For that?"

"I told them, cost less if I prang out here, considering the chances aren't good I'd get back in time anyway."

This talk made the boy uncomfortable and the man saw it, so he said, "It's that spectrograph stuff, eh?"

Manuel nodded. "That fragment. Hard to believe they could get so much information out of it."

"The dating? That's a nonresult, you ask me."

"I don't see how the Hiruko labs could come up with no date at all."

Old Matt shrugged. "The ratio of various isotopes—that's the only handle they ever get on the age of a thing. That little piece had all kinds of isotopes in it, but they all give contradictions—different ages for each ratio. Sometimes even impossibilities—more of the decay product than could be, ever, if it was just coming from the parent radioactive atoms in the material."

"So it's something they haven't seen before. So? They have such big heads, *al norte*, they think that's impossible?"

Old Matt smiled lightly. "It means the thing is not made up of naturally occurring stuff. It must keep reshuffling its own atoms all the time, to keep them so scrambled."

The old man seemed to regard this as important, but to Manuel it was a detail. "Thing is, the *big* thing is," he said, "it's not made of rock, even if it looks like it is."

"Yes?"

"There's a lot of metal. I added up all the elements in it that're good conductors, from the mass spectrograph printout they sent us. Then I figured how much other atoms there are." He leaned forward earnestly. "That fragment, it's a good conductor."

"Ummmm. That piece was from inside. We know the Aleph is not a conductor on the skin. So it must be different inside."

"Right! And a conductor, it can be a channel."

"Channel?"

"The man from Hiruko last time—like the one this year, too—he fired an e-beam at it."

"Sure. Just bounced off. Always does."

"Right! The Aleph knows how to defend its outside. Its skin does the whole job."

"Not always. It picked up The Barron."

"The Barron was a dog. It came too close. Could be it was sucked into the Aleph, the fields tore it open."

Old Matt studied the far end of the shack, as if listening to the background talk, or the wheezing of the pumps, or the gurgle of pipes. His liquid brown eyes seemed to absorb light from the shadowy, dank bunkroom. "It was studying The Barron, I'd guess. Turning it over, like a man looking at a funny-shaped pebble, and by accident he dropped it and it broke."

The boy went on, impatient: "Something like that, sure, but the point is, an electron beam carries an electrical current. Conductors are like mirrors—a current comes by them, they make an image current, only reversed. Same as when you look in an ordinary mirror, you're left-handed."

"I'm left-handed already."

"Then in the mirror you're right-handed. What I mean is, one thing you learn early in power engineering is, a current's repulsed by another current of opposite sign. Right? That means an e-beam bolt, running by a conductor, kind of sees a repulsive current in the conductor. Its own image pushes it away."

Old Matt sat back, eyeing the boy with mingled amusement and new respect. "So the e-beam stays away."

"Right!"

"Which means e-beams aren't much good against the Aleph."

"Not if you fire it point-blank, the way that Hiruko guy does. The way everybody has, near as I can tell from what my dad says. But suppose you get the beam into one of those openings."

"Then it's in a kind of metal pipe. It gets pushed away from the walls. So? Still does you no good."

Manuel gestured and waved with his hands. "No, *no*. The e-beam, it's flying through the hole, nearly fast as light. It can't run into a wall, because every time it gets close to some bend or fork in the tube, it sees its own image."

"Which it finds repulsive." Old Matt smiled, his face crinkling.

"So it goes on! See? It turns corners, it twists—all to get away from those images of itself. Beautiful!"

Old Matt closed his eyes for a long moment, his nostrils collapsing and expanding with each slow breath, the face masklike. Then he opened them again and his expression was different, as if a moment had arrived which he had expected without knowing he was waiting for it. "The e-beam works its way into the Aleph."

"And when the metal plays out—*if* it plays out—the beam smacks—zap!"—Manuel clapped his hands, making heads turn in the bunkroom—"into whatever's there. Anything nonmetal."

"Into whatever's there."

"Right. Far back into the thing."

Old Matt closed his eyes again. He nodded sleepily. "A man, then an animal, then a gun. Now we have all three. Either it is enough or it will never be enough."

Manuel was excited by his inner pictures of the e-beam jetting powerfully into the thing, snaking and finding its way, darting and striking at the soft, vulnerable things deep inside, things no one could even guess, and he scarcely heard what the old man said, or thought about what man Old Matt had meant.

PART III

LONG PURSUIT

1

Old Matt woke him early. Ganymede's dim night would later give way to dawn, a process stretching on for hours, as though all things here must be of larger-than-human scale. It was Manuel's turn to connect power cables to the crawlers and walkers, and fire up the fusion generator. He dressed sluggishly, still halfway into sleep and its foggy shapes that ran and loomed and roared against a slate-black background, a dream he knew so well now that the meaning seemed obvious, like a fact, more real than daylight. His lungs and heart felt leaden, reviving, and he shivered as he dressed in the thin but inert layers they all wore, even inside, against the perpetual sucking cold. In the bunkroom men yawned and grunted. Some stumbled to the back and urinated loudly into the open-mouthed cyclers. Shucked of their suits, their flesh was porcelain white, rubbed red where the insulating layers bunched or wrinkled. Some showed blotchy calluses and big blue veins where pressure flaws had sucked the blood to the surface. Others had patches of glossy frostbite replacements. Not a man was without mark. Their insulating sheaths fended off the brutal facts of this world, the cold and dark and scalding chemicals of the melting mountains—but shielded imperfectly, so that the men wore their ugly mottlings with a pride, a sign of having gone beyond the warm, comfortable Settlements.

He suited and left the gathering heat of the cabin. Jupiter overhead cast blurred shadows everywhere, and the moons gleamed beneath their ancient scars. He crossed the field to the fusion dome, threading among vehicles parked this way and that, dark boxy shapes on a plain glowing with a wan blue. The world lay inert beneath a rigid night, and he tasted already the coppery hot, his mind racing ahead of this slow climb out of sleep. The fusion generator's mindless *whump whump whump* seemed like an eager animal greeting him. He dragged the cables to the vehicles and socketed them and watched the black ice begin to melt from the chunky treads and wheels as the kiloAmps surged through, restoring life.

When he clumped back into the embrace of the cabin it was stirring too, the heaters cracking and spitting, men swearing at clothing damp with yesterday's undiscovered ice, their breaths already fogging the windows, pipes rattling as heat came to them again, the swarming smell of frying meat layered in the air. Old Matt sat at a table, hunkered down over a steaming bowl, chewing meditatively.

"Want to try the aim again before we put it in the crawler?" Manuel said, sitting down beside him.

"No. It's good, doesn't stray. The beam spreads a little, but you can't help that. You should try firing one—we used to use them for welding—without any air around at all. Electrons all rush away from each other; charge density just blows the beam apart. Like firing a shotgun. Worse, even."

Manuel nodded. He had never known Ganymede without some atmosphere—a thin whisper when he could barely walk, now a light cloak that could carry clouds, buoy up snow, drop the piercing acid rains. Generations would pass before a human sucked in a first good lungful. Now it was still thin stuff, little better than drawing on hard vacuum, but enough for an e-beam to fork through like lightning: breaking down atoms, clutching the newborn positive ions and ejecting the unwanted electrons, neutralizing the beam charge and enabling it to propagate in a thin, deadly stream. They were used for sealing dome exteriors now, enabling a man to zip shut a break from fifty meters away, if he had a good aiming eye.

Old Matt's jaws worked steadily, without hunger: food as fuel. Manuel took a bowl of broth and a corn slab from the loaded tray that arrived. "I was kind of surprised he did that," he said.

"Who?"

"The Hiruko fellow. Thought he'd ask for more money, once he saw we wanted the beam. Next-nearest one's in Fujimura."

"I only offered him the money to be polite. Always give Hiruko people a chance to be generous. They like it. That's not why he handed it over, though."

"Uh?"

"He's seen Eagle. He watches us, the ones who've been coming out here for so long nobody's kept track, even. He knows we can use it and he can't. Even though we told him about the conductivity and all. So he gave it."

They had taken two days to modify the long, magnet-ringed barrel of the e-beam projector, narrowing the darting stream down at the cost of losing some flux. Power that spattered against the invulnerable and still unanalyzed flanks of the thing would be worthless anyway; accuracy was more important than aimless force. The projector was an awkward thing, with its bulky power pack and evil-looking snout, and the two of them cradled it carefully out to the crawler, lashing it to the foredeck and covering it from the soft pink snow that had begun. The boy lashed down equipment and topped off pressure heads and then looked up from the work, at a circle of silent steady faces. Some he had never seen before. He realized this was the biggest party they had ever fielded, a motley crew squatting in the open near the scruffy vehicles: worn-out Agency shuttles, with plates stove in and antennas long since ripped away; crawlers missing steering treads and patched up with steel belts of the wrong gauge; walkers missing whole legs, scarred and pitted and with passenger domes starred so badly nobody could see out—equipment nearly as bad as their suits themselves, which wheezed as they moved, gushing air from pop-lines that their organic sealants flowed into and filled up, only to open again on the next step, their sour suit air snapping as it gushed out and froze and fell at their feet. They watched him steadily, without comment amongst themselves. Some worked and some rested. They stayed a good distance away from the big blue-and-red Eagle, which paced at the brow of the hill, watching the plain beyond and ignoring the milling men at its back.

"Today I think three parties," Petrovich said to the Colonel. "That parallel set of valleys—Major will take the left, I the right. Simple—"

"I think not," Colonel López said. "This is not a military maneuver. If it comes when we are nearby it will not attack a flank or bother with which way we are deployed. It doesn't care."

"I mean to—"

"We will proceed in parallel valleys. I will take the left. Keep pace."

Petrovich had been telling the new men what to do and it had gone to his head. He turned red but said nothing.

Major Sánchez put in, "The boy and Old Matt, they'll be slower with that e-beam on foot. I could stay with 'em, take—"

Colonel López said, "They stay in the main party. There are a lot of us. We'll give the thing plenty of confusion, all us helling around. Maybe help those two make a shot."

Petrovich cut in abruptly, "Are we pruning muties out here or—"

"Of course," the Colonel said. "Of course we are. You had something else in mind?" He grinned at Major Sánchez, and Petrovich swallowed his anger, seeing it was no use.

And so they set out as usual, though no one believed this was an ordinary day. The Hiruko man had checked with Central and found a report of the Aleph a good fifteen hundred kilometers from them, five days before, and since then nothing. But the odds were meaningless out here, and each man who rode or walked in the clanking, rumbling column felt that this day would be long and would leave them different from what they had been. None of them expected to succeed, to change the balance between men and Aleph.

Manuel watched Eagle running out ahead of them all, eager, head down as if listening to the ground, the powdery snow melting off it from the heat, its intricate articulating legs and treads scrambling and surging over black ice, shattering stubs and outcroppings as it passed, leaving a track almost as if it were a smaller version of what it hunted. Inside Eagle were heart and blood and perhaps lungs, maintained by the machines which also served to exaggerate and amplify its movements, so that in essence the soft inner zone was a fulcrum from which came the single intent focus of the thing, a concentration unlike a man's or an animal's but more consuming, purer, filled with the will to endure and strain and carry on until it could overtake and strike and slay. It was not Old Matt's or his own or anybody's, never could be, for it had been launched into a space beyond humanity, so far that it could not even report back and would forever now be silent, known only by its passion and remorseless desire. The boy felt a terror then, sitting in the cab of the crawler and watching Eagle. It was then that he understood what Old Matt had made in order to come this far: a thing between them and the Aleph, possessed of qualities both had but at bottom a thing strange and new, bereft of the Aleph's seasoned age and rising, deformed, from the churn of life.

The emptiness claimed them. They explored stark fresh gorges, flushed scooters and rockjaws and jackrabs, cutting out the muties and flaming them, or Eagle running them down, or the men potting at the scattering, panicky forms with their lasers and stunners. Old Matt rode on the side deck of the crawler and watched. Manuel paced alongside, worried at the placid fatigue of the old man, wanting to take a few shots with the e-beam but cautioned, when he picked it up, to save the bolts for when they alone would have a chance. Their crawler was the first, instead of the Colonel's or the Major's. In effect Old Matt led the party, peering forward at the gradually lightening ravines and peaked hills as the sun broke over the far ridgeline and cut blue shadows across the land.

An hour out, a mutie rockjaw did not scatter with its pack but instead jumped one of the new men. It tripped him and leaped onto his helmet as he fell. The man shouted and struck at it and rolled sideways to get it off. Somehow the thing pried open a helmet port. Vapor spurted from the helmet, blinding the man for a moment. Major Sánchez tore the rockjaw off and stomped it and beat it with his stunner. By the time they killed it the man had got the vent closed himself, but the insulator had broken down. His eyelids were frozen shut. That meant somebody had to lead him back to camp for treatment. It sobered a few of the new ones who had never seen a mutie turn like that before.

"Goddamn bad splice, you ask me, if just a li'l change an' the sonbitch goes for you. Some genetic drift, you ask me." The man who said this sat beside Manuel and the old man for the next few klicks, resting his weapon on the iron runners and trying to look as if he were surveying the terrain ahead for game, but too jittery to keep his eyes on the horizon for long.

"Got to happen," Old Matt murmured.

"How's 'at?"

"Hiruko tunes them to spread out, go for the right chemicals, breed. Determined, single-minded little inventions. Armored against the radiation. Bound to happen, now that some of the chemicals in the melt are running out. Competition. Natural selection's awful fast here."

"That keeps us, won't be safe to walk aroun' alone."

"It was us jumped them, remember."

"Huh. Huh." The man moved uneasily, as if just catching on to the idea that this was different from an amusement sim. After a few more klicks he got off and went back to find a friend near the rear of the column.

Beyond the far ridgeline an orange glow grew brighter. It was the ionized blowoff from a fusion heater. The crawler moved only a kilometer a day, but the stream of gas and liquid it vented washed out gullies and flooded the plains below. The Colonel moved the columns down a side ravine and into another system of valleys, to keep away from the mess. Rockjaws and scooters fled the floods as well, and the men spotted muties among them in the herds that poured out of the ravines and into the broad open land beyond. They ploughed forward, the excitement seizing the men so that in pursuit of the single fleeing forms they spread out, firing rapidly at the targets that dodged into the temporary shelter of craters or scrambled, panicky, into box cañons and dead-end ravines. They scrabbled frantically and mindlessly at the ice walls, dragging malformed limbs, eyes rattling in their wedge-shaped heads, shrieking and dying even as mere meters away the normal rockjaws and scooters browsed among the ponds of melt, some so dumb they did not even notice the drama, at turns both comic and tragic, that swirled around them.

The animals raged among the muties as well, running

them down and crushing them beneath clanking treads. Eagle was far out in front, leading without thinking of it, following the game as the muties heard the thin cries of their fellows down the valley and began to run away, some even back toward the higher ravines where now flash floods came down, gushing out onto the plain. Foam frothed on the surface of the grimy torrent as it carried ice chunks and stones fanning out over sheets of purple ice. The men stayed ahead of the surging streams easily, loping steadily, guns at the ready, watching the shadows for the deformed shapes. Eagle never made a mistake, never ran down or clubbed a norm. Some of the animals in their high spirits did, though, and the Colonel would see it even in the midst of the onrolling chaos—the best day they had had in a long while, rich with game and enough to make the blood sing—and would send a sharp rebuke to the offending animal, which days later would mean a day without food or sexsenso or some other punishment.

Manuel left the crawler and took part, not trying to outdistance the others, taking what clean shots he could. Old Matt stayed behind with the e-beam and so got nothing beyond a panicky stray that would have run under the crawler treads out of pure fear-blindness anyway. The old man was content to sit and watch as the crawler made its sluggish way down the broad valley, a slow bulk amid the dotlike figures of men who swarmed like bees, first on one target and then on another, their excited calls and shouts coming to the boy and blending with the higher keening yelps and clicks of the animals, all the voices layering and overrunning one another until the comm rang and clamored.

Manuel waded through rivulets of the dirty water. It steamed away or gurgled into cracks. Some muties were so addled that they kept slurping at the runoff even though the hunt was storming past, the thumps and snaps of men firing clear in the air. Manuel shot a few of these. He felt a current surge and suck at his ankles and moved to his left, toward higher ground, to get out of the main channel, but it got worse, and when he paused to look up the nearest ravine, puzzled, he saw the whole sweep of water turning toward him, gathering momentum, deepening, sheets of the evaporating grime-shot foam sliding off a rising mound of ice and rock that, as he watched it, split along a seam with a dull thunder that pulled his feet from under him and slammed his shoulder hard against a boulder, pitching him face forward into the sludge.

"Jesus Christos!" someone shouted.

The boy got to his knees, smearing the filth from his faceplate, and peered upward toward the still-rising bulge of splintering, groaning rock, the cracks spreading out from the high ground like a black spiderweb. Boulders tumbled into the yawning jagged openings.

Old Matt called, "Manuel! Here!" amid a rising jumble of noises as the animals yipped and the men shouted and the ground surged again, throwing the boy down as he took his first step toward the crawler a full two kilometers away across the buckling ice.

"Slide!" someone shouted. "Whole mountain's coming down!" but the boy got up and began to run toward the crawler, which was at higher ground, rather than away, down the valley. Old Matt was already unlashing the e-beam snout and wrestling with the long manifold. Manuel leaped high to keep above the creaking, surging land, landing and jumping again as fast as he could, pushing his servos to their maximum, running to reach the old man and the weapon, not even taking time to look down the valley and check for his father, nor especially to look behind him at the sudden roar of something breaking to the surface, ripping the ice, for he knew already what he would see.

2

Manuel scrambled up onto the deck of the crawler. Old Matt had the e-beam projector powered up and calibrated, his worn face intent upon the dials in the stock of the weapon, ignoring the buckling and heaving of the ground nearby. Manuel picked up the e-beam gun, hefting it, still not looking back at the source of the wrenching that he could feel through his boots, even standing on the crawler. Instead he gazed out over the plain, looking downvalley at the fleeing and now-ignored forms of the scooters and rockjaws. The frantic mindless stream swept past the men, who came loping back toward the slower crawlers and walkers, unshouldering weapons, and some already taking a practice aim during the long arcs of their strides, squinting through telescopic sights. Then the boy turned.

It was huge this time. The amber flanks crushed boulders as big as men as a long rhomboid section of the Aleph surged out of the erupted ice. It wallowed, pulling buttressed ribs free of the hole it bored. Groinwork appeared, rasping and screeching against slabs of nickel-iron from ancient meteorites. The rust-laced layers held, resistant for a long moment, and then crumbled with a muffled boom.

The Aleph jutted abruptly into the air, turning as the boy watched, and from the highest buttressed shoulder sprouted a twisted thing, moist like a stalagmite—angular, jade-green, writhing; first a knifelike blade that refracted the pinpoint sun into a splash of colors, and then swiftly becoming something gnarled and seething, sopping the light into dark crevices; and just as suddenly the angles of it smoothed and the projection had a bloblike head, a waving stump that might be an arm, a scooped-out cavity that might be a mouth except that as it grew it consumed the head and ate the neck, turning the thing into a body that vainly, hopelessly grew short thick legs and began to make slow sluggish motions as if it were running in a thick resistant fluid, even as its upper half was chewed and gnawed away—and abruptly, electrically, crystal facets shot through the whole of it, long tracings of embedded glinting silver that centered on the chest and fanned out into struggling, fresh-forming arms. The chest-centered web extended as the body fought, flailing, and the thin lines sank into the legs, glowing with inner light. Just then the Aleph moved, bending down toward the ground as it freed itself from the last clasp of dark ice. This movement carried the writhing extrusion out of the boy's sight.

He had seen all this in one quick glimpse, scarcely the space between two heartbeats. He blinked, and the shouting, milling voices came flooding in on him again, the comm choked with hoarse orders and exclamations and a radio hiss and swearing in three languages, "Goddamn shoulda knowed it'd come up on us just when" and "*schiessen Sie mit*" and "Over to the left it's goin' that way" and "Christos, safety's jammed on this thing" and "Get yer butt in close it'll flatten you out Lefkowitz I'm tellin' ya" and "Isn't a safety on that stunner at all you're pullin' out the *re*flex coil you jackass" and "That thing's bigger than the pictures for sure it musta growed" and "Damned if I'm gonna get any closer" and "You Hiruko guys so hard-ass let's see you corner it" and "Goddamn! Lookit! Goddamn!" and "Circle round on it give it a taste of this see how it likes a double-bore hey" and more, all blending into a babble the boy cut off sharp by punching off his comm line. He stared up at the Aleph, now fully exposed in the clear thin air, soaring above the tossed and tortured ice. It jerked free, the huge alabaster blocks of it working against each other with a deep-bass groaning. Then it simply hung a full meter above the jumbled land, unmoving, supported invisibly.

"Taking its time," Old Matt said matter-of-factly, touching helmets with the boy.

"Why doesn't it *do* something?" Manuel whispered.

"Doesn't have to."

"It should *run*."

"From us?"

"No, no, but . . . Before, it was always going. Moving."

"So? Just 'cause we hunt it, doesn't mean it's agreed to be hunted."

The boy had always dreamed of it in motion, ceaseless and yet stationary, like a running river that changes and is still always the same. Moving, and big, and now it seemed larger by far than when he had first seen it years before. He thumbed on his magneto detectors and saw overlaid on his viewplate the corona of arcing magnetic fields, a halo around the thing that—the scientists said—supported the bulk and gave off the soft curling spatters of radio noise that hissed on the comm lines.

"Nothing to shoot at," Manuel said.

"No openings, yes. Bad range from here, anyway. Let's get closer."

They jumped down from the crawler—the driver had stopped the treads and come up to the foredeck, staring—and began to walk, taking the curious long strides possible in low gravity. Manuel cradled the e-beam projector, deliberately keeping his pace slow so the old man could keep up, never taking his eyes from the hovering presence ahead. All down the valley the teams came closer, cautiously, weapons at the ready. Along the flanks of the Aleph more extrusions worked out of the amber blocks, writhing. Manuel tried to make sense of the forms, but they came too fast, being born and dying with a restless energy that played and rippled across the inert floating immensity. They caught and swallowed and warped the sunlight that struck them. Some seemed momentarily human, while others became like misshaped animals or deformed creatures or perhaps machines, all coming into being and giving forth a burst of animated life and then sinking back into the stony surface, lost.

Manuel eyed the hulk as they got closer. He switched on his comm again and heard louder static and a few scattered weak voices. To his left, Petrovich and Major Sánchez approached, and looking back, the boy saw knots of figures in the valley—men walking beside others, without the random directionless talk so usual on the comm, unconsciously coming together (as threads in a spiderweb converge as they near the focus), drawn by the slumbering mass that hung above the shattered plain.

"Hey!" someone shouted. It began to move. Manuel started running, bringing the muzzle up but finding no true target, leaving Old Matt behind.

The hulking, shadowy form began to drift, like a thing blown by an unfelt wind. The nervous darting extrusions subsided, muddied, blurred, and were gone. Manuel ran faster. He heard a laser bolt crash. The ruby-red beam glanced off an alabaster hexagonal edge and hissed into the ice. It spewed up a dirty gout of steam where it struck, leaving a near-perfect rounded hole. Manuel opened his servos and went fast, blotting out the rising clamor and shouts over the comm. There were now only a few men closer than he, and he passed the one who had fired—a Fujimura mechanic, a still-frozen arm pointing where the bolt had gone, a face with skin stretched tight by a yawning black mouth, open and soundless and studded with dark crooked teeth.

He hit the ground and gathered for a high jump to get a better look. He was watching to see which way the Aleph would go, and then without any transition at all he was skidding over the ice, face down. He smacked into a boulder and stopped, his right hip numb. Something had hit him from the side and bowled him over. He stood and saw it was Eagle, churning on, oblivious of the momentary obstruction that it had brushed aside. The boy glanced at the e-beam—the system diagnostics still winked green—and set off after Eagle, panting now.

The Aleph glided downslope, angling toward the distant valley walls, not toward or away from the gathering clumps of men but at an angle that selected no advantage, and ignored the hooting, shouting specks that converged on the wrecked land beneath it. It coasted, ghostlike. Eagle reached it then and drove in without pausing. The running thing looked slight and insubstantial as it leaped at the ponderous mass above. Eagle's claws grasped at the alabaster ribbing, scratching—and a chunk came away, turning pink at the fracture points, tumbling down with Eagle and striking the ice in a tangle with it. The boy stopped. He had never seen that before—seen a mere mortal thing rip the Aleph that way. He switched to his magneto detectors and saw what Eagle must have sensed: a fitful waxing and waning of the magnetic fields as the thing glided over the irregular ground, the fields seeking a grip on the iron beneath.

Eagle gathered itself and leaped again, arcing into a gap that had not been there when it left the ground but opened as Eagle flew up, a flickering weakness which the churning muscular form shot through. It snatched at a ribwork and again tore off a fragment. The fields shifted again and slapped Eagle down, driving it into the ice. But it sprang up again without a pause, this time a little too late to exploit a momentary ebbing in the fluxlines that hung in the air—and the Aleph slowed. Turned. Set off downvalley, turning an amber flank to Eagle. The boy gasped, sucking in air—he had been holding his breath—and Petrovich shouted, "Look at! Made it change its mind!" and the men ran faster.

The Aleph picked up speed and moved away from Eagle. An animal—Manuel saw it was a servo'd dog—coming from the side, made bold perhaps by Eagle's attack, leaped at the moving mass. It too cut through a flickering ebb in the flux—it was impossible to tell whether by accident or by design—but halfway to the Aleph a knot of magnetic turbulence struck it in the belly. The animal doubled over, and the belly blew open in a spew of tubes and rods and blood-spattered parts. It sent out a brief startled yelp in the radio spectrum and fell and sprawled loosely on the ice beneath the still-moving silent bulk.

Eagle was after it and leaped again and again at the Aleph as the two of them sped down a low slope. This time the attacks had no effect, as if the Aleph had learned better how to defend against this new thing. The men were coming at it from all sides now. Manuel still looked for an advantage, a target in the blank amber cubes. He breathed in the hot coppery taste strongly as he loped and squinted, panting heavily, his right hip now painful where Eagle had struck him. He heard the chorus of cries and orders and shouts over the comm build and surge as the men caught the meaning of Eagle's charge and the Aleph's continuing glide, spiritlike, over the hummocked terrain. It was not burrowing into the ice to elude them; no, it was running—not away from the men, or toward them, but clearly in reaction to the thing that men had wrought, Eagle. They began to swarm and hack at it now, firing their bolts and double-bores at whatever piece of it they fancied, whooping and yelling to each other as they ran and milled and exclaimed and reloaded and laughed in newly released, unacknowledged fear.

Another animal came at the Aleph, going *chip-chip-chip,* loud and lunging, off balance. It leaped, and something caught it partway and held it for just an instant. It broke apart in the air. The men did not notice the body fall. They came in closer, their weapons booming and crashing, potting at the alabaster slabs. Deep inside the blocks a mottled green now flowed. The shots inflicted no damage.

The Aleph was nearly to the valley wall, and the men fired faster, knowing they would lose it soon. Manuel still saw no target and held back, not sure it was going to be of any use at all to wait, but still unwilling to expend himself pointlessly the way the others did. He looked around for Old Matt. He had forgotten the old man and expected to see him far back, tired. He was surprised when his faceplate overlay showed Old Matt's pulsing blue dot close by. He waved, and the dry, sandy voice called over the comm, "Up here. Follow."

Manuel hesitated, wanting to follow the swarming, shouting crowd that pursued. Old Matt did not wait for him but went bounding up a hillside. Manuel ran after him. The old man moved slower, but chose his short leaps well and made good progress. They boy saw that this way took them through an easy pass, then over a ridgeline and along rumpled shelves of ice. Within moments he could no longer look back and see the valley floor. The e-beam threw him off balance as he ran through a clogged narrow gully. Then the two of them were headed down again, landing in slide cones where the dirt and gravel cushioned their falls. They plunged on, slipping on half-thawed ground, splashing across a brook of water with cakes of frozen ammonia in the shallows, then scrabbling up the bank and on. Manuel heard Old Matt's long, rattling gasping over the comm. They came out at the base of a long, high cliff. It was mostly rock, streaked with rusty seams and patches of conglomerate—pebbles, ice chips, lumps of gray metallic ore.

They stopped there. Old Matt bent over, hands on his knees, coughing: slow, dry barks from deep in his chest.

"You, you want to go on? Maybe ease up, wait for the crawler? I can—"

"No. Wait. Wait here."

The old man would say no more, just bent over and waited for the wracking cough to pass. Manuel cursed himself for giving up a chance at a shot, a last minute or two of opportunity, to come here. Probably Old Matt had meant to get a better angle on the Aleph as it neared the hills, to be able to shoot down on it where it might be less protected. But they'd got mixed up in these ravines and gullies and couldn't even see the plain. The Aleph was gone from the valley now for sure, vanished, so even if he went back it would be too—

The cliff shuddered. Stones fell and dust billowed. A tremor. The cliff exploded, showering them with pebbles. The tubular snout came first, grinding stone, extending out into empty space and then flexing down. The huge body followed, snaking, carrying fragments of the rusty rock. Its skin swirled now, patchy with blurred blues and greens deep in the amber. It erupted from the cliff in a last cascade of dirt and ice, and descended to the flat plateau, still riding an insulating meter above the land.

"Je—I— How'd you know it was comin' through to here? I thought—"

Old Matt waved the question aside. "Different," he said hoarsely, still panting heavily. He pointed. "It's different now."

"You mean the colors? I don't see . . ."

One of the patches resolved, solidified, darkened. It became a hole and the hole widened and something moved in it, and abruptly the boy saw that the thing coming out was Eagle. The head worked free and then the hulking shoulders. Eagle struggled against the irising lip, silent, and the wide-set black eyes locked on the men, not to ask for aid but as a remorseless mute statement it chose to make even at the moment when it surely felt what the men could see—the suddenly constricting grip that folded its left shoulder, buckled the main housing and the steel manifold, breaking the spinal reinforcement, crushing Eagle's big treads that ground against the amber walls. Only near the end did Eagle's hands stretch out and flail against the side, futilely, without hope but without surrender. Manuel stepped forward. Old Matt put a hand on his shoulder. Eagle struggled on. The great neck snapped. The eyes went blank. Eagle's head lolled, and Manuel again stepped forward. The opening convulsed once, twice, and then the third time, with a slithering sound, it swallowed Eagle's body whole.

"I—I—Damn! It just—" The boy shook with rage, crying out to no one but himself. "Eagle—got in—It didn't have to—Damn! To just—Damn!"

The Aleph moved, coasting toward the south, still floating a blithe distance from the ground.

"Eagle got in, had time to do some damage, maybe," Old Matt said. "That's what made the colors, made it open up those spots again."

"Yeah—yeah—" the boy gasped, mind churning. "To, to kill Eagle for, for—"

"Don't you worry about that end of it. Eagle didn't. You saw the look of him right there, the last second. Looked the same as ever. Mean as he ever was and not regretting it."

"I don't see . . ."

Old Matt gestured. "It's moving off down that way. Look."

Manuel studied the massive blocky shape, working its wedge-shaped collars and buttresses against each other as it glided, soundless and unhurried. Its surface still roiled with blue-black marks that came and went, and as he watched, one irised open.

"Still not done," Old Matt said. "Let's go."

They began to run again.

3

Old Matt went slower now. As they loped down a ravine the boy could see the lines of strain in the old, worn face. Their slick suits bunched and stretched with amplified strength, and Manuel saw the power gauge on Old Matt's back register nearly two-thirds gone. They scrambled over outcroppings of layered stone—rock laid down in the first days when Ganymede's raw crust was melting and freezing and remelting under the long hammering, when Jupiter glowed with its own accreting fires, and on the moons brief waters flowed to form fast-dying, steaming seas. They had to go slow on the slippery hillsides. The Aleph steadily widened the gap between them. Manuel checked his overlay and saw they were running parallel to the main valley. The blue shotgun pattern of dots told him the main party was spreading through the neighboring arroyos and cañons.

"Funny it doesn't burrow in," he called to Old Matt. "Never saw it aboveground this long before."

"I have. Twice."

"Figure it's having fun with us?"

"Doubt if it knows what we are, even."

"It knew Eagle, all right," he said with sharp pride.

The old man panted into his suit mike. "That it did. That it did."

He watched Old Matt as they loped after the serenely coasting ghostlike form. There was something in the old face now. It was neither excitement nor eagerness nor hope. Years later, when he was a man, the boy would realize finally what it had been: a blend of foreknowledge and a certain deliberate, grim determination. Old Matt had known something unspoken, back then when he first saw Eagle, and had made of the furious burning anger in Eagle something that, fashioned, could reach farther and strike at something in the Aleph. He had known and been pulled forward by the knowing, giving himself each year to learn a little more. *He had no share, no fraction of a Settlement*, Manuel would think then. *There were children, his own from decades before, but all of them scattered to other outposts or even back Earthside. That part of him was dispersed. He had spent his time and his substance in the orbital labs or on explorer teams or at Titan and Saturn when they were just opening it up out there. So he had never posted a bond or filed a term agreement and affadavit of intention, and so had no part of the land that he could nail down or lay claim to. He could live and work and earn in Sidon, at fill-in jobs; he even had a vote, but still was not a commune member and in sum had nothing of the territory other than what he sensed of it. He had known it before a foot had fallen on every hill, before centuries of brawling humanity wrote their name across it with Settlements and Centrals. But despite all that, he returned again and again to the land beyond man's enclaves, still felt its emptiness and unresolved potentiality.*

Manuel called to his father, got an answer he could not understand, and ran on. Then the Aleph dove into a hillside. It did not pause or even slow, just necked into a wall of ice and through it, boring on with a grinding and a booming.

"Hell! It's going under!" Manuel shouted, and slowed, but Old Matt said nothing, just kept running down the cañon. Manuel paused, panting, watching the last of the Aleph disappear into the still-splintering ice, tumbling boulders from the hillside, making the ground tremble and buck.

He heaved a sigh of defeat and slapped his side in irritation. He had lugged the e-beam this far and never fired it. He swore at his stupidity. He was starting to tire, and the best chance yet, the best chance he had ever heard of, had dribbled away, with never the right angle or distance for a decent shot. Maybe he should have fired anyway. Then at least he could have said he had done something, given it a try. But even as he thought it he knew that was bullshit, that shooting not for the target but for the talking afterward about it was wrong and would make the whole thing taste cheap in his mouth for a long time after. So he just stood there and swore.

When he looked around after a minute, the old man was clean gone. He checked the overlay and set out after him, feeling even more stupid than before. Old Matt's blue dot was angling around a bunch of low hills. Manuel set off and ran hard. He took long, high leaps, depending on his gyros to get him oriented right before he landed. Once he came down amongst a pack of rockjaws. They scattered in mad flight, though the boy hardly saw them. In five minutes he had nearly caught up with the figure, was only a few hundred meters behind, when a hillside broke open and the Aleph erupted from it, moving as before with that constant, indifferent gliding velocity.

"Manuel!" It was his father. He looked to the north and picked out the swift figures of the main party, converging. "We guessed you were following it. Last we saw, Eagle—"

"I know. Eagle's dead."

There was talk from the men as they came loping across the broad flat land. Manuel automatically waited for his father, loping a little to the west to keep near the Aleph, which was speeding on. More than ten klicks away an ice mesa reared up in its path, sunlight catching the ruddy peaks. The Aleph might be heading for it or the mesa might just be in the way, but if the Aleph bored through it the men would have to take a long route around, and Manuel knew Old Matt was not up to that. He was getting tired now too. Over the comm he could hear panting from the running men.

"It's movin' pretty damn fast," a voice called.

Another said, "Yeah, looks to be pickin' up speed."

"Too fast. You, *los ricos* wi' your extra servos, maybe you keep up wi' it but we can't—"

Petrovich shouted, "You wanting to drop out, go back get crawlers!"

Some swearing.

"You guys been jawing while this boy's been runnin' down the damn thing."

"Yeah, right."

"Uh-huh, just a kid."

"The old man too."

"*Sí*, they been showin' us their heels all day."

"Come on, you bastards!"

"It's only got a klick on us."

"Not gonna let that old man run you inna ground are ya? Ha?"

And the straggled-out bunches of men pulled together and began to run again in earnest, filling the comm with their harsh taunts to each other, their heavy gasping breaths as some sped out in front, spilling pellmell across the plain, their clamor and din swelling as ceramic and steel scraped and joined, propelling them on in a wedding of man, machine, and movement.

"Don't let the animals near it," Colonel López shouted. "They'll get snapped in pieces."

A voice grunted, "Damn sure I'm not goin' 'at close either," and a chorus of agreement came.

Major Sánchez called out, "Try to turn it!" though how anyone could do that he did not say, and no one asked.

By now the boy had caught up with Old Matt and saw the leathery face turn toward him, eyes bright, a thin, dry smile on the lips, the copper of his cheek flecked with sweat. "You'll have to . . . hit it . . . on the run," the old man called out.

"How? I— I— Those openings are small. I—"

"Get up close," was all Old Matt said, and then they both landed at the end of a leap and were off again, coming up alongside the smoothly gliding form. Manuel watched the crackling magnetic flux fork and dance around it, and studied it for advantage. Pockets opened and closed, but too fast for him to do anything about them. Eagle had been faster. Eagle had known the vulnerable warpings and had used them instantly, without the numbing fear that came on him now, a spreading chill that robbed nerves and muscle of vital split-seconds.

"Stay back from it, son!" But he pressed forward as he saw a blue whirlpool-like splotch form near a tangle of arcing and magnetic field lines. He raised the snout of the beam projector and as the blue melted into greenish dabs he fired. The bolt cut a slim, impossibly straight line through the thin air, landed with a shower of orange sparks, a full three centimeters wide of the mark, and flew off to the right, harmless.

"Ah! *Ah!*" he spat out in self-disgust. And fired again. This shot came nearer but still richocheted off in a flower of sparks, some of them glancing off the boy's arm, he was that close.

The Aleph was like a moving building to the boy, and he jumped back as it turned first toward him, as if to shrug him off one of the huge shoulders, and then away, rising a meter more from the ice. It towered over him, and the blue-green vortex faded. He refused to give ground. It accelerated away and the boy was after it in three fast leaps, eyes searching, Old Matt's voice in his ear: "We got to turn him more!" —and the boy saw the old man was on his left, craning his neck to look at the underbelly of the thing. The grainy amber roiled with flecks and seams of washed-out colors, as if something liquid churned just inside the skin, but the ponderous blocks looked solid and hard like deep rock too.

"One's starting over here!" Old Matt called, and lunged forward, pointing at a vortex swirl of mottled colors. A condensing magnetic knot came out of the whirlpool and struck him in the chest, and he went down. It laced up his chest and around his head, a snakelike swarming tangle of interthreading ruby flux lines, arcing and licking at him. Manuel saw him slump and go on his knees. But the boy also caught the vortex colors deepening and swung the snout toward them. He fired. Missed. Thumbed the stock to recharge the capacitors. And looked for Old Matt. The magnetic knot had started to ebb, withdrawing into the Aleph. Old Matt was still down, not moving. The boy leaped forward, further under the vast weight that worked and labored, and raised the projector again and shot directly into the thing at close range, the quick yellow stream crackling as it found the entrance. The churning dark colors sopped it up. It was swallowed, gone, the whole bolt sucked in. Manuel backed off, gasping, and the Aleph smoothly kept on. He saw he had done nothing. He dropped the projector and bent over Old Matt, who was on hands and knees and gasping, eyes closed, mouth open and salivating.

"You— Can you— Can I get you—"

"I'm . . . okay. Okay. Keep after it."

Manuel studied the creased, tired face for a long moment and then nodded and got to his feet, sighed, picked up the projector, checking the winking diagnostics, looked up—

The Aleph was down. It was on the ice, barely moving. The aura of magnetic flux faded and flickered out as the boy watched.

He yelped in sheer exuberance. The Aleph looked even bigger on the ground, cracking the ice where its great ribwork slid and stopped, slid and stopped.

A hand clapped him on the shoulder and he turned, expecting Old Matt, but it was his father. "*Jesucristo*," the Colonel said. "Something inside, some electromagnetic thing must have failed."

"It's crawling!" Petrovich broke in. "You got it crawling! The foot thing, see? Treads on other side too."

The long cone came down sluggishly, stolidly, stamping its blunted point into the ice. As the Aleph turned the men could see the treads bite in and push it forward, smacking and splitting the ice and rock in rhythm with the conical extrusion that struck and punched, struck and punched, leaving the delta-shaped print. Manuel felt the ground shake as the Aleph inexorably shoved itself forward, no longer serenely skating above the rough raw land that was the province of mere men and their lanky, scrambling, awkward legs. He stared. It was as massive as he had ever dreamed, and now that he saw it wounded and still struggling on with the same deliberate immemorial energy, as ruthless with itself as it had been with others, he knew it was undiminished by mere injury and still possessed the thing he sought.

Old Matt stood shakily. He merely gave one nod,

abrupt and final, a thin drawn smile slowly spreading until it reached the metal of him.

The men were yelling and pounding Manuel on the back and raising their stunners and lasers into the air, and in his ears the human voices rang and clamored like the yips and cries of the animals, echoing on themselves and filling the air of the caked plain, seeming to reflect and re-form and amplify, until the rousing volley of noise fed and built and a shot boomed, then another, now more—lasers and stunners and double-bores all raking the sides of the laboring thing that kept on, oblivious, as now bits and pieces of it began to fly off where the stronger laser bolts hit, alabaster chips spinning away into the clear air, stunners rippling the space between the milling, shouting men and their target, shots steaming off the ice and vaporizing rock and splashing against the intricate groining where colors pinwheeled still. In a moment Manuel stood alone and the fifty-odd men of the party had spread out, firing and running, circling around it.

"Stop! Cease fire!" Colonel López shouted, once, then again, then a third time as his words began to have effect.

"It's still *movin'*," a man called.

"You're just chippin' away at it," Old Matt said weakly. "Do no good. Won't even slow it down."

A man shouted, "Ha! Chippin', he says! We'll see 'bout that," and he made to raise his stunner.

Colonel López was on the man before he could fire, slapping the weapon down. "We'll see, eh? You on this, you follow what's good for us all, use your head, *sí?*"

"Well I don't see as—"

"Quiet!" somebody shouted.

"It's not going fast," Major Sánchez said. "We got time to think."

"Think what? Shooting it's all we can do," a man from Hiruko said.

"Yeah," another man put in, "us all shootin', maybe we wear it down."

"No," Petrovich said. "E-beam in the dark spots, that works. Nothing else has, ever."

"Right," Old Matt said.

"Those spots, there aren't many of them," Major Sánchez said, gesturing. There were few of the deeper mottled patches now. They moved in a slow whirlpool churn, deep in the blocks and collars and buttresses of it.

"Hard to hit," a man said. Others murmured and grumbled. None of them had e-beams. They were poor agro laborers, mostly, minimum-share men, and they wanted to be able to say they had shot the thing on this day and maybe even done something important. "We could sit here forever, waitin' for a—"

"Manuel's hit it already," Major Sánchez said.

Petrovich said, "Yes, too much risk he's taken. Enough for one day. I do the next."

"I'd say I know more about projectors," Major Sánchez said mildly.

Colonel López said, "Knowing projectors isn't it."

"Yes," Petrovich said. "Is hitting at right time that is important. You saw the boy."

"*Sí*," Major Sánchez said.

A Fujimura Settlement man demanded, "Seems like that e-beam oughtta be shared out."

"Yeah, common property, like."

"Only one, seems like should take turns."

"Come all this way, don' get a chance 'less they give us turns at—"

"*Quiet!*" the Colonel shouted. "You're not getting anything by whining for it." He glowered at the men and some steam went out of the discussion.

Someone said quietly, "Still, we got to decide."

Petrovich said, "The boy, he has whole rest of life to hunt."

"So what?" an agro man put in. "He's earned it. Him an' the old one."

Major Sánchez said, "Could be. Dangerous, though."

Manuel had been quiet, waiting to see which way the

talk would go, but now sensing what his father felt, he spoke up: "Old Matt deserves a try. It's already hurt him some."

Heads nodded; the crowd murmured agreement.

Old Matt said nothing, just took the projector and hefted it and ran the winking diagnostics through their cycle. The men watched the Aleph as it labored across the hummocked ground, making fair speed but still a long way from the jutting mesa.

"Why didn't it burrow?" Major Sánchez asked.

"Hurt," Petrovich said. "Needs time to fix self, maybe."

"Crawl away like an animal?" Colonel López said. "No. It's no kind of creature at all."

But the thing did have a valiant look to it now, wounded and still keeping on with its same remorseless energy, its deep drive to be forever moving.

Old Matt started forward, moving too with a slow, indomitable certainty, almost ceremonial, but hampered by the awkward bulk he carried. "I'll help him with that," Manuel called out, and ran after him.

The men spread out instinctively, forming a sweeping line as their ancestors had a million years before—a good way to flush game from thickets and run it where they wanted. They overtook the lumbering Aleph easily and the ragged line wrapped around, surrounding it. The pile-driving conical thing shook the ground, stamping furiously, and the great body swayed and creaked and groaned with its gravid immemorial momentum.

"Have to get in close," the old man said.

Manuel followed, carrying the projector. He watched for the blue-green motes that flickered across the flat faces. The motes swam as though the men were seeing them projected on a screen by some interior source of brilliant light, so strong it could illuminate through rock. His mouth filled with the hot coppery taste, now laced with an oily fatigue.

The two of them walked cautiously into the shadow of

it. A hexagonal segment rocked from side to side. The land shook and heaved. Manuel gravely gave the projector to Old Matt and saw the deep creases in his dark face, saw the haggard resolve there, and did not understand the thin, quiet smile.

"One good bolt will do it," the boy said, and felt absurd, giving advice. The old man nodded, still smiling, as bare meters away a great flat side like a wall hammered at the land and to the rear the cone jabbed and a fresh delta-print appeared, sunk deep in the rock, steaming.

"Watch for me," Old Matt said.

The boy flicked his eyes across the long profile of the Aleph, trying to anticipate where the next blue-green swirl would come, and for a while rested his hand on Old Matt's shoulder, as if restraining him from going closer, encased in the extended moment, sure that if they waited until the right glancing instant—

Blue-green flecks united just above, at a corner; rapidly grew; split into two larger mottled round, dark openings—

"There!" Manuel shouted.

Old Matt got the snout up and fired at a forming spot. The yellow bolt lashed at the edge of it, showering gaudy orange sparks down on them.

"Get it?" Manuel cried. Old Matt shook his head. He fired again. The discharge boomed in the thin air. *Another near miss*, the boy thought, but he could not tell exactly, and a green electric aura now flickered at the mouth of the opening.

The shaking, struggling mountain rocked harder, shuddered, boomed, and leaned over toward them. "It's . . ."—and the boy tried to pull Old Matt back, away, seeing the Aleph tip further, the laboring blocks struggling all along its length. Old Matt lurched away, intent, and raised the projector toward the teetering wall. The boy shouted, "Wait— Get out—"

Too late. The Aleph fell. Half-turned to run, Manuel

saw the spreading dark blue patch plunge toward him and at the last instant felt a spongy clasp around him as he cringed, braced hopelessly against the weight—

And was encased in a muffled silence, utterly black, even as he felt the shattering crash of the Aleph's impact through his boots, which still stood on the ice while the rest of him had entered this cottony blank emptiness. He was inside the blue portal; it had fallen on him. He reached out for support and found nothing but a slickness, a resistance that brushed his grip aside and imparted some momentum to him.

He felt his boots leave the ice. Lifted—

He called out, but his comm gave nothing but a hornet's buzz of static. Ahead—he knew he moved, but could not tell how—a green glow rippled and forked into the mouths of tunnels. He was gliding down a tube. Something dark scissored regularly in the diffuse light and he saw it was a pair of legs, a human form turning in the glow, and as he came closer he saw it was Old Matt, one arm up in what might be a wave, the helmet lit only by the wan green luminescence.

As Old Matt turned, the boy saw the face for an instant, uncreased and pale, smiling, looking straight at him with eyes unblinking. Old Matt said something, his lips moving slowly, silent, and the boy tried to make out the words, but a dull roar came into the tunnels then and disturbed his concentration. He was now smoothly passing by Old Matt in the glow, so he raised a hand and waved in a timeless gliding moment, and then he felt a push, a gathering acceleration, and with rushing speed fell away from the still-turning silent form. He blinked, struggled against unseen forces, and heard random crisp noises swelling as if he were coming closer, yells, swearing—

Dark ice rushed at him and he hit solidly, painfully, rolling, pinwheeling, arms flailing, voices shouting as pandemonium burst in on him. He fetched up against a boulder, slamming his shoulder into it, purpling his vision—gasped, and for a moment could not get his hands and feet under him to get up.

He clutched against the boulder and stood. He was a dozen meters away from the Aleph and could make out the gouge in the ice where he had hit, falling straight down from a yawning green opening in a hexagonal collar. He'd left skid marks. The Aleph lay absolutely still and silent. It rested on ice that had cracked beneath it. The conical delta-puncher was cocked halfway up in the air, pointing at the horizon.

Men ran back and forth around the Aleph, hooting and jabbering and yelling to each other all sorts of claims—"Didja see 'at one I got it smack inna head" despite the fact that the Aleph had nothing you could call a head, and "Shot it three times three good uns" and "—figure it was me an' Raul did it, see, we timed our bolts so they hit together on that big rib cage up 'ere" and "Damned if I did'n know it, soon's we opened fire when it was buckin' aroun', the sucker just gives up, that's all it took was some more shootin'—" and "just wore it out is all, nobody's run it down the way we have, kept after it steady" and so on, the boy standing dazed as this washed over him and the throbbing ache spread in his shoulder. A Hiruko man jumped up on the gray flank of it and stamped down as if to test how solid it was, and yelled, "One small step for a man!" and laughed and climbed on up to the top of the buttress, toting his stunner and jabbing down with his boots. Manuel gazed around. It looked to him as if he had been dropped about a hundred meters from where he and Old Matt had been. He started walking back that way, and that was when he saw the crowd. They were standing around two figures on the ground. One of them was large, an animal. The other was a man, lying face down on the ice and not moving. It was Old Matt.

4

Manuel stumbled forward and pushed his way through the men crowded around. A jagged tear ran down Old Matt's suit from shoulder to hip. Somebody had slapped an instant patch on it, and through the translucent gauze Manuel could see blood oozing out. The suit was raked all down one side, too, with shreds of it hanging out and insulation showing and fluids dripping. Gingerly Petrovich rolled Old Matt partway over. There was no damage to the front of the suit. The face was leached of color and the eyes were closed. His backpack showed life functions weak but steady.

"Did he hit on something when he came out?" Manuel asked.

Major Sánchez stared at him. "Came out? It crushed him when it rolled over."

"No, we both got picked up by it. It fell over on us. The openings, they sucked us in. *Madre*. That must be how Eagle got trapped inside too."

The men looked at him without comprehension. Colonel López said, "Old Matt's been here all the time."

"No! I saw him inside. Then the thing, it spat us out again."

Petrovich shook his head rapidly. "It started rolling over, we shot. I saw. Aleph hit the old man"—he smacked two fists together—"threw like rag doll."

"No, it had us both. Inside. It must've carried me longer, that's all. I *saw* him in there."

The men stared at him again blankly. His father said, "Look, son, you're shaky. Sit down, take a stim pack. I got to deal with this right now."

Manuel peered down at Old Matt and tried to remember just what the old man had looked like inside. The same, only not hurt. He was going to say something more when a man came up to him and said emphatically, "*Finito!*"

"Uh, what? Finite?"

"*Finito.*" The man drew a finger across his neck.

"Finished?" Manuel gazed at the hulking inert mass. "I . . . guess so."

Another man broke in with "Uh, 'at thing—it's got some systems up, but most of 'em are hopeless."

"What? What thing?" Manuel looked to where the man was gesturing. The animal lying nearby was badly mangled. He walked unsteadily over to it, halfway knowing what he would find.

Eagle's head was intact, but the neck turned at a wrong angle. The strong steel-jacketed trunk was mashed and leaking pus-colored fluid. Something had shredded and ripped its treads.

"We got to get it back to camp," Manuel said.

Petrovich had followed him. "Now, Eagle, it did come out—*poof,* like you. Maybe that's what you saw in there?"

Manuel shook his head.

Petrovich said, "Not good chance for this one."

"Animal like this, you can save it if you don't let the cold get into it or the systems lose minimum power." Manuel wasn't talking to Petrovich. He stared at the crushed Eagle and didn't seem to notice when other men came up and said something, marveling at the damage and how long Eagle had lived in there.

Major Sánchez said, "Look at it, all that time, and being carried along and all."

"Where's a crawler?" Manuel said abruptly. He went over to his father. "We need two, three crawlers."

The Colonel said, "I sent Fuentes back. Already radioed them."

"He, he's bleeding in there." Manuel stood and watched the bright red seep out of Old Matt. Without a pressure dome there was nothing any of them could do but stand there and watch it.

Petrovich said, "No leaks—I checked. But don't like his temperature."

"He's bleeding."

"Not so bad."

"Not so bad, *goddamn*. He hasn't got much in him. He's worn out already."

"Shock is worst. Worse than bleeding." Petrovich said it flatly, not coloring the facts with the sound of his voice.

Manuel paced restlessly between the two clusters of men. The bulk of the Aleph loomed over them like a ridge of rock thrust up from the ice. Motionless, it seemed a piece of the broken terrain. Manuel looked at it for a moment, not thinking of anything but merely trying to take in the enormity of the great bulk now still and dead, free at last of its duty. He tried to think of what had happened, but could not. There was a deadness in him. Then the harsh sounds of the men yelling and scrambling over the Aleph brought him back from the empty part of him and he went to his father. "Which way the crawlers coming?"

"They have to go around through some ravines," the Colonel said. He showed his son the route on the map overlay.

"That'll take too long."

"Two hours, I'd say. Petrovich thinks—"

"I'll carry him. Go up over this ridgeline here. Meet them down where the cañon necks. Cut the time in half."

"Carry him? Son, you're tired out. I can't—"

"Let's ask Petrovich if it'll hurt him."

"You'll do as I . . ." Colonel López paused, looking at his son for a moment while the boy gazed off at the crumpled form of the old man. Then he went and asked, and Petrovich thought about it and said maybe so, if Manuel took it easy, no jumps, just climbing the ridge and then coming down the far side easy, nothing fast—

"Good. Good," Manuel said.

Major Sánchez got him a power reserve pack from one of the Hiruko men who had a spare. The man argued for a while about giving it up until he saw the scowls around him. The boy did not think badly of the man; without that reserve the march back would be a long labor of sweat and ache. He ignored everyone and concentrated on slinging a harness to carry the body in his arms. He secured it against jolts with a strap around his neck. His father watched and knew with a mild surprise that it would do no good to say anything. In that moment of letting go of his son he passed into a new time, and began to accumulate a sadness and an anger fueled by loss that he would not feel consciously for months to come.

Manuel picked up the old man carefully. He glanced at the circle of faces without recognition, saying nothing in reply to the advice and warnings, already turned inward and preparing himself, and then turned and set off at a steady pace, taking each step with a rolling gait to cushion the body. He stopped once, a kilometer away, to look back and get his bearings. It seemed he was gazing back over a great distance. The men were shrunken dots, random specks milling about the flanks of an enormous carcass.

He started up the slopes of loose gravel and rock shelves. As he rose and could see further he realized how far they had run. He did not think about what had happened but just kept on, concentrating on the gently swaying loose-limbed body. Once Old Matt opened his eyes and looked up at the black sky for a time, and then shifted himself minutely, the eyes gazing out at Manuel, liquid and glistening in the pale yellow sunlight.

Manuel tramped stolidly along the rocky ridgeline. He watched clouds boiling up from the south where a fusion aura glowed, yellowing the vapors. The banks of moisture roiled and tumbled over each other and grew blue-bellied. They soared over the ridge, rising, and then a rain came down, bringing a false dusk that made the boy go slower so as to be sure of his footing. The first hour passed. The body creaked in his arms. He covered sixteen klicks on the level ridge and then started down, which was the hardest part. The gravel and moist soil gave suddenly and unpredictably, making him lurch to keep the swaying body from feeling the full shock. Old Matt's eyes opened momentarily and then the face descended into a kind of collapsed sleep.

It was into the third hour, and he could not feel his arms anymore. He went on through the gathering dull dusk, across a slumbering landscape lit by breaks in the clouds, hearing in his helmet the regular *ping ping* of the directional signal the crawler sent. He angled downward to meet it. Innumerable times he slipped and caught himself and slipped again, starting small slides and avoiding the rattling showers of gravel that cascaded down. Through the streaming gloom the spaced signals came to him like a constant calling of a mindless thing, the only presence besides the crunch of his boots on snapping ice.

He found the lead crawler making good time down a streambed. It stopped, and he put the body through the lock. Two crawlers and a walker passed by in the sleeting darkness, going on to the main party. By the time he cycled through, the body was hooked into the small medical monitor. He sat with three men and watched the diagnostics flicker and resolve. "He's holdin' on," one of the men said. "Have to get him back to camp to do any fixin' up, through."

So the crawler reversed and backed out of the valley until it could turn around without risking getting stuck in the ponds and melting ice. The falling rain carried energy stored in it by a fusion-reactor robot southward, and in recondensing now released the heat, spreading change across the face of the land.

It was a long ride back. Manuel found the men studying him and realized he had exhausted himself. His suit was on the red marker at the bottom of the dial. He sat in a sling chair and let the swaying lull him but did not sleep. Hailstones clattered on the hull. The men here had dropped out of the main party, mostly from fatigue, and did not ask much about what had happened. He was glad of that.

They covered the last distance into camp as the rain and hail lifted and the sun cut through the remaining pink fog that hugged the gullies and ice arroyos. The crawler speeded up then, growing, toward the *bip bip bip* of the ranging beacon that seemed to Manuel like one long calling, each pulse lingering in his mind until the next joined it and blended in, a hollow ringing as formless and remorseless as the fog. A dozen men waited in a little clump as they came into camp. A medical tech had come out from Sidon on Colonel López's orders. He was a thin man with uncertain, always-moving green eyes. The men helped bring Old Matt inside, carefully turning the stretcher to get it through the crawler lock without jarring. When they got his suit off, the walnut-brown body lay inert, nearly hairless, seeming smaller than the boy remembered.

The medical machinery and the tech did things to the body, patching and splicing in replacements, cleaning and disinfecting where suit fluids might have gotten into the body cavity, working on the main problems and leaving the rest for later.

"God, lookit him," the med tech exclaimed.

Manuel asked, "Exhaustion? The wound doesn't look so deep."

"Exhausted, sure," the med tech said. "Shock pretty bad too. But mostly it's the cardiovascular. Seized up somehow. Lot of neural damage, too. Can't figure how that happened. Just wore out, maybe. Doesn't response to the usual stuff."

Manuel asked quietly, "How many functions can you save?"

"Most. For sure, most."

"Replace the rest?"

"I'd say prob'ly. Some of the organs died, though. Liver, kidneys, some smaller stuff. And the small blood vessels—they've broken down all through him. Costs a lot to replace that."

"How much?"

"Dunno. I don't see many cases like this, guys this old. Most of 'em are in Hiruko."

"They'll have to take him there?"

"Prob'ly. Those blood vessels, it's not the parts, it's the labor. Lotta bench time."

Old Matt opened his eyes then. He looked out as though from far back in a hidden place, and his eyes moved slowly over the faces of the men gathered around. His face was dry and chalky, but the eyes seemed to brim with a moist fullness. He opened his mouth, but no sound came out. Then he closed it without his face showing any expression of concern.

"Some kind of control function is out," the med tech said. "Not surprising, with a spine injury."

"Can you fix it?"

"Look, I told you. Funny neural damage in there. That's not field-type work."

Manuel nodded numbly.

They let the medmonitor work on the body then, humming and sloshing and snuffling and clacking to itself. Manuel sat up watching it and then slumped over on his side and slept for a few hours. He woke when the main party hauled into camp and some men called into the cabin for help getting Eagle off the deck of a crawler. Manuel went outside and saw his father and the others dismounting, all pale and with that careful slow-moving way of men working in suits that are drained of power. He joined the gang of men on the nearest crawler. They got the lip of a forklift under one end of Eagle and worked it onto a makeshift ramp and pushed Eagle down, aided by the slippery ice that the hail had left on the ramp. They hooked it to the crawler and towed it over to the outside medical and hydraulic station for the animals.

Eagle lifted its head and tried to turn it. Steel screeched and sparks jumped. The great head crashed to the side, dangling. It shuffled its hands, and its treads clashed and jammed against each other. It struggled deep inside itself, Manuel could see that, and after a moment it shuddered and the hands relaxed and it went still again. He thought he could see a slight regular motion, as if from lungs laboring far down in there.

The med tech came out, looking harassed by the men who'd come piling into the cabin, men with pulled muscles and sprains and a few broken bones. He ran a series check on the crushed and mangled thing. He cut away Petrovich's clumsy patches and sealed on new ones, stopped fluid loss, and gave voltage boosts to the internal systems that still had life. Then he shook his head. "Can't work miracles," he muttered.

"You can goddamn try," Manuel said harshly.

"I done what I can. Got no equipment for more. Not outside stuff, anyway."

"I could take it back to Sidon."

"Don't think you should move it, not anymore."

"You going to just let it lie there?"

"Look, that's deep internal injuries there. Either the living part's going to pull through or not. Only way to help it is to pry open the shell and take it out and keep it alive until you get it to Hiruko. They know this kind of work. I don't. So I say we just leave it rest, see if it pulls through."

"How long?"

"Day, two days."

"Then?"

"Take it to Hiruko if it looks strong enough." The med tech's mouth twisted in irritation. "Look, I got men to work on. Animals come last, you know that."

"This's no animal."

"Yeah, okay, you read the regs, kid. You just read the regs." The man went back inside, fidgeting at his tools. He was having to deal with more injuries than he'd ever seen before on just a little pruning jaunt and he didn't like it.

Inside the sprawling cabin the men were eating or boozing or else lying across their bunks half-undressed, already sunk into sleep, mouths open, some of them snoring, faces dark with week-old beards and dirt. The boy sat awhile, not saying much to anybody or listening to the wandering, tired talk around him. Old Matt lay still, and his diagnostics held steady. The boy fell asleep again; but when he woke, tangled in his bunk with a blanket wrapped around his head and nothing on the lower half of him, he felt no lifting of the slow fatigue and ache in his arms and legs.

He went out then to look at Eagle. It was near noon in the long Ganymede day, and the sun had burned through the layers of mist that formed high up, where the new atmosphere was boiling out into pure dead vacuum. The dot of a sun cast sharp shadows among the men and women who were coming in now—pipefitters and agro hands from Sidon and further-away Settlements, miners from one-dome places yet unnamed, contract laborers, women widowed years before—all with a debt real or imagined that had now been paid. They came in walkers or on foot, following the same incessant *bip bip bip* and coming into the big clearing where Eagle lay facing outward, toward the distant line of slumped and folded ice hills. There must have been a hundred of them sitting in amongst the vehicles when Manuel came out. He watched them as they went up to the big crushed thing and stared at the caved-in carapace, never daring to reach out and touch it, speaking to each other in low voices that didn't carry on comm line, making their own private ritual of it. They asked to go inside and see Old Matt, too, but Petrovich wouldn't let them. They asked about Manuel, but nobody among them recognized the boy—they had only heard of him—so Manuel stayed close to Eagle and they did not bother him.

Eagle was holding steady. Every few hours it would lift its head and wrench the neck around painfully, each turn of angle like a rachet jumping forward a notch. The black eyes peered out at the gathering people and gave no sign of its inner torment. It studied the far hills, not with the ferocity it had shown before, but as if it wanted to be sure the broad, stretching wastes were still there, still lying beyond the ring of human faces. Manuel watched it then, sensing its adamant refusal to compromise, to give any sign of what lay wounded inside. Eagle was not of man and could not be reconciled with man, but was out of Earth and knew that, too. It had done its job, a task in the end self-imposed, and was now free. It died at noon.

5

Major Sánchez was the first to leave. "Got to get back. Work to do. I stayed too long already," he told Manuel.

"Most of us'll be hauling out tomorrow," a Sidon man said.

An engineer from another Settlement put in, "My men are kind of drug out. No more for us."

Colonel López nodded. "A few should stay with Old Matt until he's ready to be moved. I'll do it."

Manuel watched the people disperse from around the cabin. Most were going back to their Settlements. Some were mounting up to go out to where the Aleph was, though there wasn't much they could do besides stare at it. "I'll stay, too," he said.

"*Sí*, we got it, eh?" Major Sánchez said, slapping Manuel on the back. "After all this time."

"We'll have celebration, back at Sidon," Petrovich said jovially. "We wait for you to come in, though."

"Fine," Colonel López said, watching his son. "I imagine it won't be more than a few days. The med tech says Old Matt'll pull through."

Major Sánchez said, "*Sí, sí*. He is a tough old one." He stamped his boots to warm up, and waved at a nearby crawler. "I want to get going. Need some help getting Eagle back up on the deck and lashed down."

Manuel asked, "What'll you do with it?"

"Recycle. It's Sidon property. Lot of scrap. Some good motors 'n' servos left for sure."

"What about the body?" Manuel asked sharply.

Major Sánchez glanced at Colonel López. "Body? Animals, well . . ."

"Animals, they get organic recycle," Petrovich said.

Manuel said, "It's no animal—you don't know that."

Colonel López nodded. "As I remember, Hiruko said something about its maybe being human. Or part human."

"But Dad—"

The Colonel turned to Manuel. "When they open it up, we'll see. Sure didn't *act* human, did it?"

"That's not the point."

Colonel López smiled. "You know we value human life over everything. We're going to do all we can for Old Matt. But there was just no way to help Eagle. It was too embedded in the machinery."

Manuel said nothing. His father had always taken a lot of care with medical monitors. It was part of New Catholicism—that people should be kept alive in whatever form possible.

Major Sánchez shrugged. "A small matter. Probably very little of anything in there. Big machine, was what it was, *sí*. Now, who's to help? Eh?"

They got Eagle onto the crawler, and by the time the job was finished the field was nearly cleared of people.

Most of the main party mounted up then, calling to one another about things they didn't want left behind and things already lost and who would beat who back to Sidon. The boy heard little of it. He worked at the loading and watched the clear sky. The sun slid behind Jupiter's rosy clouds, haloing the planet, and then the gloom of eclipse descended. He watched the crawlers roar and buck and start out of camp, Major Sánchez leading. Eagle's body shook with the vibration as the crawler clattered over an outcropping, and to Manuel the body seemed reduced, loose, a heap of parts. He watched until it was out of sight.

The party left their bedding all rolled on the bunks, ready for next year. The cabin would freeze up solid while they were gone and take a full day to thaw out when they returned, but with everything sealed or rolled tight not much moisture would get in and things would be dry when the next party came to do some pruning. They left some supplies and scraps of past meals, all ready to go on the fire. Manuel helped here and there, always keeping an eye on the grizzled body encased in the gently buzzing medical monitor. The med tech was finishing up the minor injuries and telling them to stay off the gimpy legs and sore backs they had accumulated.

"That was some run you had out there," Manuel heard the man say to a patient. "All to turn a moving artifact into a dead one, hey?" He chuckled, shaking his head. "Bang yourself up just to add one more. We got plenty artifacts strewed all 'round the moons. Can't understand a one of 'em. Won't figure out this one either, I'll bet."

Manuel didn't say anything to that, didn't even know what he would have said. He just kept hauling and cleaning up and loading and not thinking about much of anything. He helped tamper down the fusion plant, listening to the stutter of it die to a slow *chugg chugg*. The eclipse was deepening as he went back inside. Five Sidon men were staying over until the morning, resting up, and with the med tech and his father, Manuel and Old Matt were all that were left. They had a silent, weary supper and turned in without anybody mentioning smeerlop or liquor. Manuel had scarcely pulled a blanket over himself before he was asleep.

Much later, he heard the dry voice. It called him. At first he thought it was a dream, but then it came again. He got up, feeling aches in his legs still, and moved through the corridors of pipeframed bunks, feeling his way in the dark. Old Matt called again, and Manuel reached out in the blackness and found the cool hand, the fingers callused and the palm worn to a glassy hardness.

"How long since . . . since . . ."

Manuel answered, "Two days, almost."

"Eagle?"

"Dead."

"So . . . it . . . gave him back too."

"Just like us."

"Like . . . me."

"Sure scared me, in there."

"You saw me?"

"Sure I did. The others don't—"

"Stayed in there long enough . . . I could tell . . . feel . . . you were scared."

"*Sí*, the ones outside, they think—"

"Stay long enough . . . scared . . . it'll learn you."

"Won't be so dangerous next time, though. It's dead, we got it—you knew that, didn't you?"

"I know it stopped."

"Soon's we get you back to Sidon and move you to Hiruko, get you patched up, you and me can go out there again and have a real look at it."

A rasping laugh came. It turned into a ragged, choking cough.

Manuel whispered, "Go up in those holes, y'know, see what's in it, what made it."

"Not me. You, maybe. If they let you."

"*Let* me? What the hell, you and me, we *got* the thing, we— But hey, what you mean, not you?"

"I been lying here . . . feeling . . . what's left of this body. Not much."

"You got your voice back. Other stuff'll come back too, once they—"

"No, it won't. I heard the med tech talking . . . to the Colonel. Too much deterioration. Nerves . . . muscles in the arms and legs all shot. . . . I'll never get enough back to run servos, even."

"Look, if it's money . . ."

"That's part of it. Always is, somebody my age. Sidon can't sink a big investment into a hanger-on. Times are hard. And I got no shares to sell."

All Manuel could think to say was "You shouldn't think that way. Let 'em try at least."

"And end up a stomach and a brain and not much else."

Manuel's hand followed down the old man's arm until it met the ceramic and metal of the chest.

"That's right," Old Matt said. "You're thinking I'm part replacements already, right? Sure enough. But there's a point . . . you don't want any more."

"Look, the money part, I can talk—"

"You thought much about what happened, Manuel? Why you figure it let us come back?"

"The others, they were firing at it. Hurt it, must've. It couldn't handle all of us."

"I figure . . . it had enough of me. It's you I'm wondering about."

Manuel smiled. "We're both too mean, is all."

Again the dry laugh. Then the hand Manuel was holding moved, and the voice came, relaxed and solemn: "Think you could fix me something from the kitchen?"

Surprised, for he knew the medmonitor was feeding the body, Manuel said, "Sure. Sure."

He made little noise in the kitchen, putting together some cold meat and cornbread. He came out with it on a tray and picked his way among the bunks to the wall where the medmonitor was. He put down the tray and was going to click on a small light nearby when he sensed that the monitor was empty. He felt, and the pallet was still warm. A strange foreboding filled him. He should turn on the lights, he knew, but instead he found his way in the near-perfect darkness to the lock at the far end of the cabin. There, by the safety lights, he saw a figure lying on the floor, nearly finished with putting on an emergency suit.

"What the hell are you—"

"The eclipse. I want to see it again."

"That's crazy! How'd you get here?"

"Crawled. Legs nearly worthless. Arms not much better."

"Hold on, now; I'm going to lift you up. . . ."

As Manuel raised the surprisingly light body, Old Matt got the seals aligned on the suit and closed them. The helmet pophole was still open, though, and through it the gravel voice said, "I'm going to ask you now. I want you to think before you do anything. Before you take me . . . back in there."

"Listen, I can't—"

"I'm telling you I want to see the eclipse one more time, from outside. Not on some damned screen, which is the way I'll be looking at it once they patch me up."

"But that's just, just . . ."

"I . . . you remember back there, when we went up to it for the last time? Remember what I said? I needed help then. 'Watch for me,' I said."

"Right. Watch for you. I don't see—"

"Think about that later. When you have time."

"Yeah, okay, but look, I—"

"Right now I want you to watch for me and be sure nobody stops me when they hear the lock cycle. I can crawl out and down the ramp okay without you. But I'm going to need somebody to stall them if they come looking. For a few minutes, is all."

Manuel studied the old face in the dim ruby light. The eyes still had that quality of seeming to catch more light, of moving with a refracting, watery intensity. He knew what the old man was saying. He said aloud, but to himself, "Watch for me."

Old Matt smiled. "That's it." The strain showed in his creased cheeks.

"Go on, now," Manuel said.

He helped the old man get into the lock and put him on the automatic conveyor used to carry goods outside. Then he went back inside and cycled the lock at a low rate, to keep the throb of the pumps down. The outer door opened. The conveyor whined. He waited long moments, facing the control panel, thinking about nothing, and then heard footsteps coming, ringing on the metal deck.

"What— Were you outside?" His father.

He turned. "No. Old Matt's out there."

"Old Ma— and you *let* him? Where's your head, boy?" Colonel López snatched at the control lever. He yanked the outer door to and started a high-speed fill. "Goddamn if I ever— what— why'd you let him? You know he's . . ." and then he snatched a suit off the rack and stepped into it, his mouth compressing into a thin line.

Manuel suited up silently. The lock popped open and the two of them went in. Pumpdown started. Colonel López flushed it at fractional pressure to save time. The lock swung open. A wind blew dust past them onto the shadowed plain, howling as it died. The Colonel stepped out first.

The body was sprawled at the base of the conveyor belt, face up, the eyes still glistening, the pophole open, the ice of Ganymede already settling on the ruined face. Old Matt had unzipped the whole front, too, letting in the full dead breath of Ganymede. Coming that suddenly, the awful cold would pop open cells as they froze, riddle him with ruin.

"*Mierda!* Vacced like that, we'll never get him back!" The Colonel whirled on his son. "Dead! He's dead! And you helped him!"

Colonel López stopped, eyes suddenly wild. He jerked back to look at the body, stooped to pick it up. Both of them heard it snap as he lifted it, cracking the frozen skin, opening fresh cuts into the body so that a plume of vapor escaped out the pophole, and the ice of this world invaded Old Matt more.

The father stared at the son. "You killed him. For good. Eternal death. You know that, don't you?"

"I . . ." He blinked, but the wetness seemed to be coming from everywhere, like sweat. His chest heaved and had no air in it. "I did. . . ." He sobbed.

"You killed him. Just as sure as if you blew him open yourself! An old man, not knowing what he was doing, crazy from being sick. And you helped him!"

Manuel's body shook and trembled, and the sureness he had carried in him dissolved. "I— Father, I—"

"Killing, that's it, *sí?* Killing everything that's old . . ." He gasped, congested with words. "Yesterday wasn't— wasn't enough, uh? You had to—"

"*What?* Kill—you mean Aleph? I was just—"

"We hunt it, *sí,* but to—to—" The Colonel shook off the thought with a physical gesture, pushing it away with his hands. "But to— Old Matt!—"

His jaw muscles bunched. "No son of mine does a thing like that! None of mine!" The eyes were wild and hard, showing too much white, flashing with a rage that once come would not depart. "No son of mine!"

PART IV

HIRUKO

Six Years Later

1

Manuel made his way through the slick iceworked corridors, distracted, not thinking about much of anything. He kept his fists balled up and tucked into his jacket pockets, even though it was not at all cold in these places. This section of Hiruko was always well heated, so the women who liked to wear skimpy clothes would be comfortable when they went out for short trips. It was a sign of something—he had never figured out what—for people to go around without the reflex reaching for a coat, casually ignoring the steep temperature gradients.

His boots made no sound on the matted insulation, but the rattle and hum of buried factories came through the walls. He rounded the corner onto the Rotonde plaza. Two young men were loitering there, dressed in faded pants and fiber shirts that looked rough as burlap. One was short and intense-looking; his small eyes flicked nervously over all the passersby. The taller one eyed Manuel and then stood up straight and held up a fist. "De—," he said with an elaborate, overbearing accent, opening the palm, "—liver."

"What?" Startled, Manuel stopped, took his hands out of his pockets.

"You got plenty of nonesses there, friend."

"Non . . . ?"

"Nonessentials—is the way—the Council phrases it," the short one declared in staccato rushes of words.

Manuel said irritably, "What the hell's that?"

"Anything not required for—immediate health—or safety—that smacks of luxury—of privilege."

Manuel had read something about that, some collective resolution, but he couldn't fetch up a memory of what it meant. The tall one brushed hair out of his eyes with a slow, confident Anglo gesture. He drawled to his companion, "'Nother citizen not keeping up with the times, Enrico. Guess we'll have to educate him."

Manuel said nothing, just inched his feet apart and loosened his stance, unlocking his knees.

"See, the Council finally reacted to the will of the people, the real people, and admitted we had too damn much conspicuous wealth aroun' here."

"You want wealth, you got to ask somebody else, boys."

"Possessions—luxury possessions—they're an insult—to the collective."

"Didja inherit that sweater ya got on?"

"This?" Manuel looked at what he was wearing—he never noticed what he pulled on in the morning—and tried to recall. "No."

"Inherited goods—possessions gotten by private dealings—dealings in the market—they are all symptoms of chance advantage." The short, dark one seethed with energy as he spat out this list, clenching and unclenching his hands. "That sweater—made with wool—looks to me like market goods. Definite—market gains. You bought that—*sí?*"

Manuel backed up a step. Now he was remembering. The Council had gotten a bad review Earthside, and three of them had been demoted, pushed back down into a laboring category. It wasn't supposed to be a failure for them, just a readjustment and a natural recycling of workers onto the Council, but everybody knew it was because Earthside didn't like the sociometric profile of the Jovian moons. Now, with three Earth-approved replacements, the Council was erasing the effects of neocapitalist inroads. To smooth out the harsh contrasts of luck and exploitation, the Council had authorized each citizen to demand any possession that reflected this past error. And you could ask it of anyone, any other citizen.

"Ya don' want to be a posser, do ya?" the tall one said ominously.

"What's that?" Manuel asked, stalling for time.

"False possession—profiting from another—enslaving him with contractual labor—*that* is a posser—for sure—and you look to be one."

"No. I got this sweater fair. I got the yarn through usual channels and I knitted it up myself."

He knew he could cover that claim because he had an entry for yarn on his last month's billing. It wasn't for this sweater, but they wouldn't know that. Or be able to prove him wrong. *But prove it to who?* Manuel thought, and realized there wasn't any authority he could go to.

"Huh!" The tall one shifted his feet and his face hardened. "We hear that one a lot, friend. Give us—"

"No—wait." The short one held up his hand in caution. He wasn't going to be thrown off. The Council gave them the right to demand only one item per citizen. "Gaudy—ete-catching—bright colors—bangles, even—looks like market goods. But he could've made it up—so obvious, yeah—to look that way."

"Tryin' to sucker us?"

"Maybe. These guys—think they're smart. Here—what's that?"

Manuel didn't move, just looked at them. The short one's hand leaped forward and grabbed his belt buckle.

"Getting friendly?" Manuel said sarcastically.

"Getting our due, citizen. That—the belt—market, right?"

Manuel couldn't prove it wasn't, which to these two

was good enough proof that it was. In fact he *had* bought it on the black market—the only market—when there was a clothing shortage. Everybody did. You couldn't wait for a Supply Commissioner from Outsystem Control to approve a new batch of longjohns; you'd freeze.

"Suppose I say it isn't."

"Well, we just check up on it for you, citizen," the tall man said, casually brushing back his hair again and shifting his weight, this time meaning business.

"The Council lets *mierda seca* like you hang around, taking—"

"Redistributing—that's the fact—redistributing."

"Don't think I like what you said there, citizen," the tall one muttered, moving closer. Anticipation filled his face. He folded one hand into the other, making a fist and cracking the knuckles. Manuel could tell he didn't know what the curse meant, but the tone had carried the intention. The short one's eyes began to dance around. Manuel carefully tensed himself and then weighed the odds. Not good.

Manuel took off the belt. "Okay, okay." He handed it to the short man. "Now what's to stop me taking it back from you, huh?"

The tall man snickered, and the short one said, "In principle—you could. But we have—the Council gave—special orders. We are special designates. We collect—redistribute—penalize the exploiters. Until the envy—and malice—are gone."

"Soldiers for equality, uh? Glad you warned me. I'd have thought you were just thieves."

The tall one said threateningly, "Now, you watch what—" but the nervous, short one held up a hand.

"We are working for you—citizen—we're your friends. And remember that—the Council—they are not timid."

"What's that mean?"

"They will strike—boldly—and prevail."

Manuel swore under his breath: "*Qué gente estúpida!*"

"What was 'at?" the tall man said, his face clouding.

"You've got your booty—get out of my way." Manuel brushed by the two and went on, not looking back.

He thought of stopping, a block further on, and yelling back into the Rotonde plaza, *Me cago en la leche de tu puta madre!* But that was the sort of thing a boy would have done, and anyway might have brought them running after him. Instead he turned right and walked on toward the Basquan Café. He had thought of going to the Quondon Stande, where there was a ring in the middle of a lush garden and the boxers served as waiters between the matches. But the mood had passed; he did not want to see women pounding at each other and breaking and bloodying their smooth skins, even though the injuries were healed or replaced before the customers had recovered from their hangovers.

The Basquan Café was big and hot. Bars were always overheated here, in perpetual rejection and denial of the everlasting chill beyond. Only in Hiruko had he seen corridors kept as toasty warm as a living room back at Sidon; here there was energy to spare. People came for a two-year rotation and never felt the sting of the true world outside, never left this pocket of humanity.

He went by the crowded tables, through the illusion smoke, and out onto the sweeping veranda. It was cooler out here, even tolerable if he took off his jacket. He liked this place best, under the pungent eucalyptus trees that were always shedding bark and leaves. He chose a small table near the statue of Romérez, a bulky figure holding perpetually aloft an ice pick and a map. The face was clouded with concentration, peering forward as if trying to see further into one of the alien artifacts Romérez had uncovered and dissected and catalogued but never figured out.

He ordered an infusion and watched the great beams of yellow light pull dust motes from the fragrant soil beyond the veranda. An unseen skylight sent blades of sunlight, reflected from Jupiter, down the large air shafts, where it dispersed among riots of greenery. He liked this garden; it had jacaranda and jade trees and dry, still air. Gardens sprouted every third of a kilometer in any direction, keeping the air clean, each reflecting a different locale back on old Earth. He watched the light change and redden in the tall stringy eucalyptus branches as the sun came nearer the limb of the planet, reflecting from the mottled pink clouds. He thought of getting one of the empty-spined books from inside and filling it with a trade-manual cartridge he should be studying. Like everything in the café, it was free. Back at Sidon he had spent his own pay to get hours on an interactive book—it cut your study time and was more fun—but for the moment it was very fine to sit and smell the fragrant breeze that came off the luminous garden, carrying away the buzz of the café behind him.

A door opened to his right and someone came out. He turned, hoping, but it was a man, and worse, somebody he knew.

"Ah, knew you'd be around." It was Ortiz Gutiérrez, and he was breathing heavily through a drooping mustache. He wore a cape that looked like velvet but that Manuel knew was made from fuzz-fiber grown in the hydroponics. There were scarlet slashes across the velvet in a rakish Spanish design that Manuel recognized from a popular Earthside show.

"May I sit with you while you wait?" Gutiérrez asked, sitting down with a swirl of the cape that fanned up a little breeze, bringing Manuel a trace of the man's smell. Some of it was a cologne and some of it wasn't.

"How you know I'm waiting?"

"You're a creature of habit, Manuel. Don't think you go totally unnoticed, my boy."

"I was kind of hoping I would."

Gutiérrez took no notice of Manuel's meaning, because he was turning to left and then to right, waving for a waiter. "Will you have a drink with me?"

Manuel had nearly finished his iced infusion. He saw

that the best thing would be to have one more and then get away somehow. He had learned that you never turned down an invitation here. For parties it was easy: you always said you would be glad to come and then later you could be sorry, could have something come up that made it impossible. For a chance meeting like this, though, there was no easy way out. "Sure."

The waiter came over and Gutiérrez ordered a cup of mulled wine. Gutiérrez turned to Manuel, who ordered another infusion. Then Gutiérrez said, "No, no. Make it a rum *adopolc*."

"Rum *adopolc:* I see." The waiter went away.

Gutiérrez noticed after a moment that Manuel was wearing no belt. This led to an explanation, which Manuel was halfway glad to relate, because it gave him something to talk about and also because he still did not understand the whole thing. After he had finished, Gutiérrez said, "So you simply weren't prepared. Don't you pay attention to the Council?"

"Don't see the point."

"Well, if you want to be stripped in the streets—"

"They said nonessentials. They can't—"

"Get them nasty and I wouldn't speak for how far they will go. A word to the wise." He tapped his forefinger to his nose significantly.

"Why doesn't Earthside keep their *chingado* faces out of here?"

"Why, they cannot. It is implicit in the dynamics of society. Earth is fully socialist. Earth understands itself scientifically—the first society to do so. Let me tell you how to look at these things, Manuel."

Manuel gazed out over the oval garden with its stands of slender trees and the baked, hard-packed sandy soil. He had come here to watch the light, had looked forward to it all day. It was a thing you had to watch carefully. The eclipse of the sun by Jupiter had come, bringing amber glows, and he had missed the change. Gutiérrez went on.

"Every civilization up until now has evolved because of internal contradictions—conflicts within it that forced change. Capitalism proceeded by contradiction to produce socialism—it was inevitable."

"Uh-huh." He was watching the light.

"The Marxists thought that under socialism, alienation and class warfare would stop. They ignored the fact that the dialectical model of change *never* predicted an end to contradictions, or to evolution. Socialism requires a bureaucracy, and that means an administrative class. The administrators faced a problem Marxism never discussed: how *well* socialism works, versus capitalism. What is the good of being exactly equal to everybody else, if that means you have to be poor? The last century has taught us—or rather, Earth—that socialism is less efficient than capitalism at producing goods."

"Uh-huh."

"So to stop socialism from sinking into the mud, the bureaucrats had to promote expansion—off-planet, out into the system. But socialism is an historical necessity that arises when you get a certain density of population. Once people spread out . . ." He opened his hands. "The population density in the new worlds is low, of course. The dynamics of economics drives them to adopt individualist, capitalist measures. They must, to survive and prosper in harsh places. So the internal contradiction of socialism is that it must expand, to make up for its own inefficiencies. Expansion, though, produces capitalism at the frontier. Your Settlement is really a small, communal capitalist unit. It interacts with Earthside through a market, not by edicts."

The waiter came, and Manuel reached eagerly for his drink. This was worse than he'd thought it would be. The waiter put down the rum and Gutiérrez corrected him. "It wasn't rum *adopolc*," he said helpfully but severely. "I wanted mulled wine."

"It's all right," Manuel said. "I'll take the rum. I'll pay. Bring what he orders now, please."

"What I ordered," corrected Gutiérrez.

The waiter returned quickly with the mulled wine. They sat in silence, one drinking of the cold, bronze, finely textured infusion, with its malty aroma and sweet-clean, yeasty flavor; the other lifted the cup of swarming warmth and drank off half of it in one long swallow, his Adam's apple bobbing. Manuel hoped there wouldn't be much more of the social theory—it all sounded like Earthside chat. Gutiérrez was influential, he knew, and it was a puzzle why the man paid any attention to a petro-worker from an obscure Settlement. There was the Aleph thing, but Manuel refused to talk about that and he hoped that everyone had by now forgotten it.

"And therein lies the true comedy," Gutiérrez went on, picking up the thread as if there had been no interruption. "You see, the Marxists always assumed the next step would complete the cycle of contradiction and change. It is so amusing! Because they could imagine no further change beyond socialism, they assumed—without thinking—that there would *be* none. They didn't notice that the dialectical model predicts *no* Final Revolution. From a materialist perspective, there need never be a Final Revolution. There is instead an equilibrium between the two forms. So we get humankind—with refined, humanitarian socialism in the older, crowded core. And capitalism sprouting up like weeds at the edge."

"So to fix that, punks hold me up in the street."

"Not if you anticipate them!" Gutiérrez swept his cape in a half-arc, smiling and showing fine, even white teeth. "This I made, totally. The only market clothes I wear are undergarments." He laughed merrily. "You must learn to swim with the currents, Manuel."

Just then a gaunt man, dark-skinned and with angular cheekbones, passed on the walkway below. He was with two other similar men. They all wore flowing robes of somber green, of a kind Manuel had not seen before. The man glanced up at the veranda and their table and then waved, lifting his arm halfway. Then he looked away and the three kept walking.

"Did you see me brush him off?" Gutiérrez asked. "Did you *see* that?"

"No. Who did you brush off?"

"That one, that new Earther. Piet Arnold." He laughed. "*Did* I snub him."

"I saw him wave."

"Yes! I glanced at him, so he would know I had seen him—"

"And then looked away. Without waving."

"*Sí*. So you did catch it."

"Why snub him?" Manuel started on the rum.

"My, you Settlement types do drink a lot."

"Sometimes. When it's rougher than usual. Why did you snub him?"

"He comes from a political faction—the Codonzenites—that opposes the existence of men on Ganymede at all."

"How come?"

"The artifacts. They want to preserve any world where an artifact exists, to keep it intact and unblemished until the artifact is completely understood."

"Huh. Sounds crazy. So you ignore him because you disagree with him?"

"Only if he is a figure of comparable stature."

"Stature?"

"*Sí*. What is the point of snubbing someone you would not ordinarily acknowledge? The point goes unnoticed."

"I see. You have to know them first."

"Indeed. And by the way, you do not simply ignore them. You deliberately refuse to recognize them."

"An important difference. So you know him."

"I met him at a state reception yesterday. He is in charge of an Earther team. They are here to add to the staff studying that artifact, the one that you—"

"I see. An important man."

Gutiérrez showed the brilliant white teeth again and

drank. His mustache dripped with mulled wine. "I spend time only with important people."

"Then why are you drinking with me?"

He blinked. "You are better known than you may think. After all, you are doing well in the petrofacs. Now that we have lost our edge over the 'roids on food, it is doubly important to mechanize, make our own lubricants. You chose a good field."

"I didn't choose it. I had to come here in a hurry. There was a job. I took it."

"Well, for whatever reason. Of course, I might never have noticed you if it had not been for your earlier exploit, the—"

"It's pleasant to be recognized by such a person as yourself, Señor Gutiérrez. I am scarcely even a member of the *lumpen intelligentsia*, after all. Ummm . . ." Manuel made a show of looking at his fingernail. "Getting late. I'd better go see if something's wrong."

"You always meet her here, don't you? I see you on my way home."

"I didn't think you had a home. People in your section, they voted to make their apartments—"

"Living units."

"Okay, living units—make them communal. So you don't have a home. You shift around every day."

Manuel had guessed right. He had gotten the conversation away from the Aleph without being nasty—it had taken him a long time to learn how to do that, in the first years—and then away from whom he was meeting, and now onto something Gutiérrez liked to talk about. If he let the man run on for a few minutes Gutiérrez would forget the earlier subjects and then Manuel could look at his watch again and leave without any trouble.

"I stick to the same half-dozen living units, for convenience—the ones near the locker containing my clothes and so on. Mind, I'm not speaking against the idea. It's a wonderful way to break down the territorial instincts. In time, those instincts will be transferred from individual property to the Hiruko community as a whole. Just as they've done Earthside. We're even making progress in getting families to participate."

"Why bother them?"

"Because we've got to start developing ways of bringing up children that don't depend on the family. Because the family in modern times is rooted in romantic love."

"So?" Another few minutes and he could go. The slanting light among the jacaranda now dimmed into a ruddy glow like smoldering embers as the eclipse came on. He had been watching the subtle changes, enjoying them despite the talk.

"It is now easy to see, in historical perspective, that the stress on romantic love came about to make a refuge for the psyche—a shelter from the strains of competition under capitalism. And the capitalists knew this—if not consciously, at least by shrewd guess. To take attention from the inequities of capitalism, what could be better than to focus everyone on internal problems?—defining yourself by your relationship to *one* other person. Wrapped up in 'love,' you forgot about your place in the pyramid of capital. And if romantic love dims, there is always the torrent of entertainments—gaudy distractions, another hallmark of the past. But take away the competition, introduce socialism—and suddenly"—he spread his hands, grinning, confident—"you find you see women as they are. As economic and political entities, without a false aura."

A soft but determined voice said, "Falseness is in the eye of the beholder."

Gutiérrez jumped, startled. Belinda stood beside him, her full mouth cocked in a wry grin.

"Please do not mistake me. I did not mean . . ."

Belinda smiled, forgiving and dismissing the man in one glance, her black hair tumbling across her shoulders. She plainly did not listen to the rest of Gutiérrez's explanation, but instead walked around the table and put a hand on Manuel's shoulder. He saw a small line of concern between her eyes, but ignored it. He was full of relief that she was here and they could leave. He began a sentence that would allow them to exit, but she cut him off:

"I am late because there was a call for you. To me. From your mother."

"What? I told you, I don't want to hear anything—"

"She knows that. I spoke to her, I heard things in her voice—"

"I don't want to discuss it here." He got up, knocking over the chair. *She's like the others,* he thought. *Talking, babbling of such things, in front of anybody, anywhere—*

"No! Listen! It was not like the other calls she made. Those stopped years ago. She—"

His face was hot with rage. "No!" He started to walk away.

"Manuel! She called me because she knew you would hang up. She had to get word to you that—your father, he is dead."

PART V

COMING HOME

1

Manuel surveyed the train station. He felt an echo of half-forgotten emotions as he watched the crowd waiting for the sleek liners, remembering the only other time he had been here: coming into Hiruko six years ago, with only a pack on his back, silent and intense, smoldering with anger and defiance. Then, the laser-polished stone columns had seemed to taper away into infinity, far higher than any building he had ever seen, even taller than an agro dome. Dust motes of considerable size had floated high up among the glassy struts, catching the amber beams of light that refracted through the serene pillars. Thick air had gathered in his chest like fine warm fleece, the first tangible sign of Hiruko's opulence. The ladies nimbly climbing stairs in their lacy fashions, the men clean-shaven and slim—all had seemed exotic, compared with the heavy, parka-clothed figures he was so used to at Sidon. Here no one carried a few extra kilos of fat at the waist or in the shoulders, as protection against cold or exhaustion. Here a coat or vest was fashioned for the eye, not the metabolism.

He had left the station reluctantly, still awed by its majesty. The crowds bore him off, and he had spent hours in the endlessly intertangling passageways and corridors, ashamed to knock on a door and ask directions. The impossibly broad boulevards and avenues he at first mistook for temporarily empty assembly areas, since they wasted so much space. At each major intersection, elegant, periodically spaced crystalline rhomboids towered over the passing throng; it had taken him another hour to realize that these were the computer interfaces he sought. Their grandeur seemed extravagant, and he had hesitated to ask for a map display. Only after he had found the Labor Coordinator and made his availability known had he felt relaxed enough to stop and timidly order a drink and then a bowl of soup at one of the sidewalk cafés. Then, finished, he had tried to pay, and been the butt of laughter. He still felt a twinge of the helpless young man's tongue-tied rage. It all seemed so long ago.

"I still believe you should have said something more to your mother," Belinda murmured, shutting off his memories.

"I told her I was coming back to Sidon. That's what she asked for, isn't it?"

"She seemed so shaken."

"It wasn't a pretty thing."

"No. Did you *have* to call up those coroner's pictures?"

He grimaced. "*Sí*, I did. I had to know."

"Know that he died in pain? An icequake knocking him down in front of that laser beam? See him torn open like that?"

"It's something a son has to do."

"A son who . . ." and she bit off the words. He knew full well what she had nearly said: *A son who had not spoken to his father for six years? A son who refused all their calls, their letters? Who brushed aside the friends from Sidon who casually dropped by and tried to bring the subject up?*

"Right. All that is finished now. There was a thing between us. Now it's gone. When he is dead you treat him as the father who brought you into the world. You don't let the last trouble count for everything."

She said softly, "I see."

A train shrieked into the station, rattling the tracks. Electromagnetic propulsors caught it, sucked away its momentum, and stored the power. Porters grunted, levering up the ice-breaking frames around each exit, shattering the shiny cloak, releasing the passengers. The rest of the sheath would melt from the train before departure time.

"You forgive him, then?"

He stared at her with flat incomprehension. She was the only person he had ever talked with about it. That was part of what bound him to her, he knew. To find she still understood so little . . .

"There was nothing to forgive. I didn't wrong him, he didn't wrong me."

She frowned. Beneath the filtered, watery light her dusky skin still held a magic quality for him. He put both hands to her face and then around, burying his fingers in her glossy black hair. Her full mouth, never far from a smile, registered uncertainty.

He said, "We disagreed. He . . . couldn't see it any differently. I couldn't either. So we each knew it was better if we kept our distance." *Strange,* he thought, *to be able to put it so coolly now. The Manuel who came into this station, big-eyed and angry, would never have said it like that.*

"I . . . are you sure you don't want me to go?"

"No. My mother . . . One thing at a time."

"I'll have to, someday."

"This first. When I've gotten things settled . . ."

"All right. Goodbye."

She kissed him fervently and then let him go, stepped back, gave him up. He grinned at her, feeling a return of the old awkward boyishness, an embarrassment at private things made public. Then the porters barked the departure call and he swung aboard. The slender passenger car was nearly filled. He stowed his pack and found a seat and waved to Belinda, who stood looking oddly alone and vulnerable on the platform. Only then did he notice that across from him sat the three Earthers he had seen from the veranda yesterday.

They went out from Hiruko Station with a rapid surge, and then a lethargic clashing of slack couplings traveling backward among the cars. The pulsers thumped, boosting them up with deep, long thrusts. Loading platforms streamed by; open yards; mills half completed; stacks of nickel cubes with McKenzie emblems stamped in their gray faces; immense pulse-forming circuits laid out for the new flinger that would hurl cargo directly into orbit; parabolic antenna fields; a raw slash of strip-mined rock. The jumbled, sprawling petro factory rose, loomed and dwindled; Manuel glimpsed the neon yellow of his prefractory tower, responsible for high-temperature bearing lubricants, made directly from Ganymede's raw ices. Then they brushed aside the last confused edge of Hiruko and ahead the track made a wide swooping curve. Manuel watched the train's head vanish into the expanses, dragging its length like a picture he remembered of a snake—a creature he had never seen, not even in the Hiruko Zoo, and thought of as mythical, like a unicorn—wriggling smoothly into the distance.

Their speed built with a clattering energy as they shot down from Hiruko Mountain and across a barren plain where the robot orbiters were parked at the end of long purple skid lines. They climbed now amid rumpled hills, and startled a flock of gippers—the new bioforms Central had designed to help keep down the bewildering profusion of mutated rockjaws. The gippers were nuzzling at the crossties of the rails, sniffing and pawing, and the train came up on them nearly soundlessly in the thin air. It turned the slow ones to pasty spots on the nearby boulders where they landed, and sent the rest in cawing frenzy down the gullies, legs kicking uselessly in their panic. Manuel wondered why Central always produced such stupid and repellant animals, and decided it was because they regarded these hapless things as throwaways, soon to be replaced by other animated chemical processors.

Electromagnetic fists seized them and flung them on with an impatient *snick-snick-snick*, between twin walls of impervious slumbering emptiness. Ice began to creep from the corners of the big windows. Manuel thumbed on the embedded web of heaters and the scum cleared. He watched the silent unfolding land, his eyes automatically surveying for darting movement, for some sign of recent passage of something huge and land-gouging, doing this while his mind was blank and preparing him for the days ahead. Slowly a pressure, unnoticed until now, began to ease in him.

A quiet voice asked, "You know this area?"

He looked at the Earther who had spoken. "Some."

"I am Piet Arnold. I gather you are from Sidon?"

"Was."

"I am of Earth."

"I know."

"It is that obvious?"

"Your clothes."

"I purchased them, thinking . . . Ah, they are too opulent, is that it?"

"Could be. What is that stuff, the pants?"

"Corduroy."

"Never saw it before."

"I am sorry. My friends"—he swept a hand to include thirteen of them, all identically dressed, seated down one side of the car, their eyes on Manuel—"are here under my guidance. I judged badly in selecting, I see that. We do not mean to place ourselves apart from you who live here. It would have been kinder to requisition clothing at Hiruko and discard our—"

"No, look, I don't care."

"We are hoping for full-hearted cooperation from the people of Sidon."

"You'll get it."

"We are here to study the artifact."

Manuel kept his face blank. "Uh-huh."

"The Aleph. Do you know much of it?"

"You'll be out at the site, right, not at Sidon?"

"Yes. The preliminary survey is done. We have studied carefully the borings and unfoldings of the structure."

"Unfoldings?"

"Yes. You do not follow the reports? There have been many." Piet spoke with a mild, reassuring cadence. He studied Manuel, undistracted by movement in the car or by the passing land outside.

"I don't get much time."

"You should take the trouble. The artifact that once moved is perhaps the most important discovery of our time."

"Uh-huh."

"We must know more of it."

"How much do you need to know?"

"One cannot know too much."

Manuel fidgeted. He reached for something to lighten this conversation. "Like sex, huh?"

Piet's face went blank. "What do you mean?"

"Like a friend of mine says, only too much is enough."

"Oh. I see." A thin, joyless smile crossed Piet's still-solemn face and, once the gesture had been made, vanished suddenly, like something collapsing.

Manuel saw he had offended the man. "So you're here to study," he said lamely.

"Yes. Study without harming. We mounted this expedition at great cost. We on Earth can ill afford many such explorations, I assure you."

"I guess it's not like the glory days."

"Glory?"

"When Earth had lots to spend. You know—the Americans and Russians and Chinese and all. Spreading out here, measuring everything. Pretty rich times for you."

"Ah." Piet's face became stony. "The high-bourgeois culture."

"Yeah, I guess."

"An unhappy time. Rootless, with the false consciousness of late capitalism—"

"I thought it was pretty good for you. The movies—"

"I assure you, we do not regret the loss of those times. Just as no one now envies the self-indulgences of the courts of monarchical Europe, or the Saturnalia of Rome."

Manuel didn't know enough Earth history to tell what the man was talking about. He frowned. "Uh-huh. You, ah, going to be here long?"

Manuel looked around the car, but there were no empty seats. He didn't remember Piet's being across from him when he sat down, but maybe the man had moved while he was looking out the window.

"Perhaps for the rest of our lives."

"What? how come?"

"The return is expensive. We can transmit our findings. Samples, once we dare to take some, can be shipped. There is no need to return us bodily to Earth. We can remain here, to undertake the long-term investigations."

"Never go *home* again?"

Piet smiled wanly. "It is the price a scientist must pay."

"Uh-huh." Manuel had no idea what to say next. It was the worst damn luck in the world to run into this. If he had to spend the hours of the trip talking—

An expression crossed Piet's face. The man smiled again and said softly, "You must excuse me. We are still not adjusted to your time schedule here. I am tired, and need to rest a moment."

Manuel nodded. Piet folded his hands, closed his eyes, and was at once deeply relaxed, the lines of his face disappearing. The other Earthers also leaned back in their seats, faces going slack, and in a moment their silence isolated Manuel in an island of calm. He decided they had some kind of implanted command that Piet had activated. He had heard of such things: economical ways to stretch out food resources in times of famine—a common Earthside need.

He was relieved to be freed from conversation. It did not occur to him that perhaps Piet had seen this, and had withdrawn. The onmarching land beyond held his attention as the pulsors thumped regularly, keeping up their speed. He let himself think about what lay ahead for him. His thoughts were as directionless as the unplumbed wastes outside, unwilling to focus themselves, and that is why he did not notice the first sideways lurch of the car. The next one came suddenly, wrenching the couplings so they screeched and people stirred, exclaiming. Manuel felt it solidly shove him against the arm of the seat. His head jerked up, searching for a cause, and his eyes met the blue, still eyes of Piet Arnold for an instant. Then the big one hit.

The crash came through his boots first and then threw him across the aisle, against a row of seats. He felt the car tilt far over. The air was filled with flying stuff and a huge, rolling noise like grinding.

He held onto the seat back near him. Somebody slammed into him and fell away. Shouts, cries. A high-pitched, piping alarm signal rose and abruptly shut off. The car shook, turned on its axis, rattled—and screeched to a dead stop.

Manuel got to his feet. He found he was standing on one of the Earthers. He stepped away, finding a place among the jumble of people crying out and struggling to get up, clothes and luggage strewn all among them. He ignored the noise and listened. No high hiss of escaping air, no pressure drop. Another trembling came, making some people fall again. A woman screamed. Manuel held on to a seat and waited. Another, just barely noticeable. Then nothing.

"Hey! Quiet!" he shouted. He did it again and the ones in the back shut up. "Somebody back there, pick up the comm phone."

White faces turned but nobody did anything. "You!" He pointed to a tall man at the other end of the car. "Pick it up."

The tall man did. He looked at Manuel. "Is it live?" Manuel asked. The man nodded. "Wait for the lead car to come on. They'll tell us the situation. The rest of you, shut up."

It took a long time to find out. The Earthers helped put a woman's broken arm in a sling and they all waited tensely. The lights stayed on, but no air came through the vents. When they got word, it was as Manuel had suspected: the ground shocks had thrown two freight cars clean off the tracks. Nobody was badly hurt in the two passenger cars. To get the train moving again they would have to pull the freight cars off the tracks.

Something was blocking the air feed. The heaters also were running at low power. Until they got the passenger cars back in alignment on the tracks, it would be hard to tell if the trouble was serious.

There was never any talk about waiting for help. It would take hours to get crawlers out from Hiruko. If there was damage to the life-support systems, it was better to be moving, even at reduced speed, toward Sidon.

Nor was there any question about who would do the work. The train captain walked through both passenger cars, picking people at random. One of the women chosen was married, and her husband jumped up, angry, protesting. So the captain let the husband stand in for her. Otherwise, there was no trouble. It would take most of the passengers to do the job, and everyone knew time might be important.

Manuel had trouble finding an emergency suit that fit him. He was late getting out the lock. He stumbled down a gravel grade, moving clumsily with the suit's unfamiliar power amplifiers. Five cars ahead, the grade had shifted and slumped. Manuel studied it, trying to see what had happened. He gazed down the valley that the magnetorail line ran through. Raw dirt and ice had spilled down into the plain. Slopes were cut and cracked by dislocations.

"What caused all this? Is it typical?"

Manuel turned to find Piet Arnold standing nearby, looking uncertain.

"I don't know. But you shouldn't be out here. You don't know how to work in this gravity."

"We do our part," Piet said simply.

Manuel saw six more of the Earthers moving awkwardly among the work gang. "Damn stupid," he said gruffly, but with some grudging respect.

The two freight cars were a hundred meters ahead. The grade had slumped under them. The sag wasn't bad enough to permanently disrupt the superconducting fields; Manuel could see the magnetic aura running firm and true. The ramrod-straight, red-dish halo held the freight cars in midair over the slumped gray grade.

"Fields musta rippled when that shake came through," a voice said over comm. "Let go the cars for a second, then grabbed 'em again."

The freight cars looked strange, hovering, caught in the act of tumbling out of the magnetic depression that cradled the train. They hung over the slope at seemingly impossible angles, frozen above the heads of the laboring men and women. In the pale light the work gang shoveled gravel and fashioned supports for the superconducting web that lay along the magnetorail bed.

"How shall we free them?" Piet asked.

"Have to pulse the fields again," Manuel said, taking a shovel from the pile. "Weaken them so's they drop the cars."

"Why dig?"

"Got to realign the bed some. When the fields collapse at one spot, that sets up a strain all along the line. We'll have to support this part of the train mechanically for two, three seconds."

Piet nodded and went to explain to his men and women. The captain was giving orders, telling people where to dig and how to wedge the steel bars into place on the slippery, unstable slope. Manuel began digging, glad of something to do, feeling the muscles in his back pull and ache. Working in the petrofac had softened him some. He started sweating heavily. He worked with concentration, forgetting everything, slinging the stones into piles with a steady, swinging rhythm. His breath echoed and roared in the narrow helmet. Around him the braces and wedged rock foundations took form. Engineers worked to make sure the stresses would be right, that angles and vectors were aligned. He preferred to leave the planning to them, to simply dig where he was told and think about nothing other than keeping his footing on the loose slope. Some of the Earthers worked alongside him, but he paid them no mind, did not even speak except to answer orders.

An hour passed. Then another. The maintenance crew could not get the air system back to normal. Carbon dioxide buildup in the passenger bubble could be controlled, but only by venting. That put a deadline on everything. Hiruko had dispatched three crawlers, but nobody on board wanted to go back to Hiruko and wait until the line was repaired. That would take a while, anyway—the seismic shocks had done damage everywhere, and all available labor was going to be scarce.

At last the frame was ready. A crude cage of rods, stripped from the freight cars themselves, held the superconducting web from below. They uncoupled the freight cars. The local current monitors were downtrack, and the captain unlocked them. He gingerly inspected the panel and then waved the work gang away. The party clustered on the other side of the grade, away from the teetering cars.

Manuel was tired and uncomfortable in the ill-fitting power suit. He sat down on a boulder that had tumbled from the hills beyond the rail grade. The slippage here was worse than any he had ever seen. He wondered vaguely where the epicenter had been. He said nothing when Piet sat nearby. Together they watched the last preparations.

"You think it will work?"

"Should. Always trouble to fool with big magnetic fields like this, though."

"Oh Earth, we would wait for help."

"Might die, waiting."

"I suppose so." Piet looked doubtful.

The captain checked with Hiruko and called a warning over comm. Figures backed further away from the grade. From where he sat, Manuel could barely see the two cars poised in midair, slanted toward the other side of the slope. A dozen meters away five Earthers clumped together, as if for security.

"Ready! Flux change of five kiloGauss, duration of ten seconds. One, two, three—on!"

The pulse came rippling down from both directions. Manuel could see it rock the cars, sweeping by them, leaving the big, sleek compartments bobbing like boats under a gentle swell. The two waves met exactly at the center of the jury-rigged frame—

And the freight cars spun apart. One tumbled down the far slope and was gone in an instant. Through some reaction, its mate tilted backward. The silvery car rebounded off some unseen fluctuation. It spun lazily in the fields, end over end, then faster—

Manuel jumped to his feet. The car shot out of the magnetic trap like a ricochet. It plunged down the gravel slope toward the work gang. The field lost it then and it fell heavily, cracking open. It spilled crates, skidding across the ice.

To Manuel it happened with a liquid slowness. The

sleek skin of the car wrinkled and split and the crates crashed out and the thing came toward them, skating on the ice, and he gathered his feet under him, arms out for balance, waiting for the right instant—

The car smacked into a boulder; split in half; burst open, slinging crates; but kept on coming, now a mass of flying bits, a wall like a breaking wave—

Manuel leaped. He gave it full power and shot up fifty meters. Below, most of the others jumped too, rising above the tumbling tide. Not all. Some dashed to the side. But one—Manuel watched a crate catch the woman full in the chest, throwing the body backward, rolling over it without pause, and finally fetching up against a rise in the ice. He changed his gyros and came down near the body.

She was an Earther. The chest was caved in, and she stared up glassily at nothing.

"Erika!" Piet cried, kneeling beside her.

"Get her into a med stabilizer!" the captain called.

Amid the shouting the Earthers gathered silently. Each took a portion of her weight. They lifted her high and carried her down the long line of cars, toward the lead car where the medical unit was. Manuel followed. He watched the Earthers and listened to their low, murmurous song that came faintly over the comm.

They got her into the freezer, but it didn't look good. There was a lot of massive, expensive damage. She had gone down to Ganymede temperature pretty fast, and that was a help, but the systemic shock effects registered near the top of the indicator. Manuel studied the Earthers as they heard all this, crowded into the little cabin at the front of the train. He walked back with them. They said little and showed no obvious signs of grief.

Maybe they were holding it all in, or maybe they had just had it trained out of them by their years on Earth, he thought. It was hard to tell. He rummaged back through his education for a comparison. With a mild shock he realized, *They came here out of duty. Not from a yearning, but because their commonweal decided. They're like priests, not explorers. Priests.*

There was a stoic, grim side to them he had never seen before, a kind of stolid acceptance. In a way he envied it, without wanting to be that way himself. It did put you beyond the terrible things that happened in the world.

But—he felt this without thinking it—it put something between you and the high, grand moments, too. That was a big price.

2

The funeral was held in the oldest agro dome. Manuel waited stiffly beside his mother and concentrated on the heavy musk that filled the air, and how it settled in his lungs with every breath.

"It is lovely," his mother said, "how they built it to look out over the valley."

"*Sí*, it is." He scuffed his toe in the rich loam. The two of them stood a little apart from the main party. Around them, like a stubby forest, were the white markers of laborers hopelessly ground up in machines, cancer-riddled cases caught too late, outbackers who had not reached a freezing unit in time, malformed children left to die at birth, old men beyond repair. And his father: the slab of rough-edged stone stood directly before them, across the yawning grave. Its flat face was mirror-smooth, glossy with a careful e-beam polish. The precise letters would notify the world for millennia that here lay remnants of Colonel Francisco León López. It seemed odd to have such a mathematically exact tribute to a man who had been wrinkled and leathery, smiling, smelling always of dirt and sweat and grease.

The ceremony had been as bad as he had feared. Some relatives had come, people remembered from Sunday afternoon reunions long ago. He remembered them: vague presences who sipped beer while he played outside with his cousins. They had been with this mother by the time he arrived. They had contrived to make of the funeral a solemn, sweet-smelling ceremony, like the ones he had known as a child. He had never seen a complete one before, because he had always twitched and whispered and finally had to be sent out of the room. This time he had sat stiff-faced through the whole thing: suffocating wreaths of flowers (a rare sight, quite expensive; some of the family had money, somehow); aunts in black lace that rustled as they knelt; candles; gleaming satin; incense; even a priest, brought from Zanakin Settlement, swarthy, red-nosed and unsteady from midmorning wine, sprinkling holy water randomly.

Now the last part. Men and women from Sidon made up the big crowd, slightly further away than the relatives. Four of them carried the cellulose box forward. It had a brown polish like walnut. The priest said some more things. Manuel tried to concentrate on the words, but the steady drone kept slipping away from him and he would find his eyes roving over the valley beyond.

Slides had covered some of the pipes, but otherwise the quake had not hurt Sidon much. Most of the damage had been in the south. The cracked domes and popped sluice lines there were nearly fixed already. The magnetorail beds would take longer. He would have to stay at Sidon until normal runs were resumed.

". . . into that great reward that comes to us all in . . ."

Manuel shut his ears to it and tried to think of the man inside the cellulose box. That was the hard part, had been hard all the years at Hiruko. To see your father finally as a man, bound on his own path. The rage had boiled between the two of them and finally spilled out, souring everything in the family. Even now he did not fully understand it. He did know, though, that it had to be put away now. It would be only a burden from here on. The Colonel—he still thought of his father with the title, unused for decades except to lend a certain authority to his father among the men of Sidon—had never been able to understand that moment outside the cabin. He had seen only one principle, a human one, life as precious beyond all else.

And Manuel had never been able to show the Colonel anything else. They had not gone back into the wastes again together. There was no time for that. The two of them had learned fast enough that they could no longer live in the same apartment, nor even in the same Settlement. His mother's tearful attempts at reconciliation had failed within days, every one.

So Manuel had finally cut it off and fled to Hiruko. If he had been thinking about his career, it would have been the smart thing to do, anyway. Most people had assumed he was merely following his own interests, since Sidon's trade was dropping off and shares in the Settlement were not going to be worth earning until things got back in order, a few years further on. Publicly, there was never any reason to think otherwise. Neither man had spoken to anyone else about what had happened out at the camp. Old Matt was entered in the log as "accidental death while deranged." So this crowd around the grave knew nothing of why the son had never been back to Sidon. They genuinely mourned the Colonel and the era he had stood for in their minds: the hard decades of raising domes, and triple shifts, and horrifying accidents, and the slow-earned, grudging return from the land that at last had begun to yield something resembling prosperity.

Now the Colonel was in amongst all the crosses and carved angels that Manuel now watched through a hazy dim light. He had not noticed the slow gathering of his tears. He could not make out what was plucking at his sleeve. It was his mother. She led him, mute and stiff-legged, to the graveside. He took the shovel that Major

Sánchez put in his hand. The Major stood ramrod-straight and looked at Manuel with concern.

Manuel bent and took a spadeful and tossed it in. It scattered over the cellulose with a hollow thump. In a few days the cellulose would decompose and let the body begin to seep into the rich loam. Within a year the slow downward convection of this dome's soil would begin to cycle the materials into the terraces and the farm domes. In the first days of the Settlement they had buried their dead in the ice. The heat of the buildings had gradually caused some slippage and the bodies sometimes surfaced, undecayed, unnatural, grotesque—skin stretched taut and ice-blackened over a cage of bones, the faces silent, grimacing in reproach, exiled in an alien land. So as soon as the Settlement could afford it they had dedicated one dome for the processing of their own. About it had accumulated the thirst for ceremony that humans carried with them everywhere, so that nearly every cross or sculpted angel had a wreath of grass or flowers, regularly renewed. Each time he stood up to pitch dirt into the hole, he glimpsed those colorful spots among the bleached white markers.

At last someone took the shovel from him. He turned, found his mother. They walked away, down a blurred corridor lined with faces he knew but had not seen in years. Next would come the small reception; the low murmuring talk with the relatives; the business of his father's estate to settle; and finally, some days with his mother. Whenever he thought of her there was some pain, but he would not face the question of her yet. He would get through that too, but not now.

3

Manuel paced beside the towering iron-webbed building. High overhead, the pressure dome diffused yellow sunlight over the irregular, slanted roofs of homes and workshops. Originally the Settlement had been laid out in a maddeningly rigid geometrical plan, but as soon as families could afford separate homes they broke the pie-slice pattern of the districts. Near the center the streets were radial or circular, but further away they began to meander into loops and tangled cul-de-sacs, until near the perimeter of the dome the avenues had a spaghetti sprawl the eye could not follow. Immigrants, unpersuaded by promises of efficiency, had made their neighborhoods convoluted and comfortable. Patches of green marked unplanned parks. Homes varied from steel-ribbed spires to crouching bungalows of stone and plaster. Manuel liked the effect. Hiruko's sensible rectangular streets had bored him.

He teetered back on his heels and peered up at the rising strutwork of the Council Hall. It had a solemn mass, unnecessary and plainly intended to give the effect of weighty matters being looked after inside. The riveted iron made black diagrams of elementary geometry across pearly organic walls.

Impatiently he paced again. A young woman passed in a purple cape and long white dress. She eyed him slightly longer than was proper. Her shoes clacked on rusty paving stones. Low gravity allowed steepness and ornamentation; her minareted heels slid and torqued with each swivel of hips, engineered to attract first the ear, then the eye with their impossible angles. They led the eye inevitably up to the line of seamed blue stockings. Manuel watched her until she turned a far corner, thinking not of her but of Belinda back in Hiruko. He pondered for a moment, then grimaced in irritation.

He returned to the large arched doorway and asked the woman there, "How much longer?"

The short, swarthy attendant grunted. "No limit on discussion. Your business comes last."

"Look, it's just a formality."

"Syndicate has to approve it as a body, Manuel."

Manuel blinked, surprised that this woman he didn't remember recognized him, even recalled his name. "Uh, maybe during a break in—"

"No breaks. They've been jawing about the new hydro plant for ten hours now. The families who'll run it want a better inhouse overhead, an'—"

"They've got to stop sometime."

"Never went to a syndicate meeting before, did you?" The dark lined face screwed up, remembering. "Shoulda come with your father, saints preserve him."

"I was too young."

"Kids can come in. Can't talk, is all."

"My father took care of all that."

"Now it's up to you, handling the inheritance. Don't worry, the syndicate'll take their half, sure—and then they'll issue a proclamation and send flowers to your mother and issue her extra work vouchers for a year, you watch. They all remember the Colonel."

Manuel slapped his hand against the iron girders in irritation. "*Sí*, I won't argue. I just want it *done*."

The short woman shrugged. "Going to be a Settlement man, you got to learn to wait people out. Hear what they got to say. Not enough to have a majority rule, y'know. Otherwise, the minority won't be convinced and they won't support the plan. No point havin' people at your elbow who're against what you're doin'. So we just got to talk it out Quaker-style till ever'body agrees. More efficient in the long run."

Manuel snorted. "They take much longer, I'll go back to Hiruko."

A new voice said, "Not soon, I hope."

It was Piet Arnold. Manuel glanced at him warily. "Soon's I finish up family business."

"I would like to buy you a drink while you wait."

"I've got to stick around."

The short attendant put in, "No big rush here."

"Don't want to miss my turn."

"I'll hold 'em. They like to trade gossip after, anyway."

Piet said, "I heard on the comm that there'll be rain in three minutes."

Manuel looked up at the layer of purple clouds crowded into the crown of the dome. "I forgot. Well—*sí, sí*. One drink. Then I either get in to see the almighty syndicate or else I leave. I've still got things to look after for my mother." He glowered at the attendant as they left, even though he knew it wouldn't do any good.

Dollops of rain spattered them as they clumped down an alley. Each day the insulation at the dome crown was relaxed, chilling the air so that droplets would form in the clouds. It was an easy way to clean the Settlement and it gave a semblance of real weather. In Hiruko, Manuel remembered, there was an amusement park where you could walk through rain, nude or clothed, any time of day. He had gone there once and nearly gotten the flu.

They found a small, greasy bar nearby. It was run out of the back room of a house, mostly for neighborhood types, with a zinc counter and warm beer on tap. There was a tiny restaurant, featuring fresh food displayed for selection before cooking. Piet stared at the small yellow animals like miniature pigs, glassy-eyed in death; strings of red sausages; root vegetables for salads; crosscut slabs of lurkey; ribbed chest and flanks of some anonymous creature; peppered sections of meat; even an incredibly expensive side of beef. Piet gulped and moved quickly away to a booth. Manuel remembered that the man was a vegetarian, like nearly all Earthers.

"Odd little place," was all Piet would say. The room was crowded and noisy. A man sat nearby, cadaverous and silent, methodically pouring a brown liquid down himself. Manuel hailed the bar. A waitress came bearing dark bottles and freed them from wire tresses, uncorking them with the same gesture. She smirked at Piet's odd clothes as she was paid, then made an obvious show of counting the money. Piet frowned at this. "It's all there," he said formally. The waitress nodded and moved away.

Manuel said, "She was making sure you hadn't given her a tip."

"Well, I would have, but the sight of those—that dead animal flesh—"

"No, look. Here nobody takes tips. It's a point of honor. They know Earthers leave something extra, so she was checking."

"Ummm. Curious idea." Piet sipped his beer cautiously and wrinkled his nose. "On Earth the bars are large, the seats far apart. A thousand customers, perhaps. Economies of scale."

"Cheaper this way."

"A passing phenomenon," Piet said. "Like the Settlements themselves."

Manuel avoided that with "Uh-huh. Beer's not bad here. Lot of malt."

"Quite." Piet pursed his lips and said carefully, "I wanted to inquire about a man named Matthew Bohles."

"Yeah?"

"You knew him?"

"Some."

"I came across some material on him in my investigations. On Earth we received only the scientific reports, you understand. The people behind the facts . . . that is another matter."

"You been a scientist all your life?"

"Yes, of course. I conducted the original laboratory study of many of the outer-system artifacts. My isotopic analysis gave the first reliable dating of them. Also, my team discovered the inlaid circuits that allowed the artifacts to function whenever the sun struck them. I am Chairman of the Institute now, but I keep up my research. Lately I have been interested in certain mathematical properties of the artifacts. Aspects bearing on pure number theory."

"You came out here to have a firsthand look?"

"Yes. Someone with the proper credentials had to lead. It was also useful in acquiring funding. My wife died two years ago, and I had few ties remaining. My life's work is actually centered out here. All my research had been done secondhand, so to speak."

"Uh-huh." Manuel was drinking his big mug of beer steadily, trying to finish it off quickly without being obvious. "How do you live down there, in all those crowds?"

"Easier than you do here, in these extreme conditions."

"They're not so tough."

"Life seems difficult for some. For Bohles, I would say it was."

Manuel took a long pull of beer and said nothing.

"You are waiting to get approval of the Settlement for the inheritance of your father's estate, correct?"

"*Sí.*"

"Why should you get anything at all?"

"My father wanted us to."

"This dynasty-forming—it is not allowed on Earth."

"Dynasty! Spare equipment, tools, some shares in the machine shop where he worked part-time, the apartment—"

"Private wealth in the long run will—"

"You don't hand down anything, how you going to remember who the hell you *are*?"

Piet raised his hands, palms out. "I assure you, I meant no offense. Truly. Ah, would you like more of this beer?"

Manuel shook his head.

Piet said carefully, "I noted in my researches that Matthew Bohles had no estate."

"He never bought into the Settlement."

"So he did not share in the profits? Inexcusable."

"His choice, Dr. Arnold."

"Surely no one chooses to die in poverty."

"Old Matt just spent his money different."

"On what?"

"I don't know. Spent time out on the ice by himself a lot. Contract hunting for muties, I guess."

"That paid adequately?"

"He never poormouthed."

"Never protested?"

"Wasn't his way." Manuel noticed that these few days in Sidon had restored to his sentences a cagey slowness, a stubborn calm which withdraws before the rapid rhythms of the city.

"You did not exclude him from your, your hunts. Even though he was not of your class."

"Never thought of it."

"Perhaps his age? A sort of elder of the tribe? At any rate, there are a few details in the reports from the early sightings of the Aleph, suggestions that Bohles was there. I gathered you relied on his knowledge?"

"Sure."

"Did he tell you of his past?"

"He taught me things, that's all. Look—"

"I found records of him from long ago—more than a century old. He grew up on one of the first Jovian orbiting stations—did you know that? After that, few traces. I surmise he came here. I must say you keep rather poor records in the Settlements."

"We're not clerks."

"Still, the evidence suggests that Bohles knew a great deal. Nothing quantifiable, nothing of direct scientific use, but perhaps if we could pinpoint—"

"Look, I got to go. Thanks for the beer."

"I see. You Settlement men drink quickly."

"Part of the diet."

"Yes, the cold requires many calories in your intake."

"No, we just enjoy it." Manuel grinned nervously.

"Matthew Bohles was an interesting person. Perhaps sometime I can ask you further about him."

"Lots of people knew him."

"Fewer than you might imagine. Or so they say."

"Plenty here in Sidon."

"I won't be in Sidon. We are working out in the field. I'm going back there today."

"Good luck, then. I'll be back in Hiruko in a few days. Got a woman waiting for me," he said with hollow heartiness. He murmured goodbye quickly, awkwardly, and left the bar.

The rain was ebbing into drizzle outside. It had drained the clouds so that now no haze collected in the crown. Following the winding avenue back to the Council building, he noticed a large mottled brown animal shuffling along, patiently sweeping the slick street. As Manuel watched, the bearlike thing upended a garbage can into a cart it pulled. It had a stolid, earnest drive to it, oblivious of the passersby. It sniffed noisily, as though it had a perpetual head cold. *Looks like Petrovich's old idea*, Manuel thought. *Wonder if it still knocks people out of its way. No, they've probably worked the bugs out of it by now.* He went on.

Beneath the wrought-iron bulk of the Council building the attendant sat on a stool, reading a manifesto. As Manuel approached she held up a crimson admittance pass.

"You're lucky. The Schlickeiser family finally gave in. Got a unanimous vote two minutes ago. You can go on in."

Manuel took the pass and pushed open the massive door. He swallowed, still tasting the dark beer, and walked into the strong, enameled light of the Council chamber, already feeling the weight of the past beginning to lift from him as he prepared to end in a formal way the echoes of his father.

4

Manuel knocked on Major Sánchez's door. He heard slow bootsteps coming and then the familiar bronzed face appeared, lighting up when the Major saw who was there. The Major slapped Manuel on the back and offered him a drink, and they talked the slightly loud, boisterous way men do when they are not totally at ease with each other but know they should be.

They had another drink of the concentrated brown whiskey that made the breath warm and burned the back of the throat. The Major took him away from the living area, after Manuel had paid his respects to the women and answered the usual questions and eaten something although he wasn't hungry, and nodded and smiled. The two of them went back into the Major's own office—the big, airy, picture-lined space Manuel remembered playing on the floor of when he was a small boy. His father, out for a walk with him in the terraces, had often stopped by for a talk on the long summer afternoons and, of course, for some of the whiskey. Beyond the curtained windows, he knew, lay a railed balcony overlooking O'Hara Square; he had discovered the fact while crawling back there one day, when he was scarcely able to walk. Why the Major kept the curtains drawn he never knew. This time he asked. The Major shrugged.

"I like to look at the pictures there"—he gestured, mouth twisted into a grin—"and the people outside, always at my back, it disturbs my concentration." Then he gave a little laugh. "Crowds. You see them all day. Seems there should be a place where you don't have to."

Manuel nodded. The Major asked the questions he had expected about how his mother was doing and what he planned, and Manuel got through them all right. Then he said, "I've been going over my father's accounts."

"Good. Try to keep the Settlement from getting it all."

"Not much I can do about that. They get half of the property, my mother the other half. She gets to live in the 'partment."

"How they expect a man to feel he's done anything when at the end they snatch it all away from his widow . . ." The Major's face clouded, and his eyes glinted.

"Can't allow private property to accumulate," Manuel said mechanically. "You should see what they take in Hiruko. And back Earthside—"

"I know, it's incredible. We had some of those passed through last week, you know. Earthers. Funny-dressed."

Manuel nodded again. "They came out with me from Hiruko."

"They talk to you any?"

"Some."

"About the Aleph?"

"Not much."

"They sure talked a lot *about* you while they were here."

Manuel blinked. "They did?"

"I heard them."

"Why?"

"I don't know. I suppose they want testimony from everybody who was there."

"They come to see you?"

"No."

"Who'd they talk to, then?"

"Some of the guys who were there. Petrovich, mostly. With the Colonel and Old Matt gone, he knows more than the rest of us. I was way back in the rear most of the time, y'know."

"You know plenty."

Major Sánchez smiled. "Well, I must admit I wasn't home a few times when they called."

"Ha! I'd do the same."

They drank some more. "I talked to one of them on the train," Manuel said. "They think we're a bunch of uncivilized capitalists."

"*Mierda*. Earthers, so pious about their social justice. Wouldn't know a syndicalist if they saw one."

"Thought we were capitalists."

The Major shrugged. "*Sí*. We have a few regs, like not letting inheritance build up—not that I think it should apply to your father, y'understand. But the Earthers would rather think we're throwbacks than admit somebody doesn't love their bureaucracy. No"—he slapped his knee—"we're small-scale anarchists, like the old Spanish syndicalists of Barcelona."

Manuel didn't know where Barcelona was, or even if it was a city or a country. All these old names and places, cultures exploded out from old Earth—they confused him. Pieces of a continent separated by mere hundreds of kilometers were projected out into the solar system, enlarged into whole worlds.

"You should come to the *bourse du travail*, Manuel. You're old enough. The syndicate, it needs—"

"Yeah, maybe after things settle down . . ."

The Major nodded. He let it go. He had known Manuel long enough to see what was possible with him and what was not. They talked for a while and gradually the older man's face grew somber. After a pause he said, "I guess you heard they've been working on the carcass."

"An Earther told me. Who's been doing it?"

"A team out of Hiruko. They hired some local people, too."

"Huh. Who?"

"Petrovich, for one."

"Goddamn. What's he do for them?"

"Works out at the site. He's a pretty fair engineer."

"Huh. You and him arrange any more pruning trips?"

The Major sighed. Manuel noticed that Sánchez was getting a little plump in the middle. The man he was used to seeing in stained overalls or a pressure suit, unshaven, two weeks from his last bath, was wearing a handsome broadcloth shirt woven in Hiruko, and pants with a crease. "No. Not really. We had a few, after you left, sure. But we all got pretty busy then. It's been a tough go around here, what with the McKenzies revving up."

"I was looking over the accounts my father kept on the prunings. Big file on it."

"*Sí*. He ran them all. Don't know what the communality will do without that man, putting himself out the way he did for ever'body."

"He kept good books, too. I checked them over. Did you know the Settlement lost money on every pruning?"

"It did?"

"Every year. Hiruko paid us some, sure. But by the time it worked through all the off-shift time for the men, and the supplies, the Settlement lost."

"Well, I'll be."

"Sure you didn't know?"

The Major paused. "Well . . . I might have suspected, sometimes. It took a lot of time."

"Why do you suppose he did it, then?"

Major Sánchez leaned forward in his chair. "I figure, he thought we needed it."

"Needed what?"

"The going out. Out there. You can't just sit in a hole in the ground all your life. Or under a dome."

"That was all?"

"No. No, it was the thing itself. It was . . ." The Major rubbed his jaw, distracted, staring off into space. "So the Colonel ran it at a loss all that time, eh, over forty years? And the Settlement never caught on, eh? Damn!"—he slapped his knee, face suddenly bright—"I like that!"

* * *

They had taken several more tumblerfuls of the dark brown whiskey when Madam Sánchez came in and whispered, embarrassed, in the Major's ear. Her dress crinkled as she bent over the big chair the Major filled. He muttered something to her, frowning. He gazed up at the pictures on his wall, big glossy ones of domes half-completed and crowds of workers and, nearer the heavy metal desk, lonely vistas of ice and rock framing the pink and white bands of Jupiter.

"It's Petrovich."

"Come to visit?"

"Not me. You. He found out from your mother where you were."

Manuel was puzzled. He took another sip of the smoldering brown liquid and sudenly Petrovich was there, bigger than Manuel remembered him, his burly chest well defined by the well-fitting jump suit he wore. He was boisterous and beaming and more outgoing than Manuel remembered him. He laughed and clapped Major Sánchez on the shoulder.

"So I've tracked you down!" he cried, seizing Manuel's hand and shaking it powerfully. "I was to the funeral, of course, but I hoped to be seeing you before you return."

"Ah, sure. I've been busy." Manuel noticed that Petrovich's voice was deeper, more assured, and he did not have the same rough accent as before.

Petrovich became solemn. "I know. A terrible thing, to have to do all these business things so soon. But tell me, what have you been doing off at Hiruko? We hear reports, your mother says a few things . . ." He shrugged.

By now Manuel had a standard description of life-in-Hiruko. He slipped in mention of Belinda without giving much away and went on to his job.

"Good, good," Petrovich interrupted. "But when you come back for good?"

"Well, maybe later. When things look better."

Petrovich spread his hands warmly. "Things are already good. In certain areas."

"He means the Earthers. They're hiring." The Major leaned back, hands clasped behind his neck, enjoying Petrovich's momentary vexed look.

"Yes, they are. A little. I think, Manuel, they would be interested in you."

"Why?"

"You know a good deal about it."

"So do you. And the Major, here."

"The Major is busy. I work as I can around the site, true—but there is much to do."

"I've got a good career going in the petrofac."

"I realize that. We are all very proud of you, m'boy. To do well in Hiruko—not easy! How-ev-er"—he drew the word out—"I believe the Earthers can top that, yes."

"No. Not interested."

Petrovich cast a look of appeal toward Major Sánchez. "You have turned him against the idea already?"

"Not at all."

"Look," Manuel said, exasperated, "I make up my own mind."

"Of course," Petrovich said soothingly. "Let me make a simpler offer. We forget about jobs, about coming back to Sidon—okay?"

Grimly: "Right."

"And you come out with me for one last trip. As in the old days. The days with the Colonel."

Manuel's lip compressed, but he said nothing.

Petrovich hesitated, wiped a bead of sweat from his brow, and went on: "No pruning, no. A simple ride. That is all. An outing."

"Look, I'm . . ." Manuel began, and then stopped, mouth open. He suddenly felt an emotion, dimly remembered, coming to him strongly, the way a scent not smelled for decades will abruptly bring back a place, a time. He blinked. "I . . ."

The two men were studying him closely. He felt dizzy with the impact of the feelings, stored up for so long and welling up now fresh and brimming. He turned and saw the Major's pictures of the wastes stretching away, bleak and slumbering. He said slowly, as though surprised at the words, "I might like that. *Sí*, I might."

PART VI

ALEPH NULL

1

They went out from Sidon Settlement in one lone crawler this time, clanking and crunching over the splotched purple plain. There were new domes abuilding on the plain now, and pyramids of waste from the fermentation and harvesting terraces that marched up the hills on either side. No animals yipped and chippered beside the crawler. Teams of them labored in the distance, though, and the thin, chilled air carried the loud *rruuurrr* and heavy booms of their work. He wondered if the people back in Hiruko were right, and the animals were a kind of new class in society, a new source of surplus value, yet another source for the forward tilt of capitalism, yet another revolution simmering on the back burner. Manuel thought of names he had not recalled for years—Short Stuff, The Barron, Slicky. Of Eagle he had thought many times, and did not put that name in amongst the others.

In the crawler with Petrovich were five laborers from Sidon who worked at the site. They kept to themselves, playing cards and sleeping in the hours the trip took. Petrovich talked about Settlement gossip and the new money crops blooming on the terraces—luxury foods, an attempt to speed-grow exotic guavas and artichokes and crisp apples—and commonweal troubles and politics (the wage-labor referendum) and back to gossip again, practically carrying on both sides of the conversation by himself. Manuel nodded and smiled on cue but mostly just stared out the big clear canopy on the crawler. It was a better view than he had ever had from the caked and scratched viewports of the craft they'd used for the prunings. This one had an Earther emblem on the side, fresh and stark blue-and-white. The seats inside still had some nap on them, and the control panels didn't have their insignia rubbed off where men had leaned against them. The pan-fry rig in the back had the usual layers of grease on it, but to Manuel it did not seem to smell so bad as when he was a boy. He ate some lurkey from it, but that didn't taste as good as he remembered, either; he guessed there was a kind of trade-off, or else that to a boy all things were exaggerated. There was something about this last thought that bothered him, but he could not say what.

"See," Petrovich called out. "Europa rising now."

Manuel followed the crescent as it rose above a mountain peak. On Europa's cracked and cratered face he could make out tiny ruby dots of fusion-busters. The busters were crawling along the cracks that wrapped the moon, melting the walls away, hoping to open the old channels below the cracks, through which the churning slush below would give forth rich minerals. Jove itself, hanging eternally at the top of the sky, was now the only face unmarked by man.

Io swam at the edge of the giant planet. Each moon shone with a diffused light, a halo bright enough to smother the nearby flecks of stars. Petrovich gestured. "See, already the cap goes on."

Manuel was surprised. "The monolayer?"

"See that blurring around Io? Light scattering. They've laid the northern hemisphere already. Spun out whole monolayer from orbit, let it fall, come to pressure balance with the atmosphere. You didn't watch?"

"In Hiruko, y'know," Manuel said sheepishly, "you lose track of what's going on in the biosphere."

"They left the big holes, for the orbital craft to come in. Looks to be stable."

"Think it'll help with the warming as much as they say?"

Petrovich shrugged. "Worked on Luna. Here—maybe. To put a cork on a whole atmosphere—incredible, hey? Things changing fast, these days."

Manuel gazed at the gauzy halo around Europa for a moment, trying to remember what it had looked like before. He couldn't. Something about that made him uneasy. "Which route we following?" he asked suddenly.

"Here, to the west. Faster than the old way."

"Uh-huh." Manuel glanced at the relief map and it came back to him immediately. He could see in his mind's eye the way the ridges and gullies would be. "Look, what say we take this side detour?"

"There? What for?"

"That's where the camp is."

"Was. Haven't been back there since—since—well, you remember."

"Me either."

Petrovich looked at him strangely, puzzled. "That time, just the few of you left out there when he . . ." A shake of the heard. "He was oldest man in the Settlement. I . . . cried when I heard."

"Yeah." Manuel gazed out at the once-jagged ramparts of an ancient crater, now slumping and melting. In the lee of a southerly wind, pink snowdrifts still clung to shards of rock. "Well? You willing?"

Again the puzzled expression. "I . . . Okay." Petrovich clapped his hands, breaking his pensive mood. "I know a cut through a gorge, there"—a fat finger stabbed the map. "Not existing even five years ago."

They worked through the narrow, stream-gutted gorge and came out beneath a waterfall. The cascading ammonia-rich river steamed when it hit their canopy, sending up geysers that caught the sun. Rainbows formed high up, hanging tenuously against the face of Jupiter and then dissolving. They rocked on, lurching over fresh outwashes. One of the men sat on the deck outside and potted away at muties that wandered into range. There were a fair number of them, and Manuel asked about keeping the population down.

"*Da*, we have to do that soon. Hiruko is griping. But they do not pay enough, is the fact. We wait a little more, get their price up."

Manuel asked, "What've they been doing with the development money?"

Petrovich shrugged. "Putting out seismos. Tilt meters. Creep gauges."

"How come?"

"Still like the old days. They dumped a new animal into the bisophere, not tell us a thing—remember? Till we got to go out and prune away their mistakes. *Then* we get the specs. Same with them now—they hire gangs to put out the meters, they smile, they pay okay, they tell us zero."

Manuel grinned. "Good to see not everything's changed."

Manuel found the camp using merely the sun's position and memory, just letting the crawler follow its nose. He was not thinking of anything in particular when the land began its slight rise, and so the ramshackle profile of the camp came up out of the horizon without any twinge of anticipation in him. The north wall of the cabin had been staved in by something and patched up with a garish yellow gummy stuff. There were broken boxes scattered around, and wind-scoured old equipment, and the fusion generator was on minimum, racheting along with a *pock pock pock*, providing power for the cluster of seismos and other odd-shaped devices driven into the ice nearby.

He and Petrovich got out and walked to the hill that overlooked the vacant, neglected sprawl. Manuel found the spot not by pacing off from the crown of the hill but by feel, remembering the way the big boulders formed a nexus that pointed downslope to the little flat area.

"They wondered about this, back Sidon," Petrovich said.

"Good," Manuel said with a sudden flash of anger that surprised him.

The ice here was crusted with old snow. Manuel scraped it clear with his hands, kneeling and letting the heat of his suit sweep away the cloudiness in the top layer of ice.

Far down, surrounded by small bubbles, was a dark shape. He could barely make out the arms and legs. It was still face up.

"Ice hasn't moved any," he murmured.

"It will. Creep meter over there I looked at. It flows, hundred meters under here."

"Uh-huh." He peered into the ice as if he could see the face.

"Could still take it in for funeral," Petrovich said quietly.

"No. Sidon's not so poor it can't go without one more corpse for fertilizer."

"You know that is not why."

"Sure I know. They wanted a little ceremony, like the one a few days ago. Community's built on ceremony." He stood up abruptly.

"They have a point."

"This is one that didn't need their ritual. He wanted to stay out here."

Petrovich nodded silently. He scuffed his boot and turned back to the camp. Manuel followed after a moment. The cabin seemed smaller now, and the stanchions had sunk beyond view in the ice, as if this place, neglected by men for a while as they fretted about other, passing matters, was taking up its natural course again, blending into the generality of the wilderness, absorbed in the deep motions of the ice.

As he tramped down the hillside, the crunch of his boots on old snow faded away into the encasing silence of the place. He could squint his eyes and still see his father standing outside the lock, angry and yet letting his son take the body up the rise and lay it out carefully, and in the hour following chop out a grave in the ice, the myriad glinting chips and crystals billowing up around the bent, steadily digging figure. The Colonel had buried his anger for that hour because his son had told him a lie, the only lie that had ever passed between them, a lie that had held until they got back to Sidon: that Old Matt had said he wanted this, to be buried out here, under the progression of dark and dawn and dark and dawn again, not held fast in the ice but free in the ice. It was a lie in strict fact, but not in essence; Manuel knew what the old man had wanted, and the fact that there had not been time to say it, or the right time, did not matter. But the small, niggling deception had eaten at the son, and within a week he had told the father, and that in the end had tipped the scales somewhere in the Colonel's mind, had made it impossible for the two of them to go on as they had before. So the sudden sparking rages had gotten worse between them and this cold flat space in the side of a hill had driven a wedge between them; *No son of mine would do such a thing;* and finally it was not over the death but, as can happen between men who have loved each other, it was over the tiny matter of the burial that they had seen the last of each other.

Manuel came stiff-legged into the field, eyes watery and aimless, and the first shock knocked him off his feet. One moment he was halfway through a step and the next he was on his back, the wind knocked out of him, feeling the ground shake. He got to his knees and the second shock came. He saw this one coming as a dark line sweeping in from the horizon, rippling the snow so that facets of sunlight struck from the crest. The seismic wave shot up the rise without pause, inexorable and swift, and jolted up through his boots like a physical blow. The cabin lurched, its metal shrieked—and it collapsed, the roof caving in first and then the walls one at a time as the stresses warped through their planes and shattered the ports, spraying transparent shards into the field, sending up showers of dust and gushes of air that froze into puffs of cloud. A girder came flying out, tumbling end over end and narrowly missing Petrovich, who was balled up on the ground. It gouged out a strip in the snow and stopped.

The crawler slewed around and rocked, but did not overturn. Hoarse shouts came over the comm. Petrovich overrode them with a harsh "Quiet!—Any hurt? Count out!"

Manuel watched the horizon as the men called out their names. No major injuries, though one fellow had sprained a shoulder falling. No more waves came over the horizon. He trotted down to Petrovich and asked, "You're tapped into Hiruko, aren't you? What's happening?"

Petrovich was staring off into space, listening intently. "Confusion. Lot of damage."

"How about Sidon?"

"Some tunnels fell in. Some injuries."

"My mother?"

"No. Nobody I know."

"I should call her."

"Comm is packed." He shook his head. "Damn, was big one."

"What's going on? Two quakes in a week."

"Don't understand. These moons, they're stable."

"The melting—it's supposed to be symmetric, not cause ice-plate tectonics."

Petrovich thought, nibbling absently at his lip. "Supposed to be, yes. I heard of some cave-ins downslope from here, in the mines . . ."

"Let's get back to Sidon."

"No. They don't need help, is being done okay."

"I think we should check. Call somebody."

"Can do that on way to the site."

Manuel gritted his teeth, but nodded. "Okay, okay. Dump these men off at the site. Then we go back."

Petrovich checked the tilt meters and frowned. "Lots of slippage down there. Come on. Let us get off this gradient."

The big man started toward the crawler. Manuel paused. The cabin whose interior he had memorized was now a rubble of beams and sheet metal and plastaform. He had missed seeing the inside again by only moments. He had wanted to walk through it, see if anything had changed. Of course, if he had been inside when—

"Manuel! Come on!" Petrovich waved out at him from the pilot's couch. "We have to move. The site—no answer. But their emergency hailer is on. Putting out Mayday."

2

The volcano rose through banks of black dust and streaming orange plumes of erupting, howling gas.

"Big bastard. Blocks the way," Petrovich said, wrestling with the controls. The crawler swerved to avoid a tumbling boulder.

"We can dogleg around it." Manuel pointed. "Through that gully—there."

A rattling vibration came up through the crawler's treads. The Sidon men clustered in the rear of the cabin and muttered to each other. Petrovich brought them clanking and roaring into the gully, swerving around a caved-in rampart of rock. Vapor poured from cracks in the gully floor. Steam hissed beneath them. The crawler's lights winked on, cones of white opening to a dimmed infinity.

"This thing's big," Manuel said. "Maybe there's erupting all along the mountain range."

Petrovich thumbed on a satellite overview. In the visible spectral range the whole area was awash in smoke and clouds. He clicked to infrared: pinpricks of bright, violent activity all along their route. "Damn."

"Look there. The ice—moving."

The infrared image displayed velocity vectors in the valley floor. Arrows clustered at the center, snaking southward. "Pretty damn fast, too," Petrovich murmured.

They lurched out of the gully into the open, caterpillar treads slipping in mud. Green vapor steamed from cracks ahead. For a moment a chance wind cleared the air down the valley. Silently the men watched a slow churning motion sweep rocks along. Blue-gray blocks of ice slid into view out of the low ground haze, sank, rose—and cracked apart with muffled crashes. Splinters speared upward and toppled. Crevasses groaned open and abruptly slammed shut. The ice heaved and thrust and was swallowed in turn by more ice sliding down from the far hills.

"*Madre de Dios*."

"The whole region is out of balance," Petrovich whispered.

He angled them along the valley wall, away from the grinding march of the ice. Above, the new volcano was wrapped in mist against a black sky. Through shifting clouds they saw ribbons of white water turn brown as they gathered up dust, and then plunge down to roaring rivers. The fluids ran off the hills and into yawning cracks in the fractured, shifting ice.

They topped a rise and crossed over into a side arm of the central valley system. "This way, we can try. See? No velocity vectors along this line."

"Maybe it's stationary?"

Petrovich raised his eyebrows. "Maybe."

On a distant flank of the volcano the ice was pressing upward, driven by pressures in the valley below. It jutted up the raw black stone slopes, melted, vaporized, and then froze again as it rose, wreathing the peak in fog. Manuel could see the red flare of the cone's summit, pulsing like rich arterial blood and bright enough beneath the pall of dust to throw crimson blades of luminescence down the shadowy, smoking slopes.

"I am afraid our Hiruko friends, they have miscalculated."

"The fusion crawlers?"

"*Da*. It is a delicate game. To build the atmosphere, but at same time keep land in balance."

"Maybe they made air too fast."

"Is not the air, is water. This world is one spherical glacier, with nowhere to go, no place to run downhill. The ice cap, it rests on rock beds—rock from meteors, that sank partway down as the crust was freezing. Melt the ice, it relieves pressure on the rock. Rock then expands, opens up pores. Fine. Extra water from the melting, water that did not turn to gas, seeps into the rock. Rock acts like sponge. Hiruko was counting on the rock sopping up this water."

"What if it didn't?"

"You fill up the sponge, the extra water moves into the joints between rock slabs. Into fault lines. That much water moving down deep, the mass pressure, plus it lubricates the fault lines . . . Zip! Old cartoon of man stepping on a banana peel. Ice on top skids along on the water below."

"Hiruko was doing it too fast."

"A very difficult calculation. Many uncertainties."

"Any more word from Sidon?"

"They are not bothering with us. They will not bother about the site either, for a while."

Manuel said grimly, "I wonder what the Earthers make of all this."

Outside, the volcano roared and fumed and sent its lancing crimson into the thickening shroud of dust.

They approached carefully across the broad plain. The ice mesa reared in the distance, its steep sides cut by slides and slumped terraces. Deep cracks laced across it. But the ice plain was firm and the crawler made good time. Behind the tiny speeding figure, an ebony volcanic dust cloud flattened as it rose into altitudes where the buoyancy of the thin air would not carry the particles. Soon it stretched from horizon to horizon, an immense black anvil.

"Don't see anybody," Manuel said.

"Probably inside the housing."

Petrovich pointed to seven half-cylinders arranged in neat rows, their walls a crimped bronze. Two had caved in. Beyond them was a tall structure of girders, rods, beams, struts, and cross-supports. Shocked, Manuel realized that this was an outer frame for the Aleph. Through the web of metal he could see cool alabaster. He compared it with the last time, when he was hurrying and had turned and looked back, carrying Old Matt. It was in the same place, as near as he could tell, but the long shape seemed broader.

They throttled down and stopped beside the half-cylindrical huts. A lock opened and two figures came out, waving, beckoning them inside. Manuel carried in the medical pack. The first person he saw inside was Piet Arnold.

"I am so grateful that you have come on," the man said, "rather than turning back to Sidon."

"Your comm is out, except for the Mayday."

"Ah, good—we did not even know if that worked. Of all our huts, the two that collapsed were the most vital. Terrible luck. Two died."

"You got them cooled down okay?"

"Yes. You can take them back as well?"

"What happened to *him?*" Manuel gestured toward an Earther inserted halfway into the hut's med monitor, feet first.

"A broken leg, some blood loss. I am afraid the blow drove bone fragments into the muscle."

"Painful. How'd it happen?"

"He fell from the scaffolding around the Aleph."

"A monitor that size, not enough," Petrovich put in. "Cannot remove deep fragments."

"I'm aware you will have to take him back to Sidon. He should rest a bit first, however. And you will need to study the route back, I should imagine." Piet spread his hands in smiling welcome. "You can surely spend a day or two here. We appreciate the company."

Manuel studied the man. "We'll be leaving tomorrow," he said flatly.

"I am sorry your arrival has been in such dreadful circumstances. These events . . ." He shook his head.

Manuel grimaced. "Don't worry about anything but setting up your comm again. That's vital. Whole damn crust's shifting, near as I can tell. You've got to stay in touch with Hiruko. Come on—I'll start on it now."

In the morning there was a hovering silence in the hut. No one was awake. Manuel got out of the fiber blankets as quietly as he could, dressed, ate a bar of food, and suited up. The lock made a lot of hydraulic noise as he went out, so he was not surprised to see another figure emerge from the hut ten minutes later. The man came trotting toward him, where he stood in the shadow of the Aleph.

Piet said nothing as he approached. The two simply

eyed each other, and at last Manuel said severely, "Why'd you talk to me on the train?"

"You were a fellow passenger. You seemed lonely."

"You knew who I was."

"That does not change anything. You still appeared lonely."

"You, Petrovich—I'm not going to tell you anything, you know."

"Have I asked?"

"Look, it's *dead*. Let it alone. Or at least let *me* alone."

"Why are you so sure?"

Manuel blinked. "Sure?"

"That it is dead."

"*Look* at it. We killed it, Old Matt and me."

Piet smiled broadly. "Yes, do look at it."

Manuel turned and studied the strutwork. "You've boxed it in."

"To make precise measurements."

Manuel sniffed. "I took its measure."

"In a way, yes. One measure of it."

"Nobody ever knew what to do about it. You read the records, right? It killed a lot of people in its time."

"Yes. By accident, apparently."

"Accident or not, we had to stop it."

"Was that it?"

"Huh? Protecting people? I don't know. I just came out here; it was . . . Ever'body . . . Every year we came out, the guys always talked about it . . ."

"Why? Why did you kill it?"

Manuel gazed at him without understanding. "Why? It . . . Look, you don't know anything about this."

Piet said, "You set about that comm repair like a demon. It took you nearly the whole night."

"So?"

"As if you were avoiding something. Talking to me. Or coming out here to the artifact."

Manuel glowered. "I came out here on my own just now."

"Yes, alone."

"Wanted to have a look at it. Got to be heading back soon. Want to start early. Could be a lot of trouble getting through, what with—"

"There will be time, I expect. From what I gather from Hiruko, these quakes are temporary phenomena."

"Listen, don't take that Hiruko flak for gospel." Manuel moved restlessly back and forth. He paced in the shadow of the Aleph, a cooler zone cast down sharp and clear on the mottled, boot-trod ice.

Piet smiled again. "Shall we go in?"

"*In?*"

"You really should have kept up with the reports, you know."

"You can go inside?"

Piet spread a palm toward the hulk inside the webbing of rods. "Four years ago a scientist from Hiruko found a peculiar wedge-shaped formation near the tail. Irradiated with neutrons, it yielded a high return flux. A method of resonance absorption—using neutrons of high energy—made the structure break down. The entire object unfolded. As if on command."

Manuel frowned. "Thought it looked fatter."

Piet raised a gloved finger. "There's the point. It unfolded—the big blocks came crashing down on the ice—but as nearly as we can tell, the net volume of the thing did *not* increase."

"Uh-huh. So?"

"The Hiruko people ventured in. Not far—but they retrieved a great deal."

"Enough to get you to come out here from Earth."

Piet nodded. "Yes. More than enough." He extended his arm toward an opening in the rodwork. "Come inside. You, of all people, should."

They walked in, stooping to get through the enclosure. "You wanted me out here all the time," Manuel said. He was still confused and uncertain, and yet . . . and yet . . . however much he distrusted the man, Piet

Arnold seemed to have a sense of the thing that he had not found in Major Sánchez or in Petrovich or even in his father.

He stopped abruptly at this thought. His father—and up from some recess came an outwelling of emotion that took him by surprise, filling his throat, choking off his breath. Emotions swirled in him, blotting out the present. It was grief and something beyond grief, a yawning abyss of loss and failed opportunity that could never be undone, a sense of passing, of moving finally beyond—

He gulped, and gave no sign of this, but walked on, following the bent-over form ahead of him.

They passed through a wedge formed of two huge alabaster blocks. A luminescence churned in the blocks, casting shadows on the taut tanned skin of his face. His boots went *chunk*, *chunk* into the ice.

"Damn big," he said uselessly.

"You would know," Piet replied, turning back, smiling.

They came out into a chamber of hexagonals. Here the light glinted from moving shards like mica. The ice floor was littered with equipment. Probes studded the smooth surfaces of the room. Meters and analyzers registered data with blue and green dials.

"We have made a thorough study here. The Hiruko data were of course essential. We knew what to prepare for. Thus, only a few days of more sophisticated observation have confirmed their results, and added a great deal."

"Uh-huh." Manuel stood, arms folded, looking at the dim patterns that formed in the deep slabs of the thing.

"It is, in a sense, mere stone. The lattice structure near the surface confirms that. . . . But below . . ." Piet touched a control and the worn rock seemed to Manuel to peel away, revealing a mottled design.

"Below, it constantly remakes itself. The molecular composition changes. The blocks are always mechanically strong, surely—but constantly in flux. New compounds, new lattices. The basic crystalline design is none of the usual ones. It is a ragged, shifting thing of points and angles."

"A machine that makes its own parts?" Manuel shrugged. "So?"

"But to remake its own molecular structure! Actually, if it were only that, perhaps you would be right—a truly sophisticated machine, an advanced technology, might very well do just that. But the molecular forms, we have found, readjust because the *atomic* structure alters. And the atoms change because the particles constantly shift and move and change identity. That is it—the steady conversion of matter into other forms, like something restlessly remaking itself, forever discontented—"

Piet broke off. "I can see you are bored by such findings. Perhaps it is best to simply let you witness." With a gesture he dimmed the lights from the analyzers, and the walls gained new life. Manuel could see the shifting lights beyond the stone surface better now, and—

—fiery pinpricks wheeling—

—a warped mass of quivering lines, a silvery coiling, thrusting out toward him—

—dissolving suddenly into a billowing softness, green clouds scratching a ruby sky with a shriek—

—bright, quick, shiny surfaces—

—a scribble of sound, blurred—

—something running, so fast there was only the impression of size and speed and relentless desire—

—rotting pinks and greens, a stench of age—

—rasping, encrusted, heavy light—

—hair like snakes—

—explosion—

"Ah!"

Manuel wrenched away, covering his eyes. Yet many of the things he'd felt had come not through sight but through the other senses, taste and smell and sound and touch, stretching fine and firm as though he was experiencing them for the first time.

Piet said softly, "You see. I am sorry, but . . . You see."

"I . . ."

"The endless change manifests itself at every level. To produce effects at our level of perception that, frankly, I cannot understand or even fully describe. What you cannot see is what this apparatus reports." He waved his hands to take in the racks of equipment. "Down at the nuclear level, and even below that, the forces *themselves* alter. There is a thing called the electro-weak interaction. Several numerical parameters describe it—parameters we thought fixed since time began, since the big bang started the universe. We now know, because of Aleph, that they are not fixed. Here, they change. Always. Nothing remains, nothing is held constant."

"How's it hold together?"

"I honestly do not know. The artifact is like a Rosetta stone—you know some Earth history?—which recapitulates all the laws of the universe. Somehow, it knows how to *make* laws. There is a scheme to it, of course. As I interpret the data, the artifact seems to be saying that the physical laws were not always the same. When the universe was young, the laws were young. Now they are somewhat aged. Our fundamental constants of today will not always remain so. So natural evolution does not apply only to life—it applies to the laws of the universe as well. The *laws*." Piet clasped his hands together. "I hope you understand what a profoundly unsettling notion this is."

"Uh, yeah."

"Perhaps you do not fully grasp the point." Piet leaned forward earnestly. "You see, physics holds that particles are created by fields—the electric field, the nuclear fields, and so on. But suppose that there was something that created *laws*. What does that? How"—he seized Manuel's arm—"how do you store the information that contains the laws? In the particles? But they are made by the fields, and thus by the laws themselves! Circular! How do you convey the information? *What makes the laws?*"

Manuel gazed at the walls, still flashing with color and light. "Well . . . I don't . . ."

"Suppose the artifact is *in* this universe, but is not *of* the universe?"

Manuel shook his head, disturbed by the thoughts this man brought up. Piet at once saw his confusion and relented, backing away. "I am sorry."

To cover his uncertainty Manuel assumed the gruffness he had used outside. "Look, why'd you show me this? I can't help you understand anything about—"

Piet held up a hand, palm outward. "Come."

On they went, through narrow passages of somber rock, up tight corridors, crawling through odd-shaped holes, down slides slick with ice. It seemed to Manuel that the Aleph could not possibly be as big as this, as complicated. The walls were dead cold stone and they stretched on, seamless, without end.

They reached an open corridor where Manuel could stand. Piet said conversationally, "Do you know who named it Aleph?"

"No."

"Some Jew, I gather. An interesting choice. You know what it means?"

"First letter of the Hebrew alphabet, an uncle of mine said. He's Jewish."

"Correct. The interesting point is that it means quite a few things in the sciences. For instance, in geometry, it is written so"—he fetched a pad from a pocket and drew on it the sign $\aleph$—"and means a point in space that contains all other points. All angles, all perspectives. And in another branch of mathematics, the number denoted by aleph null"—he wrote the sign $\aleph_0$—"is the basic transfinite number from Cantor's *Mengenlehre*—a number which has the curious property that any part of it is as large as the whole."

"That's crazy."

"Perhaps. Perhaps. Come along."

They had to crawl again, and then inch up a cleft that

seemed to be metallic. Manuel slipped on the slick mirror surfaces. Other rounded passages opened along the sides. A memory tugged at him. The walls reflected back his frowning, drawn face. The tube narrowed, and a glow from ahead grew diffuse and white.

"Here—get in front." Piet pushed him ahead.

Manuel stood in a narrow space and looked around. Weak fields clutched at him, but could find no grasp. Ahead—

Something spun in a halo of light.

"Matt!"

He stumbled forward and hit cushiony air that yielded softly and then resisted. He fought at it but could not get closer.

The head was shadowed somehow, despite the white glow around it. He could not read anything in the face. One arm was upraised—in salute or greeting, he thought. Old Matt was not in helmet and suit, the way Manuel had seen him inside the Aleph before, but rather in loose-fitting coveralls. The body spun very gradually to the left, and then the shadows on the face lifted a little and he could see the lips were moving with aching slowness. Manuel tried to make out what the words were, but before the parched lips could fully close and define the movement, the shadows—*But shadows of what?* Manuel wondered—fell again on the solemn face that peered out, unblinking, pale and uncreased as though relaxed and pensive. Manuel remembered that dry voice saying, *Watch for me* as they had walked toward the Aleph with the e-beam, that last time. *Watch for me*.

The body turned further. The diffuse halo glow was cast on the shoulders and back. Was the hand moving, a fraction of a centimeter? He strained to see.

Beyond it was something more. A vague figure of about the same size turned even more slowly, arms halfway raised at the elbows, dark running and swirling through the body so that only the outline was clear. In the fog of light he could tell this form was less detailed, blurred like a hazy image from only a fraction of a holographic print. It was helmeted, legs apart as though captured while walking, head turned—Manuel gasped. The light seeped into the veiled helmet and he saw just enough to catch the half-smiling mouth, the eyes—

"What"—he backed away—"what are these?"

"We were hoping you might know."

"Me?"

"You saw something like this before? Petrovich reports that—"

"*Sí*, something. After we shot the Aleph, while I was inside it, I thought I saw Old Matt, but when I got outside . . . I . . ." He stepped back again, mouth rigid, grimacing. "That other thing. That's *me*."

"I believe so. That is why we so wanted to speak with you, to learn how these . . . copies . . . came into being."

"I don't know." Manuel began to tremble.

"You felt nothing that time? Something holding you, extracting information somehow . . . ?"

"No!" He retreated again, squinting, eyes fixed on the far figure. "Nothing."

Piet said soothingly, "I urge you to think of this again, once you are through this first reaction. Consider—you are a Christian, are you not? Our files indicate so. Consider how closely linked the idea of preservation, of arising again in a similar but transmuted form—how closely linked this is in your culture. It is the Christian vision of resurrection and salvation. Also, it is the image of horror at the walking dead, the zombie. Try to think of it in the positive sense, if you can. I—"

"Let's get out of here."

Manuel stumbled away. Piet rushed after him, down another passageway lit by a flickering green glow. Manuel stopped suddenly.

"My God, what's that?"

The bulbous, distended shape beyond had things like

arms and a slanted head and long, spiky things jutting out from the eyes.

"Don't go near it!" Piet called.

Manuel stepped closer against spongy resistance—and the thing turned abruptly. The huge head seeming to click forward in the harsh, blinking light. Sudden terror filled Manuel. He turned and fled, running straight into Piet.

"Come on!"

"No need. It is a bit of a shock at first. Here, this way."

"What's it doing here?"

"Staying where it is," Piet said mildly. "Men are not the only beings preserved, apparently."

"But that thing, where's it from?"

Piet shrugged. "The classical definition of aleph, a thing that contains all other things . . ."

"In a place this size?" They were making their way back along a route he knew, and Manuel was calmer, beginning to think.

"Ah, but what *is* its size? That which appears to us from the outside? Or what we measure on the inside? A geometry containing other geometries . . ." Piet chuckled. "We have not yet counted all the passageways. There are many of them—or at least, it *appears* that way."

Manuel said nothing. He frowned and grimly forged ahead, his face unreadable. He was nearly to the next turn when the wall began to shake violently. With a loud crack the ice split under him. He fell through.

3

The split was deep. He grabbed at a jutting shard of ice and hung on. The stonework walls cast dim light down into the break, and he could see after a moment that it went down twenty more meters. *It's started,* he thought. It was natural for the ice to split first under the greatest weight. The whole plain outside would go next.

"Here, let me help you," Piet called. Manuel looked up. Piet was eight meters above. But the man was still judging heights with his Earth reflexes.

"Back away!" Manuel shouted. He swung up onto the ice shard. He gathered himself and then leaped the distance, even clearing the edge to land on his feet in the passageway. "Come on, we've got to break camp."

"I'll get the equipment in here," Piet said, turning back.

"Leave it! This rock will be the first thing to go."

Piet said firmly, "People invested immeasurable effort to make it and bring it here. I am obliged to see that their labor is conserved."

Manuel put a hand on Piet's shoulder. "Look, be sensible—" Piet brushed it off and walked away, not looking back. "All right, dammit—crucify yourself for your goddamn commonweal!" But Piet was gone before he finished the curse.

He found his way out alone. The ground was shaking steadily now, and the rock buttresses groaned and creaked. He had to crawl over a mound of ice in the last passageway. When he looked up, the plain beyond was a vast jumble of broken white and blue masses.

He stood up slowly, blinking, shocked. Every hut had

collapsed. The crawler was gone. Three Earthers were picking at the wreckage of the bunk hut.

He ran to where the crawler had been. It lay at the bottom of a crevasse. It was on its back and the treads were broken, the chain parts scattered all down the thirty-meter drop. "Hey!" he called on general comm. Nobody answered. He switched to suit radio.

"—five of them under there. They had no suits on. Inbody medical reads negative on all of them," an Earther voice said.

Manuel ran over to the bunk hut. "Where's Petrovich?"

The nearest one looked up. "He was moving the crawler."

"Damn. Probably unconscious. I can't get in the hatch with it overturned."

"Help us here."

"Sure. Where's your full medical equipment?"

"In the third hut, there."

"I'll start digging it out. You'll have to cool all these guys down fast."

So began a blurred, deadening time of hard labor. He helped uncover the bodies. They got several of the medical stations back in operating order. He saw Piet appear at the entrance of the Aleph, hauling equipment out and safely beyond. Manuel found working with the Earthers frustrating; they moved methodically but without imagination, meticulously removing the debris in an orderly way, not usually the fastest and most effective way. The huts had split and vented their atmospheres, pinning the inhabitants until they died, sucking vacuum. The three Earthers had been outside when the quake hit. Petrovich was outside too, heading for the Aleph after Manuel and Piet. He had tried to move the crawler away from a spreading crack, and failed.

Beyond, the valley churned with shifting ice. The shelf was beginning to flow southward.

They got the bodies sealed up all right, but some of them were badly damaged—snapped spines, guts spilled onto the ground, convulsive lung hemorrhage from the vacuum. Once that was done the Earthers themselves collapsed, not so much from fatigue as from the shock of it. They just sat down on the ice and refused to move, glassy-eyed, staring off into space. Manuel shouted at them, but it did no good.

He had to climb down into the crevasse by himself. He rapped on the crawler hull, but there was no answer. He figured a way to tip over the crawler body, using a hydraulic jack from the scaffolding around the Aleph. By this time he was working at fever pitch, taking each problem as it came and hearing or seeing nothing outside of it. He didn't even notice when a good piece of the scaffolding folded up and collapsed, just after he'd pulled the jack out from under it. He wouldn't have given a damn if he had. He had never liked Petrovich a hell of a lot, but if the man was dead you did what you could to save the body in time, before the damage from oxygen loss got too great. The biting Ganymede cold would help. If Petrovich had known he was dying, he could have vented his suit the right way, gradually, and chilled himself down without too much cell damage. Then the cold would stop the oxygen-loss damage. So Manuel worked with the jack and tried to turn the crawler over.

Twice the crevasse walls caved in. Snow engulfed him. Blocks of ice thumped by in the white swirl. He clawed his way out, tossing the blue ice chunks aside, chest heaving, sweating so much his faceplate fogged and he couldn't read the angle and pressure settings on the jack. He got it wedged under the body of the crawler and turned up the power to full. That was enough to tilt it thirty degrees over. Manuel worked his way under it, knowing that if the ground shook again and threw the jack off balance the crawler would come down on him. He popped the hatch and crawled up through it. Petrovich was hanging upside down from the pilot's chair.

Manuel didn't even look in the helmet, just pulled him down and threw the body out through the hatch. He jumped after it. Another quake started as he dragged the body away, and the crawler bucked over on its side and made a complete roll, coming after them. Manuel picked up Petrovich and jumped. He got halfway up the steep walls, hanging in air for a long moment, trying to figure what to do. The crawler tumbled over again below him and he had nowhere to go but back down. He landed on the turret as the crawler rocked over and tipped further and then settled down, nearly throwing him. He kept his balance and jumped again, this time getting a better purchase, and cleared the lip of the crevasse as big blocks of ice split off the walls with cracking, booming reports.

He kicked one of the Earthers into alertness and got him to help with Petrovich. The body seemed all right but Petrovich was in a coma. They inserted him into a medmon. It gave a good prognosis. It was a utility monitor, though, unable to do delicate reviving work. That would have to wait for equipment at Sidon.

Another quake hit then, throwing the monitor around. The ice mesa on the horizon slumped. The square profile broke, fractured, and let go with a roar, showering the plain with tumbling, roiling avalanches. Manuel thought then of Piet. He ran toward the Aleph.

It had fallen over. The equipment from inside was safe, strewn over the landscape, but Piet had been coming out when the scaffolding gave way. It had caught him and held him while the Aleph rolled over. He lay pinned under beams and pipes now, nearly touching the Aleph. As Manuel trotted toward him, the helmet came up and pain-squeezed eyes peered out.

"I got . . . it all."

"The equipment? I suppose you did, you damn fool."

"Please . . ."

The thin, weak voice made Manuel bite his lip at his own anger. "Where's it hurt?"

"Legs. Below the knees, I can't feel anything."

"Lie flat."

Manuel pushed him gently down. Piet gasped. There were medical inputs in the lower back of the suit, but they were Earther design and Manuel didn't have lock-ins for them.

"Goddamn. Where can I—"

"The . . . living quarters."

He ran back to the huts and scrabbled around in the med monitors for parts. When he came back the ground was rumbling again. The Aleph seemed to have sunk a little into the ice. It was closer to Piet.

"I . . . I'd have been done sooner," Piet said apologetically as Manuel worked on his back. Piet's breath came in long, wheezing gasps. Manuel clicked the lock-ins around the right number of turns and then worked them into the sockets. Piet sighed as his pain centers shut down. His body lost its rigidity.

"Took me . . . longer . . . to get out. Something . . . like syrup . . . slowed me."

"I'm going to have to drag you out from under this stuff."

"That same . . . soft . . . light . . ."

"Shouldn't hurt too much."

Manuel eyed the tangled, wrecked web of pipes and struts that hung over them. If it fell wrong it would trap Piet even more. He started pulling the pipes out of the way, and the whole structure rattled and clattered. Falling in weak gravity, it couldn't hurt Piet badly, but it would be a mess to undo. He decided to cut it away.

"I'm going after a cutter. Everything's okay. The bodies are sealed up. You just rest."

He had to rummage around in the wreckage. It took him a while, and as he came trotting back toward the hulking wreck a shock wave threw him down. He started to get back up and another knocked him over. The Aleph tipped over toward Piet, and the scaffolding came down with a crash. It didn't fall on Piet. Manuel could see him clearly. Piet's head came up, and the calm, clear eyes peered out, directly at Manuel, as the Aleph toppled over further, crunching, sinking fast now as cracks split the ice beneath it. Black jagged lines forked out from it. One widening crack passed only a few meters from Manuel as Piet cried out, not in terror but with a plaintive, resigned quality—screamed just once as the Aleph rolled over on him in a sudden fog, a hazy shower of glinting light that Manuel took to be ice and snow tossed up by the settling weight.

Then Piet was gone, and the enormous bulk settled further into the broken ice and the ground trembled. Manuel could not tell whether the deep, shuddering vibration came from the sinking ruin of the Aleph or from a distant quake.

The Aleph shifted, and Manuel stared at the place where Piet had been. The man he had known so little would lie now in this place far beyond the moon of Islam and the cross of Rome and the hammer of Marx, in a territory open and without plan, beyond man and his encasing theories, his filters, beyond the closed rooms of the civilized mind.

He walked slowly back to the crumpled huts. Behind him the Aleph slipped further into the yawning, groaning crevasses. He ignored the rumbling and the slow, gravid movement. The Earthers were laboring over the medical units. They clustered around each monitor, attaching temporary power packs. To Manuel they seemed like priests again, devoted to the sacred icons of their state-provided immortality. He felt a sour dislike for them, not for any reason he could identify, and decided it must be his fatigue.

The nearest one saw him approach. "We . . . watched Piet. That was terrible."

"Yeah."

"We were afraid to go near, afraid—"

"I know."

"There is no hope he is perhaps pinned in the ice below, that—"

"No. Forget it."

"Very well. I, I must report that the situation is quite serious."

"No kidding."

"I have tried calling Sidon and Hiruko. Our gear is not working."

"We can't raise them on suit comm at this range. We'll have to use the crawler's."

They went looking for it. The ice was moving and thrusting and murmuring in the distance, confusing his bearings. Several minutes passed before Manuel realized that the opening he sought was gone. "Closed up," he muttered. "Crawler's prob'ly a hundred meters down by now."

The Earther looked around at the steadily working ice plain. At the valley center the ice flow was perceptible. Blocks sprang up and flopped down, carried by greater pressures below. The huts were on a more slowly drifting section of the plain.

"How long until our area is torn loose?"

"No telling. We could be safe here. Could be this piece is hung up on a rock base and won't get carried along much."

The Earther brightened cautiously. "Do you think so?"

"No. Damned unlikely. Look how the Aleph's sinking."

"What should we do, then?"

Manuel stood with hands on hips, bent over, testing his muscles to see if he had pulled any. He said nothing. Then he sat down on the ice and stretched out. It felt good. He was tired, but not badly. On the other hand, only a fool doesn't take a rest when he can get it. "Could try to get up into the hills, but things are giving way up there too. That's where some of this stuff is coming from."

"What *can* we do?"

"Not much. Wait for Sidon to notice we're not calling.

I'd bet they've got their hands full, though. Prob'ly too busy to listen for suspicious silences."

"If the monitors run out of power . . ."

"Right."

"Perhaps the satellites will see our predicament."

Manuel shook his head. These men were used to insulating, overlapping backups. Safety nets.

He got up and walked toward the rubble of the huts. The clashing ice was a continuous murmur in the valley.

"What are you doing?"

"Looking for a reserve power pack."

"Over in number five there is one. I'll show you."

The other figures looked up from their labors to watch Manuel. He got the pack and swung it onto his back. As he did so, he chanced to look toward the Aleph and was startled to find that the ice had already swallowed it. The crevasses there did not seem to be widening any more. As he watched, restless motion sealed over some of the big hole where the stonework had sunk. He thought sadly for a moment, breathed deeply, and turned away.

"What is the pack for?" the Earther asked.

"You people hold out here. Move only if the ice breaks up right around you. I'm going to Sidon."

4

So he began to run. He ignored the shouted farewells and wishes of good luck from the few Earthers; he was already turning inward and preparing himself. The churning chunks of broken ice made footing difficult as he crossed the plain. It was like running across the tossing waves of a streaming river, and he took each long, loping step with enough altitude to see where he could land, coming down with a rolling gait to cushion himself in case the shelf shattered under him and he had to spring clear.

He looked back once. The caved-in huts and lonely still-waving figures were dots on a rumpled expanse of white. The area around them looked smoother than the rest, but it could break up any time, he knew, if the slab jarred free or the undersole got scraped by passing rocks. He shook his head to clear it and turned to the hills above.

The slopes were raked free of loose gravel, scoured by sliding slabs of ice, and that made the footing easier. He went up the hills fast, hydraulics wheezing, and reached a ridgeline that looked stable. Fresh black shoulders of stone poked through aged ice. In time, the iron would tinge with rust and the nearby snows would turn purplish from the runoff. Now the dark nickel-iron made good footing, and he chose his leaps to come down there. From the north came roiling clouds, steaming up from the new melt. The clouds darkened as they rose, swooping along the ridgeline so that his high, long jumps took him into the underbellies of cloying moisture. Droplets peppered his faceplate, and he nearly tumbled once from the disorientation. Flashes of orange raked the western mountains: more volcanoes, smoldering fires cutting through the murk.

He picked up the incessant *bip bip bip* of the Sidon hailer at the top of a steep hill. Sidon was still over the horizon, but the hailer gave him a fix. He was still too far away to reach them with suit comm. A dull ache was settling into his legs now and he took shorter leaps. He cut in the reserve pack. The valleys below were choked with muttering, moving ice. New gullies and arroyos gnawed at the hills. The ringing *bip bip bip* was the only perceptible sign of man in this rumbling wilderness—*bip bip bip*, patient and artificial and puny beside the huge forces working everywhere. He remembered returning to camp with his father each year, when he had accepted the benign landscape beyond the ports, transfixed by it and yet knowing that men ruled there, could pass through it with only incidental danger.

He had learned this, without being told, from his father. The Colonel had inherited an attitude, a stance, that said with every gesture: *We'll put our stamp here and it will remain*. The outward-pushing domes, the machine-sheathed animals, the crawlers, the muties which scoured the wilderness, chewing and digesting and mindlessly carrying out man's work—they had all been agents of the remorseless roll of humanity, of the boot-heel, of an end to mysteries.

As Manuel worked his way down a broken terrace of tumbled gray rock he felt the ache in his legs seeping up through him and began to pant harder, and saw that he would have had to leave Sidon anyway those years ago, even without the bitter anger he had felt. For at the camp in that dusky morning of Old Matt's death he had joined forever the other side—the wilderness, the opening-outward, the undomesticated, the country of the old dead time. Perhaps the Colonel had understood that too. Something had drawn the man, had made him lead the prunings and forge the ledgers that made them seem profitable. Something had drawn him out into the vastness, an unvoiced urging. But in the end when the Colonel saw what it meant, where it led, that death and loss were a part of it, seamless and undeniable—Old Matt's face swam before Manuel, the dry voice sounded in his ears—then the Colonel had rejected it.

Manuel now sensed a fraction of what his father had felt, that unendurably long moment outside the cabin, staring down at the stiff body. The Colonel's words still hung in the space between them: *killing everything that's old*—for his father had never truly meant to kill the Aleph, he had merely wanted to hunt it, to be drawn out by it from the cozy pockets of an insulated life, out from humanity. And in the death of the thing the Colonel had seen, with foreboding, his own end. . . .

He landed among a cowering bunch of rockjaws. They shrieked and fled, their asymmetric bodies lurching, their many-jointed legs going *clack clack clack* with frantic energy. Perhaps they too would be erased by the shifting ices and river torrents. But they would be back, inevitably. *Clack clack clack. Bip bip bip.* Once introduced into this world, life would never leave—there was no end to the explosive, consuming, voracious lust of long chain molecules to link and match and make of themselves yet more and more and again more.

Running stolidly now, puffing, sweat soaking him, Manuel watched the land dissolve into shifting planes of light. He shook his head. The world was moving restlessly now as ice parted and slammed, with only the distant crags fixed and reliable. He struggled across washed-out cañons. Creatures raced over the hills, panicked. In his gathering fatigue, Manuel looked out upon the fleeing forms as though from a great height. Life was growing and spreading here the way a disease propagates and eats and in the eating must kill. *There should be something more,* he thought. A kind of being might come into the universe that did not want to finally eat everything or to command all or to fill every niche and site with its own precious self. It would be a strange thing, with enough of the brute biology in it to have the quick, darting sense of survival. But it would also have to carry something of the machine in it, the passive and accepting quality of duty, of waiting, and of thought that went beyond the endless eating or the fear of dying. To such a thing the universe would be not a battleground but a theater, where eternal dramas were acted out and it was best to be in the audience. Perhaps evolution, which had been at the beginning a blind force that pushed against everything, could find a path to that shambling, curiously lasting state.

Manuel stumbled, picked himself up, and ran on. He felt himself now in that same detached state. The *bip bip bip* drew him on. Its steady call echoed in his helmet and to take away the seeping pain in his legs he thought of the time before, when he had struggled, cradling Old Matt, and the beacon had called—long, ringing, reassuring, each pulse carrying through the thick and streaming silence, volleying out and echoing, waiting until the next joined it, each note piling upon the last, hammering, forming a human presence in the face of the blank void. Yet now he did not find the mindless ringing *bip bip bip* a comfort. It was just an idiot wail, as irritating as the easy theories and cheap wisdom of Hiruko, as pointless as the bland understanding of the Earthers. Piet and the rest—they had not been made for the brawling raw edge, beyond their social certainties, confronting real chance and risk and death eternal, pitted against an infinity they worshiped but did not understand—

A geyser burst in front of him, spewing steam and hurling chunks of rock. He circled around, over slumped hills and folded ruins of mountains. He gasped, tasting the reek of hot bearings. It was hard to fall on Ganymede, but when a slab turned under him he did, twisting, stunned by the impact. *Bip bip bip,* they called to him, and he remembered the plaintive *ding dingding* that Eagle had tapped against its bars, a momentary reaching out that he had not had the sense or judgment to meet, to answer in the right way, and thus had lost the chance he would always remember—

He lurched up, blotting out the memory. *No.* The past was gone. He looked around him for bearings.

A towering mountain range had flattened, as if stamped down, into a shattered plain. From the edge of it he peered through shifting banks of fog and dust.

There—Sidon.

Cracks cut the eggshell domes. Dashing rapids crisscrossed the terraces. Wheat fields wore a pallor of gray, frozen. A column of oily smoke climbed from a reduction factory.

He hailed them for five minutes before they answered. The suit comm faded in and out amid a rustle of static, against a background of animal bellowings, wails, tight-voiced cries for help, and steady, mournful Maydays. The pockets of damp, flowering life sent their chorus across the cold and brittle vastness. A choked Sidon Central voice answered Manuel, took the coordinates of the site and the description of what they needed, and promised to relay word to Hiruko. In the chaos, no one knew when drones could reach the site and drop supplies, much less make a pickup from the splintered land.

"Come on in," the voice said. "We need help. You're twenty klicks out. Most of the way's stable."

Manuel remembered the bulging domes he had played under as a boy: the fat leafy greens that towered three meters high, and that you could pluck off and fold over, exposing the leathery spines that would slip free easily, leaving a floppy rich plate that, eaten last, would bring a sweet, heavy taste into the mouth. And the fruit hanging ripe and ready, bathed by crisp ultraviolet and gusts of fertilizing vapors, force-grown for Sidon's own consumption, sought after by Hiruko but never shipped. And the rank musk of fat-marbled flesh, grown in vats. And the swarming aroma of fresh grains . . .

He thought of Sidon. Of moist, enveloping humanity.

"No. No."

"What? Listen, I'm telling you—"

"They need me back at the site. They don't know scat-all how to handle themselves."

"We're your people here! You get yourself—"

He turned his back on Sidon. The choked voice called out to him, but he kept on going—into the land that moved with a flux of its own, casting off with an immense shrug the hand of man.

The end was coming, and he should be at the site. A deadening emptiness formed in him. He had lost most of his past. Many of the hands that had guided him were now stilled forever. He was weary beyond the point where he could assess his own fatigue, yet kept on, fording streams and stamping heavily under waterfalls that broke over him in rainbows, scrambling up arroyos and down spreading fans of fresh-turned gravel and soil, little noting in the rush and roar the crumpled bodies of crawlies and rockjaws strewn everywhere.

The land ruled now, not men. Its casual rippling had cast down his father into a laser's path, and by so doing had begun Manuel's own journey back to this place. Was it possible that, once the Aleph had stopped boring through the ice crust years ago, the gathering stresses were no longer relieved? So that killing it had brought all this on?

Manuel shook himself. That was crazy. Crazy.

Out here, forging some understanding was not a matter of guessing and then testing, like a scientist, but of listening; waiting; witnessing the slow, certain sway of worlds, the rhythms of gravity and ice, of warming and moisture and then ice again, thin onrushing air and dimmed burnt-golden sunlight, blunt masses and cold equations, smooth and unhurried motion—an old, necessary weariness that Piet had begun to sense. The Earthers around Piet were obsessed with death, with freezing themselves down and reaping the only reward a secular Earth had vouchsafed to them, the sole promise that society had to hold against the grave. But coming out here, seeing the revolving, shimmering things inside the Aleph, perhaps Piet had sensed another kind of promise, and without thinking of it clearly had allowed that to rule him at the end—had gone back into the Aleph to fetch some equipment, so he said, when something in the man had really been returning to a sensed completion, and so he had decided to take his stand there: a fervent hope that seemed to Manuel a blindness, a wish for translation, for Manuel wanted no refuge from this world of eternal cold, or from any other world—he had plans and ideas still, moored in the land and following its same hard destiny, unforgiving and irreducible.

He came down wrong on some gravel and twisted something in his knee. It began to swell up as he went on, and each kilometer became a torment. By the time he could see the site he shambled with a groggy, uneven pace.

He stopped several kilometers away and called over radio, "You look okay. Ice shifting any?"

"No. Not yet. The corpses are safe. I—"

"Good. Better not move."

"We were afraid you would not return. I want to thank you for—"

"Yeah. Look, I'm going to scout the valley. See where it's breaking loose."

They were safe for a while. The floe would smash up soon, though.

He didn't want to go into the camp just yet, didn't want to talk. He was bone-tired, but he felt better out here. He walked, limping, trying to clear his head.

At first he did not feel the silent pressure underfoot. He stopped, knowing something was wrong.

Great ice cakes beneath his boots rose, creaking. Rock groaned. The whole mountain range was tilting.

There was no place to run to. The hill bulged more.

His own musky smell flooded his suit, sour and defeated. He sank to his knees.

Then it stopped. A sudden silence fell upon the wild and endless territory that stretched quietly in all directions: Ganymede as it had been in the formless time before, crumpled, fresh, without encrustations of man, barren and without life, a stage waiting for the ceaseless struggle between the slumbering, inert wilderness and the endlessly chewing chains of life—all witnessed by a thing that knew everything, contained everything, perhaps had made everything, yet went on mutely amid all the clash and clamor, immersed in its creation, running, perhaps pausing but never quitting, leaving a wake of wreckage that was tragedy to men but mere passing drama to it: a huge, undeflected, ghostly shape—

The swelling ice rose again.

He was on his feet now as he understood, and watched

cracks forced wider at the center of the bulge. His mouth was open, breathing rapidly, a weight lifting from him and his filmed eyes grown brighter. Cracks forked from the tortured upthrusting mound. Ice fell away with loud crashes.

Manuel smiled.

Watch for me.

All those years, the men and animals running out here, roiling and heedless and joyful, and they never thought maybe it was drawing them out.

It was a different shape this time.

And as the first of the immense alabaster blocks broke free of the restraining land, showering stones into the air, he knew he would carry this, carry it on with him in the long decades of rebuilding and pain that must come now, through the heavy years of toil out in the territory, beyond the ever-reaching hand of man; the thought would come to him each day as he worked for his own undiminished destiny, or in the soft night when he lay with Belinda, or at dark moments when memory alone was all he had to sustain him—he would carry the certain sense that it was there, eternally, somewhere in the vastness, and he would remember.

Afterword

The Bear and the Aleph: *Against Infinity* and Tradition

GARY K. WOLFE

1.

To understand why *Against Infinity* is a revolutionary work in the history of hard science fiction, we have to start at the beginning.

When science fiction was just a kid, its readers weren't concerned much with either the sophistication of its science or the grace of its style. Hugo Gernsback, the field's first important editor, proclaimed that he wanted stories that would both instruct and delight—science lessons embedded in "charming" romances. Gernsback's idea of "science," however, had much more to do with Edison than with Einstein (or even Newton), and his notion of literature—the "charming romance" part—seemed inherited wholesale from the boys' books of Frank Reade, Jr., or Tom Swift. The tales Gernsback published in *Amazing Stories* in the late twenties often sacrificed any semblance of either scientific veracity or literary ambition in favor of outrageous adventures whose settings and machinery could be rationalized by some vague appeal to an aspect of speculative science. If astronomy had located distant galaxies, then a story set in a distant galaxy was "based on" astronomical discoveries; if the structure of the solar system resembled a little the structure of the atom, then tales of submicroscopic universes were "about" atomic theory. Gernsback's ideal of combining the lessons of science with the pleasures of literature in more or less equal measure never really came to fruition, but it did set the stage for an insidious schism that continues to haunt science fiction to the present day.

When science fiction entered adolescence, the most influential figure in the field was John W. Campbell, Jr., editor of *Astounding Science Fiction*. Campbell was not at all concerned with charming romances; he wanted stories that were consistent, accurate, and thoughtful in their treatment of scientific and technological concepts. Like Gernsback, Campbell was really more interested in science than in fiction, but in place of Gernsback's naive pulp style he preferred a more realistic, transparent prose that would not get in the way of the story's speculative content. His ideal author was probably the young Isaac Asimov, whose "Foundation" stories managed to eliminate not only most distractions of style and character, but most narrative action as well—though their overall concept and effect were magnificent.

The stories that Campbell championed have for various reasons come to be called hard science fiction, since they most often deal with the "hard" sciences such as chemistry and physics, and for decades hard science fiction has been set in opposition to almost everything else the field has had to offer: hard SF vs. "soft" SF (meaning, presumably, SF based in the social sciences); hard SF vs. social satire; hard SF vs. "literary" SF; hard SF vs. the New Wave; hard SF vs. cyberpunk; even hard SF vs. science fantasy (even though no one to this day claims with any authority to know what science fantasy is supposed to be). How can one branch of science fiction be such a polar opposite to so many disparate movements? How did it grow into such an enemy of the people? It's as though hard science fiction is less a subgenre of science fiction than a kind of family tradition against which younger generations rebel in their various ways—or a crusty old uncle who fought in all the wars and knows damn well what the family stands for.

However hard science fiction is defined, it has given rise to a number of myths about itself of varying degrees of validity. Five of these myths are of particular relevance to understanding how *Against Infinity* works to redefine and reshape this most basic of science fiction traditions.

Hard science fiction holds no truck with mysticism. Everything in it has to be accounted for, or at least not prohibited, by appeal to scientific theory current at the time of the writing. This rule usually goes out the window as soon as an author has a need to get his characters across the galaxy at faster-than-light speed, or to transport them back and forth in time—leading to James Blish's astute observation that the most important scientific elements of most science fiction are its impossibilities. (Benford, it should be noted, is unusually conscientious in limiting his use of such impossibilities.) Even Arthur C. Clarke, whose science is generally impeccable, often writes himself into metaphysical cul-de-sacs in which his narrative has no place to go except in the direction of a universal Overmind or a reincarnated Starchild. One reason for this is that the "sense of wonder," so often cited as the main source of science fiction's emotional appeal, can no longer be spontaneously generated by the mere thought of rockets to Mars. Just as horror movie audiences become inured to splatter, science fiction readers require ever larger canvases, ever greater marvels, until science fiction butts right up against theology—or against infinity, if you will. Benford solves this problem in *Against Infinity* in a straightforward and (one would think) obvious way: he makes the sense of wonder a function of character, and presents it to us through the eyes of Manuel and his mentor, Matt Bohles. The Aleph, which might otherwise seem little more than another alien menace to be fought, takes on an added symbolic weight because of what it represents to Manuel.

Hard science fiction requires fancy technology. Both James Blish and Norman Spinrad have observed that what usually passes for science in hard science fiction is really technology, and there is much to support this position. An awe-inspiring artifact such as a Dyson sphere may provide the setting for an otherwise undistinguished chase-adventure, or an ingenious technological Macguffin may set the stage for simple tales of deduction and puzzle solving. But almost always the narrative is, in the end, the adventure or the mystery or the romance; once we've seen the special effect, there has to be a story. Benford, however, *begins* with a story—an almost archetypal tale of the hunt—and his imagined technology grows out of the tale's own imperatives. In *Against Infinity,* the rockjaws, the crawlers, even Eagle, seem logical aspects of the frontier environment in which Benford has chosen to set the tale.

Hard science fiction deals with whole societies, not families or individuals. Even well-drawn characters are often presented to us not as personalities, but as representatives of a certain stage of societal development, or as rebels against a system that is usually more interesting than they are. Heroes who might have been lifted bodily from the pages of Joseph W. Campbell are portrayed as loners, isolated from family and unconcerned with (or unaware of) their own past and traditions. After all, how can one maintain a gimlet-eye focus on the future and on change if one is looking over one's shoulder? But *Against Infinity* had much to do with family and heritage, both Manuel's and Benford's and shows that understanding our past is prerequisite to imagining our future—both for science fiction's characters and its readers.

Hard science fiction is an urban literature. Its model environment is the planet-wide city of Trantor in Asimov's "Foundation" series. Yet the story most often cited as the benchmark of hard science fiction—Tom Godwin's "The Cold Equations"—is in every sense a frontier tale of sparse settlements in inhospitable environments—and even Asimov's Trantor depends upon a growing empire for resources. In fact, a remarkable number of hard science fiction narratives take place not in cities, but on colonial planets, in interplanetary mining settlements, aboard exploratory starships. The city is only half of the hard science fiction equation, as Arthur C. Clarke's elegantly titled *The City and the Stars* makes clear. (It's not surprising that Benford himself was drawn to this narrative, expanding upon it in *Beyond the Fall of Night*.) *Against Infinity* explores directly why this equation is not only aesthetically satisfying, but economically and socially inevitable.

Hard science fiction is a self-contained genre. That is, its immediate literary antecedents are other works of hard science fiction. This self-referentiality has gotten so extensive that twenty years ago Donald Wollheim, in his book *The Universe Makers*, was able to describe a kind of consensus future history in which various authors could participate on the tacit understanding that readers would share their assumptions about background. (Readers not familiar with prior science fiction, such as those encountering the genre for the first time in a college class, often do *not* share these assumptions, leading to the occasional student misunderstanding that hard science fiction is so-called simply because it is hard to read.) "Literary" science fiction, in this formulation, is something else entirely—fiction that draws upon literary traditions outside the science fiction community. Ray Bradbury may set a Thomas Wolfe story in outer space, or Robert Silverberg may do a science fiction version of Joseph Conrad, or James Blish and Brian Aldiss may pay homage to James Joyce, but these are seldom regarded as hard science fiction works, and for the most part hard science fiction has stuck to its own traditions. It is as though in staking its own claim to literary respectability, hard science fiction has found it necessary to renounce all narrative voices but its own. After all, what possible relevance could Hemingway and Faulkner have to fictions of the far future?

Fortunately, this has begun to change in recent years, and we may not be too far from the day when this traditional distinction between hard science fiction and everything else will seem arbitrary and capricious. There are echoes of Hammett and Chandler in certain of the cyberpunks, and the Hemingway tradition seems finally to be finding a science fiction home in the work of Joe Haldeman. But one of the most important works in signaling this change is the one you hold in your hands. In *Against Infinity*, Gregory Benford achieves a dazzling effect by turning to what at first seems the most unlikely of narrative traditions for hard science fiction to draw on—the rich, deeply cadenced storytelling voice of the rural South, and of William Faulkner in particular.

2.

Against Infinity is closely modeled on Faulkner's classic 1942 novella "The Bear," so much so that upon its first publication, some readers chose to regard it more as a literary tour de force than as a serious effort to extend the stylistic and thematic scope of "hard" science fiction. To be sure, the ingenuity with which Benford transforms Faulkner's late-nineteenth-century Mississippi bear hunt into a quest for an alien artifact on a moon of Jupiter is impressive purely in terms of literary adaptation, but the tale was archetypal even when Faulkner told it, and Benford's use of this classic structure provides him with an opportunity to demonstrate how the resources of hard science fiction can enlarge upon and extend some deep-rooted American myths of maturation and confrontation with the wilderness. At the same time, Benford shows how science fiction can be enriched and deepened by the rhythms and voices of a specifically American storytelling tradition. Complaining that science fiction "seldom uses its relation to our past and past literature to grow wiser," Benford reports that *Against Infinity* was his attempt to deal with this vacancy of sensibility in the genre. The novel, he says, "opens and closes with the storytelling voice I heard my step-grandfather use around the fireplace in the 1940s [Benford was born in Alabama]. . . . It specifically echoes Faulkner's wonderful novella, 'The Bear,' comments on it, reflects on what it means about long-term human destiny."

"The Bear" is part of Faulkner's complex series of novels and stories that have come to be known as the "Yoknapatawpha Saga," after the fictional Mississippi county where Faulkner set most of his tales. Early versions of the story were published in 1935 and 1942, but the version most familiar to modern readers appears in Faulkner's 1942 collection *Go Down, Moses*, and which includes a long meditation on guilt, history, and responsibility omitted from the earlier versions.

From the age of ten, Ike McCaslin has been permitted to join the annual hunt for an almost-legendary bear named Old Ben—"the yearly pageant-rite of the old bear's furious immortality." These annual hunts become a kind of initiation into adulthood for Ike, and his tutelary figure in this rite is a part Indian named Sam Fathers. At first, Ike is unable even to catch a glimpse of the bear, but when he leaves behind his gun, watch, and compass—all the appurtenances of civilization that separate him from the purity of the wilderness—the bear appears. Ike gradually achieves such a union with the wilderness that he can easily track Old Ben's footprints, at one point even confronting the bear with a pack of dogs, including a little mongrel terrier that vainly tries to attack the monster. Later, Sam Fathers finds another dog, an immense mongrel named Lion, and Old Ben is finally cornered and killed—but at the cost of both Lion's and Sam Father's lives. This action comprises the first three sections of the story.

The difficult fourth section takes up the action five years later, with Ike's coming-of-age and his decision to give up the plantation that he is to inherit from his father. Ike is upset not only at the gradual loss of the wilderness, which he sees as symbolized in the death of Old Ben, but at the discovery of corruption and incest in his own family, revealed in old plantation ledgers. Section 5 of the story returns us to a time three years earlier—two years after the deaths of Ben, Lion, and Sam Fathers—when Ike returned to the scene of the final hunt to find the graves of Lion and Sam. A lumber company has bought the land and built a railway track through it, and the wilderness is disappearing fast. Ike again begins to feel a strange unity with the wilderness, but his reverie is interrupted by a hammering sound. Nearby, he finds Boon Hogganbeck—the hunter who had actually killed Old Ben—frantically trying to patch together his gun in order to kill the squirrels that are swarming all over the tree above his head.

Cleanth Brooks, one of the first important scholars of William Faulkner's work, offers an explanation of the mystique of the hunt in "The Bear" that might equally apply for readers of *Against Infinity*:

> The urban reader may need to be told that it is the hunter who loves the game that he pursues, and that his code of sportsmanship embodies—however inadequately and however crudely—a regard for his prey which is probably much deeper than that of those citizens who have no firsthand concern for the animals of the wilderness and who would be perfectly happy to have all the creatures of the world eliminated except for such stock as might be kept for scientific purposes in properly appointed zoos.[1]

It is this very love of the wilderness—in this case an interplanetary wilderness—that informs *Against Infinity* with a sensibility so markedly different from that of most

[1]Cleanth Brooks. *William Faulkner: The Yoknapatawpha Country*. (New Haven: Yale University Press, 1963), pp. 416-7.

of what is called hard science fiction. Such fiction, as we have seen, customarily celebrates the hegemony of man and his technology, and pays little attention to what is lost as galactic empires metastasize enthusiastically among the stars. Occasionally, an alien or alien race may be treated sympathetically, but only by making them seem human enough to warrant our sympathy. Benford's Aleph, however, is a celebration of mystery and wildness on its own terms—it isn't cute or even comprehensible. Instead, it is one of those marvelous inventions of pure "otherness" that science fiction sometimes produces, like the sentient ocean in Stainslaw Lem's *Solaris* or the lunar labyrinth of Algis Budrys's *Rogue Moon*. Such images are perhaps the closest thing the scientific imagination can give us to the thrill of the supernatural, or what Freud called the uncanny. They can be studied and measured for years, but we are given to understand that the enigma that is at their center will remain forever just beyond our reach.

Set in a frontier settlement on the Jovian moon Ganymede, *Against Infinity* is organized in six parts, the first five roughly paralleling the five sections of Faulkner's novella, and the sixth extending the theme of the frontier to incorporate broader "science fictional" concerns—not only the infinitely receding frontier of space exploration, but also the scientific and even metaphysical frontiers represented by the bizarre nature of the alien artifact called the Aleph. (In this latter regard, Benford echoes Jorge Luis Borges as well as Faulkner; Borges's 1945 story "The Aleph" also concerns an artifact that seems to contain infinity. "Aleph," of course, is the first letter of the Hebrew alphabet, but it also holds a special meaning symbolizing the godhead in kabbalistic lore, and is used by mathematicians to describe transfinite numbers—numbers in which any part is as great as the whole.) Like Faulkner's Old Ben, the Aleph seems unstoppable and immortal, having for decades burrowed unpredictably throughout Ganymede, sometimes disrupting settlements and wreaking havoc with human attempts to "terraform" the satellite into a habitable world. ("Terraforming" is a common enough concept in hard science fiction, although the notion of altering planetary environments had been used earlier and may even have its roots in nineteenth-century dreams of turning the "Great American Desert" into a garden. The word itself was coined by Jack Williamson in a story published in 1942, and although its use remains largely confined to SF stories and long-range space exploration planning, it might just as well describe what Ike sees happening to his beloved wilderness in "The Bear.")

Like "The Bear," *Against Infinity* is a coming-of-age story. Manuel López first sees the legendary Aleph when he is thirteen, and repeatedly encounters it over the next several years. Finally, under the tutelage of an aging pioneer named Matt Bohles (Bohles appeared as a teenager in Benford's 1975 novel *Jupiter Project*, set nearly a century earlier) and with the aid of a mechanically enhanced part-human animal known as Eagle (a thoughtfully imagined science fiction version of Faulkner's mongrel dog Lion), he is able to immobilize it. Benford's plot is so rich in science fiction invention—terraforming, mechanically reinforced animals with enhanced IQs, alien artifacts, space colonies, etc.—that it may at first seem daunting to readers not familiar with science fiction's conventions, although Benford is among the best at providing implicit explanations that do not intrude on the narrative flow. Furthermore, all this science fictional paraphernalia is as crucial to the novel's success as is its use of a Faulknerian framework and (occasionally) style. Benford is not out merely to give us "The Bear" in outer space, in the manner in which the film *Outland* is *High Noon* in outer space. Instead, he has made the only decision available to a serious novelist undertaking such an experiment—that the novel must succeed purely as science fiction, and this success depends in large part on the degree to which Benford draws from and adds to the traditions of the genre. Apart from the passages of Faulknerian prose, the first two thirds of the novel might easily be read as an interplanetary adventure firmly in the tradition of John W. Campbell, Jr.'s *Astounding Science Fiction*. In fact, Matt Bohles's own coming-of-age in *Jupiter Project* is very much such a story, excellently done but providing little real insight into the older Bohles of *Against Infinity*.

In the last two parts of the novel, Benford sets out to make something uniquely his own out of these disparate traditions of Southern storytelling and hard SF. Part four, like section four of Faulkner's novella, is set some years later and fills in much of the historical and social background to the main action. Manuel has moved from the frontier settlement of Sidon to the city of Hiruko. Urban life brings him face-to-face with the underside of a socialist economy that has grown corrupt at its center, but that must expand in order to survive. Two men accost Manuel and demand his possessions, arguing that such demands are sanctioned through a legislated redistribution of wealth. A colleague explains to him that this kind of socialism evolved on Earth out of the contradictions inherent in capitalism, but that the socialist system itself—while efficient at handling the overpopulated condition of Earth—must exploit new worlds to maintain efficient production of goods; this in turn breeds a new kind of capitalism at the frontier. "So we get humankind—with refined, humanitarian socialism in the older, crowded core. And capitalism sprouting up like weeds at the edge."

The frontier society that has been Manuel's home, then, is less the product of a vision of manifest destiny, or of celebrating the wilderness, than of the brute economic necessity of supporting an increasingly corrupt and unstable social organization. Like Ike McCaslin in Faulkner's "The Bear," Manuel learns that his inheritance is tainted. His mentor—the propertyless Matt Bohles who had lived more than a century in the colonies around Jupiter and who apparently had no family ties (the figure of Sam Fathers from "The Bear")—is revealed as a social anomaly, almost an outcast, rather than a heroic frontiersman and harbinger of a regenerated society. Most important, the Aleph itself has been reduced to an object of scientific research, a museum piece providing employment for a generation of theorists, investigators, and bureaucrats. At this point, appropriately, Manuel learns that his estranged father has died. All that has made him recedes into the past, and Manuel is left to grapple with his inheritance on his own terms.

When Manuel returns to Sidon and meets Earthers visiting Ganymede to conduct research on the Aleph, he comes to realize that "*They came here out of duty. Not from a yearning, but because their commonweal decided. They're priests, not explorers.*" At Sidon, the frontier is giving way to civilization, even though the settlement's random sprawl still contrasts with the orderly grids of Hiruko. After his father's funeral, Manuel learns an odd fact about Colonel López, who had earlier seemed to represent the stifling order of civilization in contrast to Matt Bohles's pioneering spirit of independence: throughout all the years of Matt's childhood, the hunts that eventually brought down the Aleph had been financed by his father at a loss to the settlement's economy—not only as a kind of R&R, but for "the thing itself"—the hunter's love of the wilderness and the prey. Matt Bohles was not alone in providing Manuel his wilderness heritage; only his position as outsider gave him the freedom to acknowledge it, whereas Colonel López's professional life denied him such freedom.

The beginning of the final part of the novel echoes the beginning of the first part, with an expedition from Sidon Settlement in search of the Aleph. New domes have grown up, an atmosphere is becoming evident on the satellite, and there is talk of the mechanized animals creating a new underclass in society, "yet another source for the forward tilt of capitalism." Manuel accompanies an Earth scientist doing research on the Aleph, and learns that the Aleph has revealed secrets as challenging to physics as the space frontier itself is to society: it continually rebuilds itself at the atomic level, "like something restlessly remaking itself, forever discontented." It reveals, in fact, that the physical laws governing the universe may themselves undergo evolutionary change. "'Nothing remains, nothing is held constant,'" as the scientist explains to Manuel. At the same time, the Aleph seems to contain all it has encountered, like the Aleph of Jewish legend: venturing inside it, Manuel finds images of Matt and of himself, stored from his earlier encounter with the artifact.

Later, when the earthquake resulting from the stresses of the terraforming process kills the scientist and nearly destroys the settlement, Manuel recognizes that the wilderness can never be fully subdued—"The land ruled now, not men"—and that he himself, perhaps as long ago as Matt's death, "had joined forever the other side—the wilderness, the opening-outward, the undomesticated, the country of the old dead time." The "killing" of the Aleph not only accompanied the death of Matt, it prefigured the death of Manuel's father as well, and committed the boy to a new way of thinking, dominated neither by the economic structures of his society or the scientific mode of its progress. "Out here, forging some understanding was not a matter of guessing and then testing, like a scientist, but of listening; waiting; witnessing the slow certain sway of worlds, the rhythms of gravity and ice . . ." The universe resolves itself into a series of dialectical frontiers at various levels: economic systems generate new patterns as a result of internal stresses, stresses in the crust of a planet build and rebuild it into a kind of ongoing dialogue between what humanity seeks with its terraforming and what nature will permit, and stresses at the subatomic level of matter itself—such as within the Aleph—suggest a universe forever remade and never completely understandable, but one that will always draw certain individuals into its vastness.

More than any other novel *Against Infinity* suggests that, in science fiction, "frontiers" may take on endless layers of meaning, encompassing such diverse themes as economic expansion, particle physics, planetary exploration, and the ancient myth of the hunt. This, to me, is what gives the novel its greatest strength, and what makes it as much a classic as a popular novel can be only a few years after its initial publication. The notion of space exploration as a "new frontier" has become as hidebound a cliché as popular culture can provide, from Ray Bradbury's influential treatment of Mars as a new arena for westward migration to *Star Trek*'s portentous opening narration of "Space—the Final Frontier!" Hard science fiction itself, as we have already seen, is as much a literature of the frontier as of the city. Even Edgar Rice Burroughs's John Carter started his career as an interplanetary swashbuckler while trapped by marauding Indians in the American Southwest. But none of these writers have given as much intelligent thought to what frontiers might really mean as has Gregory Benford in this novel.

Nor have many writers so seamlessly united the once-antithetical traditions of hard science fiction and mainstream literary tradition. *Against Infinity* is a watershed novel, and one of the science fiction classics of the 1980s.

ABOUT THE AUTHOR

Gregory Benford is the author of several acclaimed novels, including *Tides of Light*, *Great Sky River*, *Heart of the Comet* (with David Brin), *In the Ocean of Night*, *Across the Sea of Suns*, and *Timescape*, which won the Nebula Award, the British Science Fiction Award, the John W. Campbell Memorial Award, and the Australian Ditmar Award. Dr. Benford, a Woodrow Wilson Fellow, is a professor of physics at the University of California, Irvine. He and his wife live in Laguna Beach.